T0273965

THE LITTLE BLUE FLAMES

and Other Uncanny Tales

THE
LITTLE BLUE
FLAMES

and Other Uncanny Tales
by A. M. Burrage

Edited by

NICK FREEMAN

THE BRITISH LIBRARY

This collection first published in 2022 by
The British Library
96 Euston Road
London NW1 2DB

Introduction and selection © 2022 Nick Freeman
Volume copyright © 2022 The British Library Board
Short stories © The Estate of A. M. Burrage. Stories sourced from the following
publications and reproduced with the kind permission of the Estate.

A. M. Burrage, *Some Ghost Stories* (London: Cecil Palmer, 1927);
'Ex-Private X' (i.e., A. M. Burrage), *Someone in the Room* (London: Jarrolds, 1931);
A. M. Burrage, *Warning Whispers*, ed. Jack Adrian (Wellingborough: Equation, 1988).

Cataloguing in Publication Data
A catalogue record for this publication is available from the British Library

ISBN 978 0 7123 5412 7

Cover design by Mauricio Villamayor with illustration by Mag Ruhig.

Text design and typesetting by Tetragon, London.
Printed in Malta by Gutenberg Press.

MIX
Paper from
responsible sources
FSC
www.fsc.org   FSC® C022612

CONTENTS

INTRODUCTION
Through the Dark Glass

During the Battle of Passchendaele in 1917, Private A. M. Burrage of the Artists Rifles had some form of premonition he described as seeing "through the Dark Glass". Shortly before his platoon was to attack the German lines, he recalled in 1930, their commander smiled at something Burrage said, and "as he smiled, I saw Death looking at me from out of his eyes, and I knew that his number was up." The bluntness of the trench slang cannot disguise what was obviously a terrifying experience. "I can't describe what I saw," Burrage continues. "It was just Death, and it made me afraid in a ghastly, shuddering way. The momentary transfiguration was just as unpleasant as if his features had melted into the bones of a death's head." The young officer was killed a few minutes later.

The notion of seeing "through a glass, darkly" derives from the Bible (1 Corinthians 13:12) and suggests something of Burrage's Catholic upbringing. It also places him in a distinguished tradition of supernatural storytelling: Sheridan Le Fanu had reworked the phrase for *In a Glass Darkly* (1872), the landmark collection containing his masterpieces "Green Tea" and "Carmilla". Most importantly however, the incident typifies Burrage's approach to the supernatural, from its everyday language to the way that quotidian realities are suddenly transformed into something sinister and macabre. In his work, ghosts manifest themselves without warning in commonplace surroundings—rented rooms, railway carriages, hotels, a party game, a holiday cottage—and are more likely to be the spirits of the relatively recently departed than malign ancient forces or nameless cosmic horrors.

They are therefore quite different from the ghosts conjured by many of his contemporaries. Burrage admired M. R. James (who grudgingly admitted that his stories "keep on the right side" and were "not altogether bad"!), but his own fiction was set in a world far removed from the academic antiquarianism of "Casting the Runes" (1911) or the Latin cryptograms of "The Treasure of Abbot Thomas" (1904), and his ghosts were more human than the "intensely horrible face of *crumpled linen*" that terrifies the hapless Parkins at the finale of "Oh, Whistle, and I'll Come to You, My Lad" (1904). Burrage avoided the mysticism of Arthur Machen, the pantheism of Algernon Blackwood, and the dreamy poetry of Walter de la Mare. His writing has something of the briskness of E. F. Benson's "spook stories", but his characters are usually less socially elevated (his work shows a notable awareness of the injustices wrought by wealth and class), and he lacks Benson's enthusiasm for the monstrous. The bioluminescent giant caterpillar of "Negotium Perambulams..." (1923) or the shadowy thing that "waved as if it had been the head and forepart of some huge snake" in "And No Bird Sings" (1928) have no place in Burrage's world.

He was also remarkably adaptable, moving from stories of gentle whimsy and sentimental reincarnations to outright horror, and at times using elements of science fiction such as timeslips and suggestions of alternative realities. The aim of his stories was modest, but his simple desire "to give the reader a pleasant shudder, in the hope that he will take a lighted candle to bed with him" disguises a writer who, at his best, was as skilful and imaginative as any of his more famous peers.

In a 1921 essay, "The Supernatural in Fiction", Burrage expressed his admiration for the perfect fusion of style and content in Henry James's *The Turn of the Screw* (1898), a story which he felt "opens up little avenues of thought, pushes us, and sets us wandering down them to go alone to the edge of places into which we dare not look". He admitted though that James was anything but an easy read and his own stories used less mandarin methods much closer to those of the popular writers he praised, such as Barry Pain (whose *Stories in the Dark* [1901] was a favourite collection), W. W. Jacobs (Burrage singled out "The Monkey's Paw" [1902] and "The Toll House" [1909] for particular praise), and Oliver Onions (whose "The Beckoning Fair One" he rightly saw as the highlight of Onions' 1911 collection, *Widdershins*). Frequenting the many pubs of Fleet Street, Burrage often found himself in the company of journalists and reporters, and he seems to have preferred their directness and economy to self-conscious literary affectation. Like H. G. Wells, whose plain style influenced his own, Burrage saw himself as more akin to a journalist than a Jamesian artist. He certainly had a journalist's ear for a good story, and several of the tales in this collection show how he exploited the reading public's fascination with sensational murder trials in the age of capital punishment.

Above all, he was a thoroughly professional writer who combined an understanding of the literary marketplace with an uncanny ability to startle and unnerve. His imagery is often striking, as when in one story here, an encounter with the supernatural makes the narrator's flesh shrink, "as you see a strip of gelatine shrink and wither before the heat of a fire". "For the Local Rag" (1930) skilfully combines these aspects of his work, in being a sideways look at his conception of the ghost story and, in its deadline-driven protagonist, "secretly proud of his calling, but used long since to be snubbed, patronized, and abused", something of a self-portrait.

Alfred McLelland Burrage (1889–1956) was born in Hillingdon, Middlesex. His father (also called Alfred) and his uncle, E. Harcourt Burrage, both wrote for publications such as *The Boys of England* and *The Robin Hood Library*, but their unceasing efforts guaranteed only a precarious prosperity. When Alfred senior died suddenly in 1906 leaving a wife and two children, his son's life changed almost overnight. Writing was in young Alfred's blood—he had already published the occasional school story—and now, rather than going to university as his father had intended him to do, he left education and immediately began making use of his family contacts, contributing to *Chums* and other boys' papers. From these he moved into the adult market, quickly establishing himself as versatile, hard-working, and extremely reliable. Burrage always claimed to be lazy, but he clearly thrived on deadline adrenaline. He soon began to see the rewards of his labours, though he preferred the swift returns from short stories and serials to the uncertainties of royalty payments. Before war broke out in 1914, he was publishing across a range of genres, from school stories to romantic comedy, throwing in tales of crime (he wrote a couple of Sexton Blake stories), adventure, and the supernatural along the way and gracing the pages of prestigious monthlies such as *Pearson's*, *Cassell's*, and the *London Magazine*. He even managed to continue writing while on active service from December 1915, recalling how an editor wrote to him in the trenches to ask whether he could, "have one of your light, charming love stories of country house life by next Thursday".

Burrage had written supernatural fantasy stories such as "The Wrong Station" (1916) during the war, but after being invalided out of the army in 1918, he came into his own. During the 1920s, the ghost story enjoyed widespread popularity, and writers were able to publish their work in anthologies as well as in periodicals and individual collections. Benefitting from the patronage of David Whitelaw, editor of the *London*, Burrage hit a rich vein of form between 1925 and 1930, publishing 28 stories in the magazine during that time. Wary of relying on a single outlet, he contributed another twenty to other magazines in the same period, some of which were anthologized by his friend, Dorothy L. Sayers, in influential books such as *Great Short Stories of Mystery and Horror* (1928). A selection of the *London* tales was collected in two books of his own, *Some Ghost Stories* (1927) and *Someone in the Room* (1931), both of which were well received. Perhaps surprisingly however, neither was reprinted despite the presence of tales such as "Smee", "The Waxwork", and "The Sweeper", and he published no further collections.

As the market for ghost stories dwindled during the 1930s and 1940s, Burrage moved into other fields, working as hard as ever. Jack Adrian, who edited a collection of his weird tales in 1988, estimated that he may have published as many as 1600 stories during his fifty-year career, with 40 appearing in the *Evening News* during the final six years of his life. His full output remains unknown, and it may be that for all Adrian's determined research—he speculated that Burrage may have written 100 ghost stories—other tales are yet to be discovered in the back issues of forgotten periodicals.

Burrage's most famous and controversial work is his memoir of his army service, *War is War*, published in 1930 under the nom de guerre, "Ex-Private X", the same name being used for *Someone in the Room* the following year. It is a vivid and often shocking book, which is openly contemptuous of what Burrage saw as a hypocritical and often cowardly officer class. It is equally unforgiving of the French civilians Burrage encountered behind the lines, its outspokenness making it a book which was more talked about than bought. Burrage was somewhat disappointed by its limited success, but he made effective use of his wartime experiences elsewhere, notably in "The Recurring Tragedy", a bleak complement to more famous wartime tales with a Christian undercurrent, such as Arthur Machen's "The Bowmen" (1914) and Rudyard Kipling's "The Gardener" (1925). This was typical of Burrage's working methods. Always on the look-out for "copy", his stories drew inspiration from his schooldays, from a dismal period of flat-hunting with his mother and sister after his father's death ("The Little Blue Flames"), his Cornish holidays ("The Running Tide"), and a trip to Madame Tussauds ("The Waxwork"), never wasting an opportunity to put life at the service of art. This imbues his best stories with a strong sense of authenticity, something helped by his eye for telling details, his realistic dialogue, and the unfussy style he used throughout his long career.

Burrage's reliance on the periodical market and one-off payments rather than royalties meant that he preferred the immediate rewards of publication to those of posterity. He did not reprint many of his stories, did not adapt them for the theatre or cinema, or succeed in establishing himself in the United States: a television version of "The Waxwork" was screened as part of the series, *Alfred Hitchcock Presents*, though not until 1959. Most of his short stories were ephemeral achievements paid at the rate that Charles Dorby receives in "For the Local Rag", 30 shillings per thousand words (around £100 by today's standards). Always at work on the next commission, Burrage gave published pieces little thought once they appeared in print. A handful survived in anthologies, but it was not until 1967 that there was another significant collection of his work, *Between the Minute and the Hour: Stories of the Unseen*, which added five new tales to work from his two books of ghost stories. This lack of visibility has meant that Burrage has received only cursory attention from literary critics, and he remains too-little known despite the excellence of his best work.

The stories collected here show the range of Burrage's talent as a writer of ghostly and supernatural fiction. Some ring ingenious changes on established motifs such as vengeance from beyond the grave, some are melancholy and consolatory, some are terrifying, while others have a subtlety that lingers in the mind. All of them show an accomplished craftsman working at the height of his powers, so light a candle or two, bank up the fire, and pay no attention to those rustling leaves outside. It's only the wind. *It's only the wind.*

NICK FREEMAN

A NOTE FROM THE PUBLISHER

The original short stories reprinted in the British Library's classic fiction series were written and published in a period ranging across the nineteenth and twentieth centuries. There are many elements of these stories which continue to entertain modern readers; however, in some cases there are also uses of language, instances of stereotyping and some attitudes expressed by narrators or characters which may not be endorsed by the publishing standards of today. We acknowledge therefore that some elements in the stories selected for reprinting may continue to make uncomfortable reading for some of our audience. With this series British Library Publishing aims to offer a new readership a chance to read some of the rare material of the British Library's collections in an affordable format, to enjoy their merits and to look back into the worlds of the past two centuries as portrayed by their writers. It is not possible to separate these stories from the history of their writing and as such the following stories are presented as they were originally published with the inclusion of minor edits made for consistency of style and sense, and with pejorative terms of an extremely offensive nature partly obscured. We welcome feedback from our readers, which can be sent to the following address:

British Library Publishing
The British Library
96 Euston Road
London, NW1 2DB
United Kingdom

THE WAXWORK

WHILE the uniformed attendants of Marriner's Waxworks were ushering the last stragglers through the great glass-panelled double doors, the manager sat in his office interviewing Raymond Hewson.

The manager was a youngish man, stout, blond and of medium height. He wore his clothes well and contrived to look extremely smart without appearing over-dressed. Raymond Hewson looked neither. His clothes, which had been good when new and which were still carefully brushed and pressed, were beginning to show signs of their owner's losing battle with the world. He was a small, spare, pale man, with lank, errant brown hair, and although he spoke plausibly and even forcibly he had the defensive and somewhat furtive air of a man who was used to rebuffs. He looked what he was, a man gifted somewhat above the ordinary, who was a failure through his lack of self-assertion.

The manager was speaking.

"There is nothing new in your request," he said. "In fact we refuse it to different people—mostly young bloods who have tried to make bets—about three times a week. We have nothing to gain and something to lose by letting people spend the night in our Murderers' Den. If I allowed it, and some young idiot lost his senses, what would be my position? But your being a journalist somewhat alters the case."

Hewson smiled.

"I suppose you mean that journalists have no senses to lose."

"No, no," laughed the manager, "but one imagines them to be

I

responsible people. Besides, here we have something to gain; publicity and advertisement."

"Exactly," said Hewson, "and there I thought we might come to terms."

The manager laughed again.

"Oh," he exclaimed, "I know what's coming. You want to be paid twice, do you? It used to be said years ago that Madame Tussaud's would give a man a hundred pounds for sleeping alone in the Chamber of Horrors. I hope you don't think that we have made any such offer. Er—what is your paper, Mr Hewson?"

"I am freelancing at present," Hewson confessed, "working on space for several papers. However, I should find no difficulty in getting the story printed. The *Morning Echo* would use it like a shot. 'A Night with Marriner's Murderers.' No live paper could turn it down."

The manager rubbed his chin.

"Ah! And how do you propose to treat it?"

"I shall make it gruesome, of course; gruesome with just a saving touch of humour."

The other nodded and offered Hewson his cigarette-case.

"Very well, Mr Hewson," he said. "Get your story printed in the *Morning Echo*, and there will be a five-pound note waiting for you here when you care to come and call for it. But first of all, it's no small ordeal that you're proposing to undertake. I'd like to be quite sure about you, and I'd like you to be quite sure about yourself. I own I shouldn't care to take it on. I've seen those figures dressed and undressed, I know all about the process of their manufacture, I can walk about in company downstairs as unmoved as if I were walking among so many skittles, but I should hate having to sleep down there alone among them."

"Why?" asked Hewson.

"I don't know. There isn't any reason. I don't believe in ghosts. If I did I should expect them to haunt the scene of their crimes or the spot where their bodies were laid, instead of a cellar which happens to contain their waxwork effigies. It's just that I couldn't sit alone among them all night, with their seeming to stare at me in the way they do. After all, they represent the lowest and most appalling types of humanity, and—although I would not own it publicly—the people who come to see them are not generally charged with the very highest motives. The whole atmosphere of the place is unpleasant, and if you are susceptible to atmosphere I warn you that you are in for a very uncomfortable night."

Hewson had known that from the moment when the idea had first occurred to him. His soul sickened at the prospect, even while he smiled casually upon the manager. But he had a wife and family to keep, and for the past month he had been living on paragraphs, eked out by his rapidly dwindling store of savings. Here was a chance not to be missed—the price of a special story in the *Morning Echo*, with a five-pound note to add to it. It meant comparative wealth and luxury for a week, and freedom from the worst anxieties for a fortnight. Besides, if he wrote the story well, it might lead to an offer of regular employment.

"The way of transgressors—and newspaper men—is hard," he said. "I have already promised myself an uncomfortable night, because your murderers' den is obviously not fitted up as an hotel bedroom. But I don't think your waxworks will worry me much."

"You're not superstitious?"

"Not a bit," Hewson laughed.

"But you're a journalist; you must have a strong imagination."

"The news editors for whom I've worked have always complained that I haven't any. Plain facts are not considered sufficient in our trade, and the papers don't like offering their readers unbuttered bread."

The manager smiled and rose.

"Right," he said. "I think the last of the people have gone. Wait a moment. I'll give orders for the figures downstairs not to be draped, and let the night people know that you'll be here. Then I'll take you down and show you round."

He picked up the receiver of a house telephone, spoke into it and presently replaced it.

"One condition I'm afraid I must impose on you," he remarked. "I must ask you not to smoke. We had a fire scare down in the Murderers' Den this evening. I don't know who gave the alarm, but whoever it was it was a false one. Fortunately there were very few people down there at the time, or there might have been a panic. And now, if you're ready, we'll make a move."

Hewson followed the manager through half a dozen rooms where attendants were busy shrouding the kings and queens of England, the generals and prominent statesmen of this and other generations, all the mixed herd of humanity whose fame or notoriety had rendered them eligible for this kind of immortality. The manager stopped once and spoke to a man in uniform, saying something about an armchair in the Murderers' Den.

"It's the best we can do for you, I'm afraid," he said to Hewson. "I hope you'll be able to get some sleep."

He led the way through an open barrier and down ill-lit stone stairs which conveyed a sinister impression of giving access to a dungeon. In a passage at the bottom were a few preliminary horrors, such as relics of the Inquisition, a rack taken from a mediæval castle, branding irons, thumbscrews, and other mementoes of man's one-time cruelty to man. Beyond the passage was the Murderers' Den.

It was a room of irregular shape with a vaulted roof, and dimly lit by electric lights burning behind inverted bowls of frosted glass. It was, by design, an eerie and uncomfortable chamber—a chamber whose atmosphere invited its visitors to speak in whispers. There was something of the air of a chapel about it, but a chapel no longer devoted to the practice of piety and given over now for base and impious worship.

The waxwork murderers stood on low pedestals with numbered tickets at their feet. Seeing them elsewhere, and without knowing whom they

4

represented, one would have thought them a dull-looking crew, chiefly remarkable for the shabbiness of their clothes, and as evidence of the changes of fashion even among the unfashionable.

Recent notorieties rubbed dusty shoulders with the old "favourites." Thurtell, the murderer of Weir, stood as if frozen in the act of making a shop-window gesture to young Bywaters. There was Lefroy, the poor half-baked little snob who killed for gain so that he might ape the gentleman. Within five yards of him sat Mrs Thompson, that erotic romanticist, hanged to propitiate British middle-class matronhood. Charles Peace, the only member of that vile company who looked uncompromisingly and entirely evil, sneered across a gangway at Norman Thorne. Browne and Kennedy, the two most recent additions, stood between Mrs Dyer and Patrick Mahon.

The manager, walking around with Hewson, pointed out several of the more interesting of these unholy notabilities.

"That's Crippen; I expect you recognize him. Insignificant little beast who looks as if he couldn't tread on a worm. That's Armstrong. Looks like a decent, harmless country gentleman, doesn't he? There's old Vaquier; you can't miss him because of his beard. And of course this—"

"Who's that?" Hewson interrupted in a whisper, pointing.

"Oh, I was coming to him," said the manager in a light undertone. "Come and have a good look at him. This is our star turn. He's the only one of the bunch that hasn't been hanged."

The figure which Hewson had indicated was that of a small, slight man not much more than five feet in height. It wore little waxed moustaches, large spectacles, and a caped coat. There was something so exaggeratedly French in its appearance that it reminded Hewson of a stage caricature. He could not have said precisely why the mild-looking face seemed to him so repellent, but he had already recoiled a step and, even in the manager's company, it cost him an effort to look again.

"But who is he?" he asked.

"That," said the manager, "is Dr Bourdette."

Hewson shook his head doubtfully.

"I think I've heard the name," he said, "but I forget in connection with what."

The manager smiled.

"You'd remember better if you were a Frenchman," he said. "For some long while that man was the terror of Paris. He carried on his work of healing by day, and of throat-cutting by night, when the fit was on him. He killed for the sheer devilish pleasure it gave him to kill, and always in the same way—with a razor. After his last crime he left a clue behind him which set the police upon his track. One clue led to another, and before very long they knew that they were on the track of the Parisian equivalent of our Jack the Ripper, and had enough evidence to send him to the madhouse or the guillotine on a dozen capital charges.

"But even then our friend here was too clever for them. When he realized that the toils were closing about him he mysteriously disappeared, and ever since the police of every civilized country have been looking for him. There is no doubt that he managed to make away with himself, and by some means which has prevented his body coming to light. One or two crimes of a similar nature have taken place since his disappearance, but he is believed almost for certain to be dead, and the experts believe these recrudescences to be the work of an imitator. It's queer, isn't it, how every notorious murderer has imitators?"

Hewson shuddered and fidgeted with his feet.

"I don't like him at all," he confessed. "Ugh! What eyes he's got!"

"Yes, this figure's a little masterpiece. You find the eyes bite into you? Well, that's excellent realism, then, for Bourdette practised mesmerism, and was supposed to mesmerize his victims before dispatching them. Indeed, had he not done so, it is impossible to see how so small a man could have done his ghastly work. There were never any signs of a struggle."

"I thought I saw him move," said Hewson with a catch in his voice.

The manager smiled.

"You'll have more than one optical illusion before the night's out, I expect. You shan't be locked in. You can come upstairs when you've had enough of it. There are watchmen on the premises, so you'll find company. Don't be alarmed if you hear them moving about. I'm sorry I can't give you any more light, because all the lights are on. For obvious reasons we keep this place as gloomy as possible. And now I think you had better return with me to the office and have a tot of whisky before beginning your night's vigil."

The member of the night staff who placed the armchair for Hewson was inclined to be facetious.

"Where will you have it, sir?" he asked, grinning. "Just 'ere, so as you can 'ave a little talk with Crippen when you're tired of sitting still? Or there's old Mother Dyer over there, making eyes and looking as if she could do with a bit of company. Say where, sir."

Hewson smiled. The man's chaff pleased him if only because, for the moment at least, it lent the proceedings a much-desired air of the commonplace.

"I'll place it myself, thanks," he said. "I'll find out where the draughts come from first."

"You won't find any down here. Well, good night, sir. I'm upstairs if you want me. Don't let 'em sneak up be'ind you and touch your neck with their cold and clammy 'ands. And you look out for that old Mrs Dyer; I b'lieve she's taken a fancy to you."

Hewson laughed and wished the man good night. It was easier than he had expected. He wheeled the armchair—a heavy one upholstered in plush—a little way down the central gangway, and deliberately turned it so that its back was towards the effigy of Dr Bourdette. For some undefined reason he liked Dr Bourdette a great deal less than his companions.

Busying himself with arranging the chair he was almost light-hearted, but when the attendant's footfalls had died away and a deep hush stole over the chamber he realized that he had no slight ordeal before him.

The dim unwavering light fell on the rows of figures which were so uncannily like human beings that the silence and the stillness seemed unnatural and even ghastly. He missed the sound of breathing, the rustling of clothes, the hundred and one minute noises one hears when even the deepest silence has fallen upon a crowd. But the air was as stagnant as water at the bottom of a standing pond. There was not a breath in the chamber to stir a curtain or rustle a hanging drapery or start a shadow. His own shadow, moving in response to a shifted arm or leg, was all that could be coaxed into motion. All was still to the gaze and silent to the ear. "It must be like this at the bottom of the sea," he thought, and wondered how to work the phrase into his story on the morrow.

He faced the sinister figures boldly enough. They were only waxworks. So long as he let that thought dominate all others he promised himself that all would be well. It did not, however, save him long from the discomfort occasioned by the waxen stare of Dr Bourdette, which, he knew, was directed upon him from behind. The eyes of the little Frenchman's effigy haunted and tormented him, and he itched with the desire to turn and look.

"Come!" he thought, "my nerves have started already. If I turn and look at that dressed-up dummy it will be an admission of funk."

And then another voice in his brain spoke to him.

"It's because you're afraid that you won't turn and look at him."

The two Voices quarrelled silently for a moment or two, and at last Hewson slewed his chair round a little and looked behind him.

Among the many figures standing in stiff, unnatural poses, the effigy of the dreadful little doctor stood out with a queer prominence, perhaps because a steady beam of light beat straight down upon it. Hewson flinched before the parody of mildness which some fiendishly skilled craftsman had managed to convey in wax, met the eyes for one agonized second, and turned again to face the other direction.

"He's only a waxwork like the rest of you," Hewson muttered defiantly. "You're all only waxworks."

They were only waxworks, yes, but waxworks don't move. Not that he had seen the least movement anywhere, but it struck him that, in the moment or two while he had looked behind him, there had been the least subtle change in the grouping of the figures in front. Crippen, for instance, seemed to have turned at least one degree to the left. Or, thought Hewson, perhaps the illusion was due to the fact that he had not slewed his chair back into its exact original position. And there were Field and Grey, too; surely one of them had moved his hands. Hewson held his breath for a moment, and then drew his courage back to him as a man lifts a weight. He remembered the words of more than one news editor and laughed savagely to himself.

"And they tell me I've got no imagination!" he said beneath his breath.

He took a notebook from his pocket and wrote quickly.

"Mem.—Deathly silence and unearthly stillness of figures. Like being bottom of sea. Hypnotic eyes of Dr Bourdette. Figures seem to move when not being watched."

He closed the book suddenly over his fingers and looked round quickly and awfully over his right shoulder. He had neither seen nor heard a movement, but it was as if some sixth sense had made him aware of one. He looked straight into the vapid countenance of Lefroy which smiled vacantly back as if to say, "It wasn't I!"

Of course it wasn't he, or any of them; it was his own nerves. Or was it? Hadn't Crippen moved again during that moment when his attention was directed elsewhere. You couldn't trust that little man! Once you took your eyes off him he took advantage of it to shift his position. That was what they were all doing, if he only knew it, he told himself; and half-rose out of his chair. This was not quite good enough! He was going. He wasn't going to spend the night with a lot of waxworks which moved while he wasn't looking.

… Hewson sat down again. This was very cowardly and very absurd. They *were* only waxworks and they *couldn't* move; let him hold that thought and all would yet be well. Then why all that silent unrest about him?—a subtle something in the air which did not quite break the silence and happened, whichever way he looked, just beyond the boundaries of his vision.

He swung round quickly to encounter the mild but baleful stare of Dr Bourdette. Then, without warning, he jerked his head back to stare straight at Crippen. Ha! he'd nearly caught Crippen that time! "You'd better be careful, Crippen—and all the rest of you! If I do see one of you move I'll smash you to pieces! Do you hear?"

He ought to go, he told himself. Already he had experienced enough to write his story, or ten stories, for the matter of that. Well, then, why not go? The *Morning Echo* would be none the wiser as to how long he had stayed, nor would it care so long as his story was a good one. Yes, but that night watchman upstairs would chaff him. And the manager—one never knew—perhaps the manager would quibble over that five-pound note which he needed so badly. He wondered if Rose were asleep or if she were lying awake and thinking of him. She'd laugh when he told her that he had imagined…

This was a little too much! It was bad enough that the waxwork effigies of murderers should move when they weren't being watched, but it was intolerable that they should *breathe*. Somebody was breathing. Or was it his own breath which sounded to him as if it came from a distance? He sat rigid, listening and straining, until he exhaled with a long sigh. His own breath after all, or—if not, Something had divined that he was listening and had ceased breathing simultaneously.

Hewson jerked his head swiftly around and looked all about him out of haggard and haunted eyes. Everywhere his gaze encountered the vacant waxen faces, and everywhere he felt that by just some least fraction of a second had he missed seeing a movement of hand or foot, a silent opening or compression of lips, a flicker of eyelids, a look of human intelligence now smoothed out. They were like naughty children in a class, whispering, fidgeting and laughing behind their teacher's back, but blandly innocent when his gaze was turned upon them.

This would not do! This distinctly would not do! He must clutch at something, grip with his mind upon something which belonged essentially to the workaday world, to the daylight London streets. He was Raymond Hewson, an unsuccessful journalist, a living and breathing man, and these figures grouped around him were only dummies, so they could neither move nor whisper. What did it matter if they were supposed to be lifelike effigies of murderers? They were only made of wax and sawdust, and stood there for the entertainment of morbid sightseers and orange-sucking trippers. That was better! Now what was that funny story which somebody had told him in the Falstaff yesterday?…

He recalled part of it, but not all, for the gaze of Dr Bourdette urged, challenged, and finally compelled him to turn.

Hewson half-turned, and then swung his chair so as to bring him face to face with the wearer of those dreadful hypnotic eyes. His own eyes were dilated, and his mouth, at first set in a grin of terror, lifted at the corners in a snarl. Then Hewson spoke and woke a hundred sinister echoes.

"You moved, damn you!" he cried. "Yes, you did, damn you! I saw you!"

Then he sat quite still, staring straight before him, like a man found frozen in the Arctic snows.

Dr Bourdette's movements were leisurely. He stepped off his pedestal with the mincing care of a lady alighting from a 'bus. The platform stood about two feet from the ground, and above the edge of it a plush-covered rope hung in arc-like curves. Dr Bourdette lifted up the rope until it formed an arch for him to pass under, stepped off the platform and sat down on the edge, facing Hewson. Then he nodded and smiled and said "Good evening."

"I need hardly tell you," he continued, in perfect English in which was traceable only the least foreign accent, "that not until I overheard the conversation between you and the worthy manager of this establishment, did I suspect that I should have the pleasure of a companion here for the night. You cannot move or speak without my bidding, but you can hear me perfectly well. Something tells me that you are—shall I say nervous? My dear sir, have no illusions. I am not one of these contemptible effigies miraculously come to life; I am Dr Bourdette himself."

He paused, coughed and shifted his legs.

"Pardon me," he resumed, "but I am a little stiff. And let me explain. Circumstances with which I need not fatigue you, have made it desirable that I should live in England. I was close to this building this evening when I saw a policeman regarding me a thought too curiously. I guessed that he intended to follow and perhaps ask me embarrassing questions, so I mingled with the crowd and came in here. An extra coin bought my admission to the chamber in which we now meet, and an inspiration showed me a certain means of escape.

"I raised a cry of fire, and when all the fools had rushed to the stairs I stripped my effigy of the caped coat which you behold me wearing, donned it, hid my effigy under the platform at the back, and took its place on the pedestal.

"I own that I have since spent a very fatiguing evening, but fortunately I was not always being watched and had opportunities to draw an occasional deep breath and ease the rigidity of my pose. One small boy screamed and exclaimed that he saw me moving. I understood that he was to be whipped and put straight to bed on his return home, and I can only hope that the threat has been executed to the letter.

"The manager's description of me, which I had the embarrassment of being compelled to overhear, was biased but not altogether inaccurate.

Clearly I am not dead, although it is as well that the world thinks otherwise. His account of my hobby, which I have indulged for years, although, through necessity, less frequently of late, was in the main true although not intelligently expressed. The world is divided between collectors and non-collectors. With the non-collectors we are not concerned. The collectors collect anything, according to their individual tastes, from money to cigarette cards, from moths to matchboxes. I collect throats."

He paused again and regarded Hewson's throat with interest mingled with disfavour.

"I am obliged to the chance which brought us together tonight," he continued, "and perhaps it would seem ungrateful to complain. From motives of personal safety my activities have been somewhat curtailed of late years, and I am glad of this opportunity of gratifying my somewhat unusual whim. But you have a skinny neck, sir, if you will overlook a personal remark. I should never have selected you from choice. I like men with thick necks… thick red necks…"

He fumbled in an inside pocket and took out something which he tested against a wet forefinger and then proceeded to pass gently to and fro across the palm of his left hand.

"This is a little French razor," he remarked blandly. "They are not much used in England, but perhaps you know them? One strops them on wood. The blade, you will observe, is very narrow. They do not cut very deep, but deep enough. In just one little moment you shall see for yourself. I shall ask you the little civil question of all the polite barbers: Does the razor suit you, sir?"

He rose up, a diminutive but menacing figure of evil, and approached Hewson with the silent, furtive step of a hunting panther.

"You will have the goodness," he said, "to raise your chin a little. Thank you, and a little more. Just a little more. Ah, thank you!… *Merci, m'sieur… Ah, merci… merci…*"

*

Over one end of the chamber was a thick skylight of frosted glass which, by day, let in a few sickly and filtered rays from the floor above. After sunrise these began to mingle with the subdued light from the electric bulbs, and this mingled illumination added a certain ghastliness to a scene which needed no additional touch of horror.

The waxwork figures stood apathetically in their places, waiting to be admired or execrated by the crowds who would presently wander fearfully among them. In their midst, in the centre gangway, Hewson sat still, leaning far back in his armchair. His chin was uptilted as if he were waiting to receive attention from a barber, and although there was not a scratch upon his throat, nor anywhere upon his body, he was cold and dead. His previous employers were wrong in having credited him with no imagination.

Dr Bourdette on his pedestal watched the dead man unemotionally. He did not move, nor was he capable of motion. But then, after all, he was only a waxwork.

NOBODY'S HOUSE

THEY faced each other across the threshold of the great door in the dimness of two meagre lights. It was just dusk on a windy autumn evening, and Mrs Park, the caretaker, had brought a candle with her to answer the summons at the door. Behind the stranger the last grey light of the day filtered through veils of dingy, low-flying clouds. Between them the candle flame fluttered in the draught like a yellow pennon, the cavernous darkness of the hall advancing and retreating like some monster at once curious and shy.

The man was tall and broad and seemingly in the early fifties. He wore a grey moustache and beard, both closely trimmed, and his black velour hat was pulled low down over a high forehead. His overcoat was cut to an old-fashioned pattern, having a cape to it, and it was perhaps this which lent him an air of—even at his years—having outlived his age.

He was fumbling in an inside pocket when the door was opened, and he said nothing until he had produced an envelope.

"I have an order from Messrs Flake and Limpenny to see the house." Here he offered Mrs Park the envelope. "I am afraid I have called at an inopportune time, but 1 missed one train and the next arrived late. Perhaps, however, you won't mind showing me over?"

He spoke slowly and a little nervously, as if he were repeating a speech which he had previously prepared. His voice was very low and mellowed and gentle. Mrs Park stood back from the threshold.

"Will you come in, sir?" she said. "I am afraid you won't be seeing the house at its best. I shall have to show you over by candle; there is no gas or electric light."

He stepped inside and scrutinized her. She was a tall, gaunt, middle-aged woman of the kind which is generally described as "superior." Nature had intended her to become matron of an institute. Fate and widowhood had forced her a rung or two down the ladder. She looked what she was—honest, hard-working, and almost devoid of sympathy.

"I'm afraid," she added in her hard, toneless voice, "you'll find everything just anyhow. I wasn't expecting anybody. Very few people come here nowadays. And a place of this size takes more than one pair of hands to keep it clean."

"It has been empty a long time, then?" he hazarded.

"Ever since—" She checked herself suddenly "For more than twenty years, I should think." She turned her shoulder upon him, lifting the candle above her head. "This is supposed to be a fine hall, and everybody admires the staircase. If the house doesn't find a tenant or a purchaser soon, I hear they intend removing the staircase and selling it separately. There is a lot of fine oak panelling, too. The library—"

Turning to see if he were listening, she saw him start and shiver and rub his long, thin hands together.

"Excuse me," he said. "I have been a long time in the train, and I am very cold. I wonder if it would be troubling you too much to get me a cup of tea."

"Yes, I could do that," she answered. "The kettle is on, for I intended having one myself. Will you come this way? Perhaps you would like a warm by the fire?"

She led the way across the hall and through a baize-covered door at the end. Turning once to see if she were giving him sufficient light, Mrs Park noticed that he walked with a slight limp. He followed her down a short passage, through a great kitchen ruddy with firelight, down another passage, and into a small room intended to be used as a housekeeper's parlour. Here there was warmth, even stuffiness. A paraffin lamp stood burning on a flaming red table-cloth. The room was full of hideous modern cottage furniture, and decorated largely with the portraits of people who ought to have known better than to be photographed. He saw at a glance Mrs Park in some kind of uniform, Mrs Park's mother wearing bustles, Mrs Park's father in stiff Sunday attire and side-whiskers. But a fire burned brightly in the grate, and a kettle on a brass trivet murmured and rattled its lid. This commonplace room, light and hot and over-furnished was at least a relief from the dark passage and the draughty, gloom-ridden hall.

"I'll give you your tea in here, sir, and take mine in the kitchen," the caretaker said.

"Nonsense. Why should you? Besides, I want to talk. Oh, here's the order to view. You see... Mr Stephen Royds—that's my name... to view..."

He was running his thumbnail along the sheet of heavily headed office notepaper. Mrs Park glanced perfunctorily at the typewriting. So far as she was concerned an order to view was a superfluous formality. She was more interested in this Mr Royds, who, having removed his hat, disclosed a head of sparse iron-grey hair. He spoke like a gentleman, but there was nothing opulent in his appearance. He looked an unlikely purchaser or tenant; but for that matter she had never been able to visualize the sort of person whom the house would suit.

"I'll remove my greatcoat if you don't mind," he said, while Mrs Park went to a cupboard for another cup and saucer. "The room is warm." He laid the coat across the back of a chair. "Do you live here entirely alone?"

"Yes."

"Aren't you—nervous?"

She looked up sharply.

"Nervous? What is there to be nervous about?"

"I didn't know. Some people cannot bear loneliness. Can you tell me why the house has been on the market all these years?"

Mrs Park smiled grimly.

"That's easy enough," she said. "It's nobody's house."

"What do you mean—nobody's house?"

"People who can afford to keep up a great house like this generally want land along with it. There isn't any land. People who don't want land can't afford to keep up a house like this. The estate was sold to Major Skirting. He's a house of his own. He's let the land and he's been trying to let or sell the house ever since. I've shown hundreds over but nobody's ever thought twice about taking it."

"Strange. It's a good house. But the land… yes, I quite follow you. Whom used it to belong to?"

Mrs Park set the cup and saucer down upon the table with a rattle.

"A gentleman named Harboys," she said; and suddenly stood rigid, her head a little on one side, in an attitude of listening.

"Do you hear anything?" he asked sharply.

"No. I'll make the tea."

"I suppose you sometimes fancy you hear things?"

She bent over the kettle, giving him no answer. He waited until the teapot was full and then gently repeated the question.

"Hear things?" she repeated with some show of asperity. "No. Why should I?"

"I didn't know. These empty old houses…"

"I'm not one of the fanciful sort, sir… Will you help yourself to milk and sugar?"

She let him see that the talk had veered in a direction contrary to her liking. There was veiled fear in her eyes, and, watching her intently, he could see that she was not impervious to loneliness. Here was a woman who suffered more than she knew. She could bluff her nerves by sheer will-power, but this will-power was steadily losing in the long battle. Mrs Park was afraid of something, and always, in her inner consciousness, fighting against that fear.

"Thank you," the stranger said, taking the cup and saucer. "Who was this Harboys? Is he still alive?"

"I couldn't say."

"Isn't there some story about the house? Didn't something happen here?"

"I don't know."

"Forgive me. I think you do."

"There are stories… You don't need to listen…"

She spoke jerkily. Once more he remarked that look in her eyes.

"Tell me," he said gently.

"I can't, sir. If Major Skirting knew I told people I should lose my job. He'd think I was trying to prevent people from taking the house."

"It wouldn't prevent me. Wasn't this Harboys supposed to have shot—"

"Ah!" She set cup and saucer down with a rattle. "Then you've heard something already, sir!"

"A little. You had better tell me all. It will not affect me as a prospective purchaser."

Mrs Park passed a hand across her forehead.

"I don't like talking about it, sir. You see, I live here all alone…"

She checked herself suddenly, finding herself about to admit to a second person something which she never confessed even to herself.

"Just so," Royds said sympathetically. "And you sometimes hear noises? What noises?"

"Oh, it's imagination," she said. "Or the wind. Sometimes the wind sounds like footsteps and voices, and sometimes I seem to hear… It may be a loose door somewhere that bangs."

He leaned forward, his eyes shining with the excitement of some strange fascination.

"You mean you hear a shot fired?" he asked, scarcely above a whisper.

Her one hand resting on the table-cloth contracted nervously.

"I've known it sound like a shot. Oh, I don't believe…"

"They say the house is haunted?" he asked eagerly.

"They say… Oh, when there's been a tragedy happen in a house people will always—"

"Never mind what people say. What do *you* say?" The timbre of his voice had changed; under excitement it had hardened, grown louder. "*Is the house haunted?*"

There was something compelling in Royd's gaze, in the new tone of his voice. She answered him sullenly, helplessly.

"I don't know. I've heard things. I tell myself they're nothing." She groped for a handkerchief. "I've *got* to tell myself they're nothing."

"You haven't—*seen* anything?" he asked in a low, strained voice.

"No, thank God! I never go near the library after dark."

"The library? So it was there. Tell me."

Mrs Park gulped some tea and replenished her cup with a shaking hand.

"It must have been about twenty years ago," she said in a low and curiously unwilling tone. "The place belonged to a Mr Gerald Harboys. He was quite young—not much more than thirty, and very well liked. Some said he was a bit queer, but there was a strain of queerness in all the Harboys. Mad on hunting he was, and one of the best riders in these parts. You'll be surprised at the size of the stables when you see them. He had them built.

"He'd married a young wife, one of the Miss Greys from Hornfield Manor, and some say he thought more of her than he did of his horses. She used to ride too, and the pair of them, and Mr Peter Marsh from Brinkchurch were always together. Harboys and Marsh had known each other since they were in the cradle. Whether there was really anything between Marsh and Mrs Harboys, I don't know. There's been arguments about that for years, but they're both dead and gone now, and nobody will ever know.

"About one Christmas-time Harboys took a fall in the hunting-field and broke his leg, and it was during his convalescence that he got into one of his queer moods. I daresay it was being kept out of the hunting-field which brought it on. His leg mended slowly, and right at the end of January he could only just get about with a stick. Mrs Harboys followed the hounds every time there was a meet in the neighbourhood and, with her husband unable to get about, she saw more of Peter Marsh than usual. But nobody seemed to know that Mr Harboys was jealous or that he suspected anything wrong.

"Well, one day at the end of January, Mrs Harboys went out hunting, and her husband brooded all day over the library fire. During the afternoon he amused himself by cleaning a revolver, which he afterwards laid aside on the mantelpiece within reach. Mrs Harboys came in just after dark. Peter Marsh had been piloting her, and she brought him with her. While she was ordering tea and poached eggs to be sent up to the morning-room, she sent Peter Marsh into the library to get himself a whisky and tell Mr Harboys about the day's hunting. He had not been in the library a minute when angry voices were heard and then a shot. The butler then burst into the room and found Peter Marsh lying dead, and Mr Harboys, still in his chair before the fire, staring wildly at the body, with the revolver in his hand."

She paused, and in the silence she heard Royds breathing heavily. His head was bent and his gaze lowered to the near edge of the table, so that she could scarcely see his face.

"Mr Harboys," she resumed, "pleaded Not Guilty at the trial and said that his mind was a blank at the time when the shot was fired. He couldn't remember anything that had happened between Marsh coming into the room and then the butler bending over the dead body. His counsel put in a plea for insanity, but the jury would not have it. They found him Guilty and added a recommendation to mercy. The death penalty was changed to penal servitude for life."

She broke off and began to muse, knitting her brows.

"That must be twenty years ago... They let them out after twenty years. He's out already, or soon will be, if he's alive."

Slowly Royds lifted his head and turned burning eyes upon her face.

"And do you think Harboys did it?" he demanded.

The question took Mrs Park aback.

"Of course! Why! How else could it have happened? There was only those two in the room. It couldn't have happened any other way."

Royds got upon his legs. His pale face was shining with little drops of moisture, his eyes aflame with a strange passion.

"I swear to you," he cried, "that I don't believe Harboys did it. I knew the man—"

Mrs Park's stare intensified and she uttered a smothered exclamation.

"—I knew him well as child and boy and man. I was at school with Harboys. I tell you he was incapable of murder! All the circumstantial evidence in the world would not weigh an atom with me against my knowledge of his character. They say he had fits of madness. Another lie! But mad or sane he couldn't have done it. He loved his wife—and old Peter Marsh. He knew that they were two of God's best and whitest people. I tell you—"

He broke off suddenly and lowered his voice.

"I'm frightening you," he said. "I didn't mean to. Oh, but think! There's Harboys been rotting in prison these twenty years, remembering nothing of those few dreadful moments. To this day he doesn't know if he's innocent or guilty. Think of it."

Mrs Park lifted her white face and twitching lips. One hand had stolen to the region of her heart. Each rapid stroke of her pulses seemed to shake her.

"Why have you come here?" she cried in a voice which rose high and querulous with a nameless dread. "You don't want the house! You never intended—"

"No," said Royds, "I came here to find out."

"What?"

"They say strange things happen in the library. I have heard stories. You tell me you have heard footfalls, voices, the sound of a shot. Don't you understand, woman? What happened in the library that evening twenty years ago is known only to God! The man who lives remembers nothing. If it be true that Peter Marsh returns... Oh, don't you understand? It is the only way of learning... the only way..."

Mrs Park stood up; her slim body made a barrier between him and the door.

"I can't let you go to the library," she cried, sharply.

"I must. I'm going to spend the night there. I'm going to wait until Peter—"

"I can't let you," she said again.

"But you must. Don't you understand? This means life or death to a man."

She backed almost to the door.

"It's madness!" she cried. "Nobody has ever endured that room after nightfall."

"I will!"

"I shall be sent away if it is found out."

"It won't be found out. I'll recompense you if it is. Here, I came prepared to pay for the privilege." He tugged a bundle of banknotes roughly out of his breast pocket and flung them on the table. "How much do you want? Five pounds? Ten? Twenty?"

Mrs Park's gaze lingered on the roll of notes. She knew the value of money. Besides, she was alone in the great house with a man whom it might be dangerous to thwart.

"Come," said Royds, "here are five five-pound notes. Take them and act like a sensible woman. Then I shall go to the library, and you will make me a fire. Is there any furniture there?"

"No," muttered the woman, her gaze still on the roll of banknotes.

"Then, if you will permit me, I will take a chair." He picked up the notes again and transferred all of them but five to his breast pocket. With these five he advanced and pressed them into the woman's hand. Her fingers closed over them.

"I'm doing wrong," she muttered.

"You're doing right. I'll get the truth tonight if I have to summon the devil himself. Now come and help me make a fire in the library."

She turned heavily away without a word and went to a cupboard, from the bottom of which she took a bundle of firewood and an old sheet of newspaper, which she dropped on top of the contents of the half-filled scuttle. Then she lit a candle in a brass stick and motioned him towards the door. He picked up a chair as he followed her.

The house was very still as they passed through the kitchen and passages leading to the hall. Their footfalls on the uncarpeted floors rang out sonorously through the hollow shell of the house. To the woman this shattering of a silence which seemed almost sacred was a new weapon put into the hands of Terror. Her overstrained nerves cried out in protest at each of the man's heavy steps. Around her, in the shifting penumbra beyond reach of the candlelight, above her in the empty upper chambers of the house, all manner of sleeping horrors, shapeless abominations of the night-world, seemed to waken and listen and draw near. The silent house seemed full of stealthy movement, and each blotch of darkness was an ambush, peopled by the lewd phantasms of her mind. The man walking behind her seemed to be without nerves, or he had so stimulated them as to bring them entirely under his control.

Evidently he knew the house, for he passed her in the hall taking the lead in the procession of two, and went straight to the library door, which he flung open and passed on the crest of the following candlelight.

The library was a long room in an angle of the house. A long row of windows fronted the hearth, and two more faced the door. The walls were of oak panels stained a mahogany colour, but in that dim light they looked black, as if they were hung with funereal trappings.

The man lingered between the door and the first of the windows while Mrs Park, half closing her eyes, hurried across to the fireplace with the scuttle. He seemed to be searching for something. Presently he found it.

"There's a hole in one of these panels," he announced.

Mrs Park's heart gave a leap.

"Yes," she stammered. "It's a—a bullet hole. The shot lodged there after—after—"

"Yes," he said, quietly, "I understand." He crossed the room with a chair and set it down at that corner of the hearth which faced the door and the damaged panel. "And that afternoon, over twenty years ago, I was sitting here—"

There was a crash as the scuttle fell from the woman's hands. All her horror and amazement expressed itself in one thin, muffled scream.

"*You* were sitting there! *You!* Gerald Harboys! Gerald Harboys, the murderer!"

He answered quietly: "Gerald Harboys or Stephen Royds—God help me, what does it matter? Murderer or not—only God knows! But I shall learn tonight. Light that fire, woman, and then leave me."

She left him and stumbled blindly back to the little vulgar room behind the kitchen. But a fascination stronger than terror drew her back to the outside of the library door, there tremblingly to wait and to listen…

Harboys, to give him his real name at the last, settled himself on the chair, and at first busied himself with the building up of the fire. Then he took a revolver from his coat pocket, and placed it upon the mantelpiece within his reach. This done he looked out across the room with a steady gaze.

The firelight wrought strange patterns among the shadows, but in the swiftly changing measures of this shadow-dance he found nothing of what he sought. Presently he began to speak aloud, quietly but very distinctly, so that the shivering woman outside the door brought her hands to her tightening throat.

"Peter, Peter." The tone was almost wheedling. "Can you hear me? I'm sitting in just the same place that I sat that evening, with my bad leg resting on a stool. Here am I, and here's that damned revolver. Now, Peter, won't you come? They say you're always here—that you can't rest because your best friend shot you. Did I shoot you, Peter? My mind's a blank—a blank! For twenty years I have been trying to remember. I have not known peace day and night for twenty years, Peter. Oh, come and tell me! I want to know—to *know*. There's something wrong, Peter. I couldn't have done it. How could I have shot you, boy?"

He relapsed into silence, his gaze never leaving the space between the door and the first window. After a long minute his voice broke out again, choked and almost tearful.

"Is it because you hate me that you won't show yourself, Peter? Was I mad? and did I do it after all? Don't hate me, Peter. I've suffered! Have pity! One way or another I want to end this agony tonight. Oh, God, make him merciful to me! Peter, we'd been friends so long. School… don't you remember Wryvern, and those long talks under the lime-trees in the Close on summer nights? And study teas? And going up to Lord's?"

He babbled on, while kaleidoscopic pictures passed before the eyes of his memory. Cool, dewy morning, and the cricket eleven tumbling out of houses for fielding practice; rows of languid boys in dim classrooms and a scratching of pens; bright sunlight, and white shapes moving on a green sward; crowded touch-lines, and the scrum forming, and goal-posts standing up stark against a grey November sky. In each and all of them he caught a wavering, vanishing glimpse of Peter Marsh.

"Peter!" he cried out again. "Can't you hear me? Won't you come to me? You *do* come back. They all say so. That woman hears you. You—in your scarlet coat, as you came in that evening. I remember… when I saw you lying there… the blood scarcely showed. I was sitting here waiting for Muriel. I heard you both come up the drive. Muriel was laughing at something. You were both talking to the groom outside. Then I heard you in the hall, and Muriel ordered tea and went upstairs. And I thought: 'She doesn't come in to see me. I'm nothing to her now I'm crocked. It's all Peter, Peter, Peter. By God!' I said, 'I've been blind as well as lame. The things I've seen which they pretended were nothing… The things I haven't seen, but heard of in whispers and hints.' All in a moment my brain caught fire. 'Damn you!' I said, 'I'll teach you to make a cuckold of a lame man!' Then… you came in."

The trembling woman outside heard him utter a hoarse cry.

"Peter! Peter! Oh, God, I'm beginning to remember! You stood where you're standing now, touching the handle of the door. That's right! And you said—I remember now—'Give us a peg, Jerry. I'm frozen. There's a devil of an east wind.' Peter! Peter! Don't look like that! I'm remember-ing… remembering. Oh, God, have mercy… have mercy!"

A hoarse scream echoed through the room, a chair heeled over with a crash, and then followed a frenzied shouting.

"*I remember… I remember… damn you! when you turned your back on me… like that…*"

A shot rang out; then another. Then silence enfolded Nobody's House, and its one living inmate, a swooning woman, who clung to the oak balustrade.

It was half-an-hour later when Mrs Park forced herself to enter the library. The red glow of the fire was still dancing on the walls and floor. For a moment one ruddy gleam seemed to take a fantastic shape—like the prostrate figure of a man in hunting pink.

Harboys lay crumpled and face downwards across the hearth, the revolver still in his hand, the ugly wound in his temple mercifully hidden. To that end had he remembered.

2 7

Where there had been a bullet hole in one of the panels, the police next morning found two. They were side by side and scarcely an inch apart.

SOMEONE IN THE ROOM

OR several reasons I believe Mrs Fairchild's story, but it may suffice if I name only two. The first and least is that I think her to be
incapable of inventing anything on a more ambitious scale than
those excuses of which, I gather, her creditors are already beginning to
tire. The last and greatest is that Mrs Fairchild hates having to believe her
own story, and quite plainly tries *not* to believe it. When she can be made
to tell it—which is not often, and only under pressure from those whose
good graces she wishes to preserve—she tries to interpolate a certain
facetiousness which falls rather flat.

I have heard tales told by well-meaning folk who wish it to be believed
that they have had experiences of the supernatural. They want so des-
perately to believe in, and convince others of, the survival of the spirit
after death, that one feels them pathetically trying to believe their own
well-intended inventions. In such matters knowledge is not always for
the seekers, for Mrs Fairchild is certainly not of this school. I know her to
be terrified of death, not because she dreads the thought of destruction
but because she dreads the thought of survival. For her, the belief that
she may have to expiate her unpicturesque sins in some terribly mixed
state of society in which she may not be considered quite a lady, is a creed
without comfort.

Mrs Fairchild, after some early struggles, had succeeded in ousting
from her mind all those thoughts engendered by a conventionally religious upbringing, which are so uncomfortable to those who make it their
only business to have a good time. In this one aim and object she had

succeeded to admiration, although, having married Michael Fairchild in his palmy days, she had the chagrin of seeing the bulk of his fortune fall through the shafts of some out-worked mines in South Wales.

After that she became a sort of professional poor relation. She and Michael had a stuffy little flat squeezed just inside the postal district of Mayfair whither they retired when through ill-luck or temporary mismanagement there was no other roof to cover them; but for ten months of the year they contrived to live in other people's country houses, on other people's yachts, in other people's Continental villas—anywhere, in fact, where there was amusing company and good board and lodging to be had for nothing.

The experience which befell Mrs Fairchild, which I am about to relate, happened some two years ago. It was in the autumn and the Fairchilds were temporarily separated while Michael joined a bachelor shooting party in a Devon farmhouse. They had both been staying with Joan Fairchild's uncle and aunt right down in the toe of Cornwall, and Joan stayed on under the avuncular roof until it was such time as she was due to join Michael at a country house near Liskeard.

On the day when she was due to depart Joan Fairchild crowned a somewhat inauspicious visit by missing the only train which could convey her to her destination by nightfall. She returned crestfallen to meet an aunt who shared her disappointment but without loss of sympathy. The house was due to fill again on the morrow, and if dear Joan didn't go when she said she was going there was no saying when the broadest hints would dislodge her.

If her aunt were anxious to speed the parting guest Joan Fairchild was equally anxious to be sped. She had some of the pagan superstitions of the age, and stigmatized the house she was trying to leave as Unlucky. For the last four days she had been made painfully aware that bridge is a game of aces and kings and that skill is of no avail against the kind of brute force which scores hundreds for aces above the line. The sooner she was gone the better. Moreover her absence from the other end would leave an odd number, and she was particularly anxious not to inconvenience the Paley-Thorntons, who had just taken a villa for the season at Cannes.

Her aunt solved the problem by consulting road-maps, speculating as to how long she could comfortably forgo the services of Cox the chauffeur and the use of her limousine, and by bribing Cox with the promise of a day's holiday some time during the following week. Cox looked doubtfully at a line of country on which first-class roads were conspicuously absent and contour lines extremely frequent and close together, but at last he said that he "reckoned he could do it." His task was to deposit Joan Fairchild safely in the neighbourhood of Liskeard in time for dinner, and return home by midnight. So it ended in Joan being lent Cox and the limousine and departing hastily, leaving her aunt moodily to reflect that relatives were an error on the part of Providence, and poor relatives a positive solecism.

Joan Fairchild travelled without a maid, and borrowed assistance from her hostesses. She had for company on the journey only a curtailed back view of Cox seen through the glass, his green-clad shoulders, his red ears and neck, and the top of his back-tilted cap which adhered to his head like a rakish halo. She had schemed to escape altogether without tipping him; and now she wondered if a pound note would evoke that dumb insolence to which, from other people's servants, she was becoming used. Probably he would linger to take refreshment at the Paley-Thorntons' and the over-fed, over-paid beast might easily warn the servants' hall against devoting too much attention to the comfort of an unprofitable guest. Since she had begun to live partly on charity and partly by her wits she had come to observe in servants certain uncomfortable penetrative faculties.

As a defensive measure she began to complain against the slowness of his driving. The roads were no better than mazes of lanes and the hills were mountainous. Cox was soon behind on his self-compiled time-table, and before half the distance had been covered it was plain that Joan

Fairchild would not arrive in time for dinner. The goaded Cox courted disaster by trying to recover lost time, and it was just as dusk was falling that the accident happened.

They were descending a corkscrew hill with occasional gradients which flung Joan Fairchild forward in her seat, when Cox took a bend at a pace which swung him on to the wrong side, to meet a Ford lorry which was toiling up, boiling water spouting from its radiator as from a geyser. Cox missed the lorry by inches and by a miracle, and Joan Fairchild bounced like a die in a dice-box. She was hardly back on the seat before she was shaken off it again. The car heaved itself on to roadside grass, plunged forward leaning at an angle, then stopped with a crash and a jolt.

When she had recovered herself sufficiently to climb out she found Cox ruefully regarding a ripped front tyre, the stump of a tree and a broken front axle. Cox's pallor of face was evidence that he thought things might have been worse. In a few well-chosen words he told her the extent of the damage.

What Joan Fairchild found to say to Cox and what Cox replied to Joan Fairchild are not on record. We are only told that Cox was quite impudent about it, nor was he very helpful when Joan asked him what he was going to *do*. Moreover he did not seem to know where he was, save that he was on the right road, nor the nearest place whence assistance could be obtained.

So far as Joan Fairchild had been able to notice, they had been passing through a tract of wild and desolate country, scarred with the shafts of deserted tin mines. Houses were few, but it happened that she had seen one on the top of the hill which they had half descended. It looked to her like a farmhouse. So she sent Cox up to inquire their whereabouts and the locality of the nearest garage and post-office.

Cox was absent about a quarter of an hour and returned with a long face.

"I've seen the lady and gentleman, ma'am, and they say that the nearest garage and post-office is five miles on."

"Oh, they're a lady and gentleman, are they?" said Joan hopefully.

"You'd be a better judge about that than me, ma'am," said Cox guardedly.

"Are they on the telephone?"

"No, ma'am; I asked."

"Well, what did they think we'd better do?"

"They said a car might be coming along the road that would take a message."

"But suppose one doesn't?"

"I don't know, ma'am."

"And even if we get help, I suppose it will be impossible to get on the road again tonight."

"That's true, ma'am," said Cox equably. After all, he was not due to stay at the Paley-Thorntons'.

Joan Fairchild stamped her foot for sheer irritation.

"Well, the best thing you can do," she said, "is to walk to this wretched village, tell the garage people about the car, and try and get a hired one to take me on."

Cox presented her with a blank stare.

"What, me walk five miles!" he said. He bent and caressed one of his calves. "Beg pardon, ma'am, but I got a packet here in the War."

"Well, we can't be here all night," said Joan Fairchild with that air of finality which she always used in dismissing unpleasant possibilities.

The dialogue was interrupted by the sound of footfalls descending the hill. A male figure hove in sight, and Cox remarked *sotto voce* that here was the gentleman from the house on the top. A closer inspection revealed to Joan Fairchild a tall, rugged man in early middle life, clad in old pale-grey tweeds which, she said, made him look like a dirty sheep. When he drew near he pulled off his cap and addressed Joan Fairchild in accents in which there were distinct traces of the Midlands.

"I'm afraid you're in trouble," he said. "Mrs Fifield and I have been talking it over and we're both afraid you may not be able to get on tonight.

If you can't, we'd be pleased to give you a room. We both know what it's like to be stranded."

Joan Fairchild gushed, and considered while she gushed. Mrs Fifield was evidently the wife of this good Samaritan, and she realized that, while they were not "her kind of people" it would be impossible to offer them money. On the other hand she would feel morally compelled to send them a more or less expensive present, and she would have to endure their company which, instinct told her, would be no small penance.

"Oh, not at all," said the Samaritan in reply to the gush. "It would be a hard world if we couldn't help each other. Besides, we don't get much company. There's a nice spare room and some hot supper."

"There's my chauffeur," said Joan Fairchild doubtfully.

"He can have the second spare room, and I shouldn't be surprised if we can find a bit of hot supper for him too."

Cox was plainly very much in favour of the proposal and remarked in a low tone that he didn't see much hopes of getting any further that evening. Joan reflected that even if she were able to get on the road again in another car she could only hope to arrive at the Paley-Thorntons' at some hour which would not enhance her popularity. Besides, she found herself already tired and hungry. So, with a graciousness and many expressions of thanks which constituted a fine piece of acting, she accepted the invitation.

The house was one of nine or ten rooms, built of Cornish granite and inexpressibly hideous on the outside. The interior was not much more prepossessing, save that oil lamps were burning, and a good fire blazed in the grate of a hybrid apartment which was neither dining-room nor drawing-room. Here Joan Fairchild was greeted by her prospective hostess, a faded woman of about forty who wore a tweed skirt and a dove-grey woollen jumper.

Mrs Fifield's greeting was at once hearty and sympathetic, but the heartiness soon died away, as if a false note had been struck in a house of depression. Joan Fairchild looked around the room and shuddered. It was a museum of all those decorative horrors which an educated taste had taught her to despise. The fireplace was small and bordered by hideous green tiles, the grate narrow, shallow, and plainly constructed for the purpose of economizing in coals. The furniture belonged to the worst phase of the Victorian era, and the pictures were mostly depressing engravings and framed photographs of people who bore the authentic stamp of such relatives and friends as she would have expected the Fifields to possess.

Much hospitality pushed Joan near the fire, then thrust her from one chair into another which was alleged to be more comfortable, then conducted her upstairs into the conjugal chamber for the removal of her hat. Then followed a leaden half-hour before the fire, during which time the Fifields and their visitor tried vainly to find some common ground on which to meet and talk.

Cox, sitting before the kitchen fire, was not faring much better with the one maid of the establishment, a taciturn Cornish girl who belonged to some eccentric religious sect, and believed that the stranger had been sent to her so that he could be saved. He resisted salvation with some energy and even lapsed further by cursing his temporary mistress under his breath. He regretted his eagerness to accept the invitation, and devoutly wished that he had walked the five miles despite the "packet" in his leg.

Meanwhile Joan Fairchild smothered yawns, and tried to appear at least polite. She had none of the picnic instinct, and no sense of humour. Nor had she, with any innocent meaning, that golden attribute of the Apostle Paul. Her world consisted of the sort of people she cared to know, and of servants. She was aware of other people existing, but had never dreamed of being forced to meet them on terms of equality and had not the vaguest idea how to talk to them. She sat on with the miserable conviction that all the funny stories which she had heard about the middle-middle and lower-middle classes must be true.

But she tried hard to hide her snobbery, without the least suspicion that she was a snob. She told herself that if they had been bright and amusing after their own fashion she could have suffered them more or less gladly; but they were about as heavy and about as interesting as two great slabs of suet pudding.

This, she thought, might be partly due to the fact of their having recently endured trouble. Fifield wore a black tie and a diamond of crepe had been sewn on to one of his sleeves. The air was heavy with melancholy, and the house itself was like some monstrous figure of grief brooding alone on the hill-top.

In the course of desultory talk Joan Fairchild learned that her host had been "in business" and had been compelled to retire some two years since on account of his nerves. That he suffered from some nervous disorder was plain, for often when he talked his lower jaw gave a sidelong twitch. He spent his enforced retirement in rearing chickens and tame rabbits, on which subjects he showed symptoms of being prepared to converse.

The guest uttered an inaudible sigh of relief when at last the taciturn maid came in to lay the table, but her heart sank when a dish of stewed rabbit appeared. She had not tasted it since she was in the schoolroom, and remembered hating it even then. The possibility that it was one of the tame rabbits, and the unlikely but unwholesome thought that it might have died a natural death, did not help her appetite when she sat down at the table. She toyed with her food and talked on any and every subject that entered her head in an effort to conceal the fact that she was not eating. There followed some tinned fruit which she was able to swallow, but on sipping from her glass she wondered why poets of the breezy, swashbuckling school wrote songs in praise of cider.

"I think you'll find your room comfortable," Mrs Fifield assured her. "It hasn't been slept in for six months, but we have kept it well aired and there has been a fire in it once a week since the cold, damp weather started. We have very few people to stay with us."

The last statement did not strain Mrs Fairchild's credulity. Whatever gratitude she may have had in her composition, and it was not her most salient characteristic, had been choked out of her by boredom and a desolating sensation of strangeness. The world was only for herself and the people who amused her. That these strangers had gone to some inconvenience to feed, house and attempt to entertain her was a matter which counted for nothing to a lady who had made a fine art of selfishness.

She sat on, wondering how soon common decency would allow her to shed a hint about going to bed. There were symptoms of the rabbit-chicken conversation beginning over again. Normally she hated her own company and would not have dreamed of retiring for hours; but anything was preferable to the company of these two incredible bores.

At last Mrs Fifield gave her the desired opportunity.

"You look tired," she said. "Wouldn't you like to go to your room?"

Joan Fairchild exhibited a smile which was almost vivacious.

"Well, really," she said, "if you don't mind I almost think I should."

"We're early birds ourselves," remarked Mrs Fifield. "And you've come a long way, haven't you?"

She said good night to her host, and Mrs Fifield conducted her upstairs with a lighted candle and threw open the door of a medium-sized room, facing south. The furniture and pictures were such as Joan Fairchild had told herself to expect; but the bed looked comfortable, and when the light was out she need not notice her surroundings.

Mrs Fifield cast a deprecating glance at the hearth. A fire had been laid and lit, but only the paper had burned.

"There now," she said, "I told that girl to light a fire, and she hasn't stayed to watch if it burned up."

Joan Fairchild smothered a yawn.

"Never mind, thank you," she said. "I shall be going straight to bed. Good night, Mrs Fifield, and thank you so much."

The door closed, but she was not left long to herself. Mrs Fifield returned and tapped at her door at least half a dozen times, bringing little things supposed to minister to her comfort. But the well-intentioned persecution ceased at last, and Joan Fairchild unlocked one of her trunks and took out such articles of toilet as she required for the night. By the time she had blown out her candle and got into bed all members of the household were upstairs and the house was still.

She says that she slept almost at once, but fitfully, and whenever she half woke she heard a kind of whispering, such as many people imagine they hear when they lie in a state of semi-consciousness. A voice which she imagined was produced by her own subconsciousness proceeded to count in a whisper and very slowly and carefully. "*One, two, three, four, five, six*," it said. It never got further than six, and then began over again.

After one of these periods Joan Fairchild woke completely, but she lay still, and smiled at her own aberration. Why had she repeatedly counted up to six? What had she been dreaming? Probably she had been playing in her sleep some absurd hand at bridge, and had been counting the cards still unplayed in a certain suit. What deplorable luck she had been having lately! That awful game consisting of three hands; three down doubled on quite a reasonable spade call, and then two little slams in no trumps made by the other side. But it couldn't go on like that. At the Paley-Thorntons'... And, without realizing it, she was half-asleep again.

"*One, two, three, four, five, six.*"

She woke again, this time violently. The whispered voice had seemed not to proceed from her own brain. It seemed to her that she had actually heard it from outside, from somewhere in the room. The breath in her nostrils turned cold. She turned over in bed and looked around her fearfully.

The moon had climbed the sky outside and lit up the room. A long flag of silvery light from the window lay unfurled upon the floor and reached to the washstand opposite. Even the shadows were not impenetrable, and

Joan Fairchild, examining every dim curtain of shade, let her breath go freely at seeing no suspicious shape. Her imagination had played a trick upon her and she was quite alone.

Then something on the washstand caught her attention. It was a stray moonbeam which had focused there on some particular object. She lay wondering what it was, but without sufficient curiosity to get up and see; and after a while discovered that it was the tooth glass which she had used and set down there before retiring. She turned over and tried once more to sleep.

This time she tried in vain. Her nerves had been more highly strained than she had supposed. She heard stealthy movements about her in the room, the furniture began to creak and rap, and all the half-forgotten bogies of her childhood returned to torment her.

Quite uselessly she asked herself what she had to fear. It was all nerves, all imagination. Something seemed to be moving over by the washstand. There were little senseless noises like the tinkling of glass and the clink of toilet-ware. But she wouldn't look. What was the use of looking when it was all "nerves" and there was nothing to see?

"*One, two, three—*"

She turned over with a muffled scream, lashing the bedclothes with her limbs. *She* had not whispered that, nor had she imagined it. Somebody in the room was whispering aloud; somebody by the washstand.

She forced herself to look, and there was nothing. Only the moonbeam was now dancing, moving up and down and to and fro, as if somebody were toying and hesitating with the glass. So it wasn't the glass after all…

And then her heart stopped, and for so long that she felt it would never start again. It *was* the glass, and apparently it was moving in the air of its own volition. Then she saw the moonbeam dim and something like the shadow of a hand encircled the tumbler.

Joan Fairchild sat up in bed and pressed two hands to a heart which rioted now like some caged and frenzied beast. A shadow beside the washstand grew out of nothing, and increased in visibility and substance. "I'm not mad and I'm not dreaming," she thought in her misery. "Then, oh God! what is it?"

The tooth glass was replaced on the tiled washstand with an audible clink. She was now quite definitely not alone in the room. An elderly, grey-bearded man in shabby grey pyjamas had set it down, and he took up a medicine bottle which he leaned very carefully over the rim.

"One, two, three, four, five, six."

She could not cry out nor take her eyes from him, but he turned and fixed her with a haggard gaze of agony, as if to make sure that she was following his movements. And in the midst of the tortures of her mind Joan Fairchild knew that her creed of materialism was all a pricked bubble, that the dead survive, that the Thing with the glass in its hand was something not of this world but yet a living and conscious entity.

She knew that he was in that state which the Churchmen call Hell, that he was vile and odious and suffering, that he had done in life the thing that he was about to do again. He put the glass to his lips, threw back his head and drank, set down the glass, and, to the wretched woman's indescribable panic, he advanced towards her.

He had not taken two steps when his eyes rolled, he clutched at his throat, swayed, writhed and plunged forward, sinking on to his knees as he clutched at the bedclothes, and burying his face in the eiderdown.

Then, for a moment, Joan Fairchild went mad. She clawed at the Horror, touching nothing. She caught at her pillow and lashed and lashed at the bowed head. Then it slipped off the edge of the bed and she saw on the floor a shapeless mass slowly melting like mist before the sun.

I don't know what clothes she put on before letting herself out of the house. She says that she ran down the hill barefooted to the car, that she dressed inside in the dark, and that she cried and moaned all the while. But some time before dawn she fell asleep for she was awakened by Cox in broad daylight.

"Good morning, ma'am," he said, trying to conceal his surprise. "The people up at the 'ouse said you must have got up very early and gorn out, and I guessed you must have gorn down to the car. Well, I've just stopped a man in a Morris up the road, and he's promised to send help along from the nearest place."

Joan Fairchild nodded without interest.

"Go back and get my luggage," she said, "and bring it down here. I can't go back. Tell the people at the house anything—anything you like. I'm not going back there."

Cox eyed her with respectful solicitude.

"Beg pardon, ma'am, but is anything the matter?"

"No, nothing," she answered. "Don't worry me."

"It's that 'ouse give you the creeps, ma'am," said Cox. "I don't wonder, for it fair gave 'em to me. They 'ad one suicide there six months ago, and I'm not surprised, although—"

"They—*what?*" Joan Fairchild cried.

"Suicide, ma'am. Mrs Fifield's father it was. Their servant was telling me all about it. He poisoned himself one night. He was a pretty bad lot from what she told me. The police were going to arrest him for something nasty. I don't know for what, because she either didn't know or wouldn't tell me. But—"

"Oh, stop!" cried Joan Fairchild, and thrust her fingers into her ears.

Cox regarded her in dismay.

"I beg pardon, ma'am. I didn't mean to upset you at all. Do you feel ill, ma'am?"

Joan Fairchild made a spasmodic movement and thrust her face into the palms of her hands.

"Yes," she cried hysterically, "I feel ill—I feel ill!"

And, with her face buried, she began to rock herself to and fro.

FOR THE LOCAL RAG

ARLY in December it was customary for Mr Marvell, the editor
and proprietor of the *Foxbridge Independent*, to edge his way into
the reporters'-room and say to Dorby:

"Oh, Dorby, about our Christmas supplement. We'll have a short story
from you as usual this year. Have it ready in plenty of time, won't you?"

And Dorby would say: "Yes, sir, thank you. The usual sort of short
story?"

"Yes; something—h'm—sentimental, you know. Holly and mistletoe,
and families being reunited and—h'm—enemies forgiving each other on
Christmas Eve."

And Dorby would go home and write something which he fondly
believed Charles Dickens would have approved, full of the Christmas
spirit, with aged and starving parents being surprised on the eve of Noel
by the return of a prodigal son or daughter burdened with hitherto
unsuspected wealth and laden with presents. For this he received thirty
shillings—which relieved Mr Marvell from the embarrassment of feeling
that he ought to have made his faithful employee a little present.

The total population of Foxbridge did not exceed eleven thousand, and
the circulation of the *Independent* was proportionately small. Like more
ambitious newspapers, it relied largely on advertisements for its revenue.
Mr Marvell had no difficulty in getting sufficient of these to make a comfortable little income. Auctioneers' notices, servants wanted, agricultural
implements, manures and land dressings, bargain weeks at the local shops,
all were grist that came to that dusty little mill set in an alley behind the

High Street. And, as Dorby could tell you, Mr Marvell kept the expenses of the paper very low.

But at Christmas-time Mr Marvell lashed out. He published a supplement as a kind of Christmas box to his readers. You could rely on finding some syndicated articles on Old Christmas Customs, Christmas Games, a revolting Household Hint or two on what to do with a stale turkey or how to make mincemeat go twice as far, and always a short story by Charles Dorby—with the title in huge Old English letters intertwined with holly and mistletoe.

Charles Dorby was the chief reporter. As a matter of fact, he was the only reporter, for you could hardly count Monkland, the pimply boy of sixteen who seemed to come to no harm through wearing canvas shoes all the year round. So far Monkland could only be trusted to report cricket and football matches. He had not yet learned to read his own shorthand, and he had a fascinating gift of misreporting speeches and, in the fresh innocence of his youth, making "floaters" which, if undetected at the office, might have involved Mr Marvell in heavy legal expenses. The bulk of the labour therefore fell on Dorby's shoulders, and he was thus overworked besides being underpaid.

Dorby was a little man of indeterminate age, and he wore the dejected air of a dog which had been chained up too long. He was secretly proud of his calling, but used long since to being snubbed, patronized, and abused. He was proud of the *Independent* and simmered under the surface in mild rages when he heard it described as "the local rag". True, it wasn't run quite as he would have run it if he had had full control. It wasn't quite so independent as it sounded. He knew quite well that Mr Marvell increased his modest revenue by accepting presents for leaving something out or putting something else in. And the world's worst poetess since Eliza Cook enclosed a postal order for ten shillings with each of her effusions.

Dorby, then, was a small man of dejected aspect, and this was accentuated by a drooping moustache, which Mrs Dorby in her maiden state had thought silky and fascinating. He had married in his intrepid youth, when he still dreamed of coming to London and editing the *Times*, a local music-teacher, who was responsible for most of the desolating noises which the young bourgeoisie of Foxbridge knocked out of their untuned cottage pianos. The Dorbys were not more unhappy than the average married couple with a family and a very slender income. There were two boys who relieved Dorby of some embarrassment by winning scholarships to the local Grammar School. He wanted them to become journalists!

In his spare time—yes, he managed to find a little spare time—Dorby wrote short stories, and occasionally these were accepted by obscure publications. Dorby's chances came when the editor of a would-be popular weekly found himself short on the day of going to press. He was a really terrible writer of the worst kind of journalese, and all the most worn *clichés* were as dear to him as his wife and family. If your eye happened first to catch the substantive you could guess the adjective. A barrister? Well, of course, he was "rising" and "young." A chasm? Naturally it was "yawning." A void? Not very surprisingly it was an empty void. And his characters all talked as if they were living in the eighteen-eighties—and proud of it, too!

But Dorby knew not of his own treasonable assaults on the King's English. In his own funny little way he was inordinately vain. If a friend met him at Christmas-time in the local Constitutional Club, and said, "Oh, Dorby, old man, that was a jolly good yarn of yours in the supplement of the local rag," he felt like a schoolboy who had just won the mile open, and forgot the offensive name by which his paper had been called.

I have been generalizing, of course, meaning all the while to come to a certain day in Dorby's life. The boy Monkland, obviously, was not always sixteen. He had been younger, and he will unfortunately grow older unless his canvas shoes lead him to the grave by way of pleurisy and pneumonia. I do not know the exact date of the day I have in mind; I only know that it was early in December and that it was snowing. The time was early afternoon, but it was already dusk, for the clouds which were shedding

45

the snow had shut out the failing sunlight. Dorby sat on a high stool in the reporters'-room, transcribing shorthand notes into longhand with the grudging assistance of a blue flicker of a gaslight overhead.

He had been to a wedding, and he hated weddings; still he had to go. The boy Monkland had once been entrusted with a wedding, and, quite innocently, had written in his report something so shocking that, but for the sharp-eyed compositor, the subsequent and inevitable legal proceedings must have ruined Mr Marvell. This had been a bad wedding, even as weddings went. The bride's people, a frugal family, had, it seemed, detailed a relative to steer the reporter away from the refreshment buffet. Dorby preferred funerals. At funerals the bereaved were generally so distressed as not to care what became of the ham sandwiches.

Dorby went through his notes. Had he a full list of presents? Yes, he had. Heavens, how many fish-slices had been bestowed on that happy couple? It looked like the shopping-list of a monastery in Lent. Could he call it "A Fashionable Foxbridge Wedding"? If he did the county people wouldn't like it, and if he didn't the townsfolk would be offended. Well, one can't please everybody in this complicated world.

Still, there was snow falling and Christmas was coming on. Dorby loved the merry Yuletide—as he invariably described it. When he had dealt faithfully by this hateful wedding, he knew that he would feel quite Christmassy and sentimental. It was about time that Mr Marvell came in and reminded him about the Christmas story.

And it was at that very moment that Mr Marvell actually came in, with the promptness of a familiar spirit responding to an incantation.

"Oh, Dorby," he said, "leave out that report about the affiliation case. The man's people have been to see me and—h'm—you know—I don't think any good purpose would be served by publishing it. You can fill up the space by writing something about the real Father Christmas who will be at Judson's Toy Bazaar. They've sent us a quarter-page ad., and it won't hurt to write them up a bit."

Mr Marvell edged himself a little further into the room. He could not get in very far, because the room was merely a cubby-hole. There was no available space for Dorby to entertain callers. He could not spread his arms beyond the margins of the narrow desk without soiling his elbows with the dust from old files of the paper which had been kept for some unknown, but probably morbid, reason.

"And," Mr Marvell continued, "you'd like to do a story for the supplement as usual, I s'pose?"

Dorby looked up.

"Yes, sir. Thank you. Same sort as usual?"

Mr Marvell screwed up his liberally whiskered countenance and rolled his eyes in an effort to concentrate his thoughts. He might have been a publisher trying to make up his mind if it would be worth while to bring out an *édition de luxe* of the works of some precious but not too popular author.

"No," he said slowly, "I think not."

Dorby had written the story for the supplement on each occasion for the past twenty years, and year by year Mr Marvell had been growing more and more conscious of an element of "sameness" about them. Prodigal sons had returned home on Christmas Eve with a punctuality highly creditable to the railway systems, which were generally disorganized at that time of year. Old enemies had shaken hands or embraced according to whether they belonged to the same sex or not. Peace children had brought the Christmas Spirit into sordid homes. Church bells had pealed out their messages of peace and good will. Modest maidens had surrendered—verbally, at least—to dashing young men while the carols were being sung. On the whole Mr Marvell was conservative, but he believed in a change now and again.

"I tell you what," he said. "Write us a ghost story."

"A what?" said Dorby. Dorby's face did not fall, because it had fallen years ago and had, so to say, stayed down; nor did his tone indicate the dismay in which the request had suddenly plunged him. It merely suggested that he thought he might not have heard aright. Mr Marvell might have said goats instead of ghosts. "A what?" he asked again.

Mr Marvell responded quite airily.

"Ghost story," he repeated. "Christmas ghost story. You know, old country houses—panelled walls—spectre with clanking chains—missing will, or hidden treasure. You know the sort of thing."

"Yes, sir," said Dorby. "Very well."

If Mr Marvell had told Dorby to write a tragedy in blank verse after one of the Elizabethan models, Dorby would have said, "Very well!" and gone home and had a shot at it; and he would have owned himself to be no journalist had he failed to produce something. Mr Marvell, quite unaware of the shattering effects of his order, then nodded and withdrew.

You must know Dorby a little better to understand why the blow that had fallen on him was indeed a blow.

First of all Dorby was proud of his old-fashioned Christmas stories. He secretly regarded himself as a second Dickens, but deprived of general recognition by the stupidity of the public and a general conspiracy on the part of most editors and publishers. He had looked forward to writing that Christmas story for the supplement and afterwards receiving the congratulations of a few sentimental old women and one or two insincere male friends. It was his star turn, and now he had been robbed of doing it by a mere editorial caprice.

In the second place, Dorby did not believe in ghosts. He believed in a great many things which leave most men sceptical, but not in ghosts. He was well-known in the town and had made no secret of his views. For so mild a man he had said some quite cruel things about superstitions and the superstitious, and said them publicly. Now there would be a great deal of ribald laughter in the town when it became known that old Dorby had written a ghost story.

Ghosts! How could such things exist? When you died you went to Heaven if you had been good, or to Hell if you had been wicked or bad, or perhaps only just ordinary. How could anybody come back? If you were in Heaven you wouldn't want to, and if you were in the other place you jolly well couldn't! This was logic. Only the subscribers to an almost unmentionable creed, and a few loose-thinking people with practically no religion at all, believed in a middle state in which souls were neither yet at peace nor eternally condemned.

Again, he did not know how to write a ghost story. He hated such things and had never read one except on rare occasions when he had been led astray by the dishonest methods employed by the author. Yet what was he to do? Refuse the commission and lose the thirty shillings? That was quite unthinkable. Besides, to do so would be a tacit confession of his failure as a journalist. A journalist, he held, should be able to write something about anything on the shortest notice.

It was then, while he continued knocking his "wedding" copy into shape, that he renewed his regrets for having quarrelled with Rennick.

Rennick was the only man in the town in Dorby's station of life whom he felt that he was meeting on terms of intellectual equality. The interests of the local tradesmen were few and material, and instead of looking up to Charles Dorby as a representative of the Fourth Estate they were apt to pity him for being an over-driven and underpaid hack. Rennick, though, was different.

Rennick was a little dried-up man of fifty, clerk to the principal lawyer in the town. He, too, was poor, for although he knew most of the villainies perpetrated by his employer during the past thirty years, he lacked the blackmailing touch, and his salary remained disgracefully small. But he was not fond of money. His tastes marched a long way with those of

Dorby. He knew his Dickens and his Trollope, and spoke highly of a certain Henry James, whose works Dorby often tried hard to enjoy, but who invariably defeated him and sent him to bed with a headache.

Also Rennick was a mine of odd scraps of local information and forgotten folklore. He knew how many horses had been stabled by Oliver Cromwell in the parish church, and the site of a battle which had taken place outside the town during the Wars of the Roses, and where the Duke of Y and Lord X had fought a duel during the eighteenth century, and the spot where the last of the fairies was supposed to have been seen by a plumber late on Boxing Night. Rennick was just the man to know of some ghostly legend which could be twisted into a tale. In that case there would be the added attraction of local colour. But three months ago he had quarrelled with old Rennick, and they were not now on speaking terms.

It has been said that only a fighting man should keep a fighting dog, because a dog of that nature is sure to lead his master into trouble sooner or later. Neither Dorby nor Rennick could have been described as fighting men, but their respective dogs were about as pacific as two adjacent Balkan States. Rennick owned an Irish-terrier which was a sort of canine Tybalt and regarded every other dog as a Montague. Dorby owned a pugnacious mongrel, with perhaps rather more bull in it than anything else, which he had bought as a pup under the delusion that it was a pure-bred fox-terrier. Of course, neither had the least control over his dog, and the result was inevitable.

The men and the dogs met one Sunday morning, and while the two men were discussing the unemployment problem the two dogs made acquaintance in the unconventional manner of their kind. Then Rennick's dog bristled all over and rumbled like an empty stomach, and Dorby's dog, having made a rude and quite unmistakable gesture of contempt, uttered distant thunder in his throat. Of course, both men shouted "come here," and, of course, neither dog took the least notice. A moment later events were moving at such a pace that it was impossible to distinguish one dog from the other.

That was perhaps how it was that Rennick came to smite Dorby's dog with his umbrella, and Dorby did violence to Rennick's dog with a rather futile little partridge cane. By why describe the childish scene that followed? Each man took his own dog's part, and each blamed the other for not keeping his dog under control. They quarrelled like a pair of flustered old hens giving each other little verbal pecks. They parted in anger, having said just enough to hurt each other. When they met again Dorby tried to look down at the drooping ends of his own moustache and Rennick looked pointedly in another direction. They had not spoken since.

Tomorrow was press day, and besides being chief reporter Dorby was also chief sub-editor and had to get everything ready for "putting the paper to bed." He finished his notes about the wedding, and wrote a few lines about Judson's Toy bazaar and his Father Christmas, to take the place of a police court case which Mr Marvell, on receipt of five pounds, had considered too unsavoury to be reported in detail. Where was Monkland's football copy? Oh, there it was. "County Senior Cup— Foxbridge's Slashing Victory." Same old stuff. Monkland was a partisan and had once been charged with the impropriety of booing the referee from the Press box. Foxbridge were always gaining slashing victories or suffering narrow defeats. Mustn't forget to leave room for a report of the Wesleyan Mission Tea Social which would come in this evening, and the Bowling Club annual dinner which would come in tomorrow morning. Thank Heaven the Wesleyans and the Bowling Club did their own reporting. It was quite slack for the day before press day. He could go home quite early.

Yes, and then he'd have to tackle that beastly ghost story!

All the while he had been attending to the needs of the paper his mind had been elsewhere. The quarrel with Rennick and the prospect of having to write a ghost story were as two weights dragging at him. The one affected the other. If he hadn't quarrelled with Rennick he could have gone round to his house that evening and said: "Rennick, old man, give us an idea with a bit of local colour in it. I've got to write a rotten ghost story this year, instead of one of the good old-fashioned Christmassy sort."

And then a happy thought struck him. If he couldn't write a sentimental Christmas story this year, at least he could *live* one. It had never before occurred to him to forgive Rennick. After all, the quarrel was very foolish and trifling. Why shouldn't he go round to Rennick and say: "Rennick, old man, it's getting on for Christmas, the season of peace and goodwill. I'll own I was in the wrong"—although he didn't really believe that—"let's shake hands and be friends again?"

He knew that Rennick would respond, just as he himself would have responded if Rennick had made the first advance. Each had been looking for a sign from the other. It would all be very pleasant and very Christmassy, and would more than compensate him for the pleasant little task of which he had been deprived. After all, it is far better to experience something delightful than merely to write about it. Then he and Rennick would go off arm-in-arm to the Constitutional Club and take something to moisten the new cement of their friendship. Or perhaps Rennick would have "something" in the house—which would be even better.

Dashed if he wouldn't do it! It was a fine idea. What funny things men were! Here was he, who had written scores of stories about quarrels being made up at Christmas-time, prepared until a minute or two since to nurse a stupid little grudge and greet an old friend with a scowl.

Dorby's heart lightened suddenly. Even the prospect of writing the ghost story was not so dismal and irritating. Certainly he would go and see Rennick. Wait a minute, hadn't he heard that Rennick was laid up, or had been laid up? A cold or a touch of 'flu or something. Well, that only made it the more likely that he would find him at home. It was quite dark outside when Dorby left the office, and snow was still falling. As he came out in to the High Street the illuminated dial of the clock outside the town hall, shining like a full moon, informed him that it was twenty-eight minutes past four. Snow was beginning to lie on the pavements, but traffic had so far kept the roads clear. Dorby lived in one of a row of villas some half a mile distant on the outskirts of the town. He set off briskly enough, but after a few moments the sight of a grocer's window tempted him to loiter.

A grocer's window, well lit and packed with crackers and dried fruits, looked more Christmassy to Dorby than any other sight in the world. For a moment or two he stood gloating over it. Then a car drew up close against the kerb behind him, and a voice addressed him.

"That you, Dorby? If you're going home I can give you a lift."

The speaker was young Mr Packham, the auctioneer, and to reach his home he must pass Dorby's. Dorby thanked him gratefully and climbed in beside him. The car went forward.

Two or three hundred yards distant, on the near side of the street, was the shop of Mr Munko, a dealer in second-hand furniture and books. When on foot Dorby always looked in at the window. It would not be safe to guess how many hundreds of times he and Rennick had turned over the contents of the threepenny box in the hope of finding a first edition worth hundred of pounds. Mr Munko, however, had other views.

The blood of nearly every known tribe of the human race was mingled in the veins of Mr Munko. It would be safe to say that none of his ancestors had married anyone hailing from within a thousand miles of his birthplace. Mr Munko, despite a tendency to scream when he became excited, had a level head. Such men are not fools in business. One never found anything in the threepenny box much more exciting than the sermons of some defunct and forgotten clergyman whose innocence had been exploited by wicked publishers. But he and Rennick had never quite given up hope.

The thought that he was approaching the shop put Dorby once more in mind of Rennick. Then, as the car drew near, Dorby was a little surprised to see Rennick standing bareheaded in the fluttering snowflakes, peering in through the shop window. Rather silly of him, Dorby thought, to stand about bareheaded in the snow so soon after having had a chill or a touch of 'flu.

Dorby had no doubt but that it was Rennick even before the little man turned and faced the street. The shape of the figure, its poise with bent head and short-sighted stare were unmistakable. An instant later the car was passing, and then Rennick turned, looked straight into Dorby's face, and gave him the friendliest of friendly smiles.

Dorby acted on an impulse.

"Would you mind stopping just for one second?" he said to Packham.

"Eh? Oh, very well. Only do be quick!"

The car stopped. Dorby clambered out and ran back. Rennick was waiting in the ungenerous light which filtered through Mr Munko's dirty windows.

"I say, old man," Dorby exclaimed breathlessly, "I want to make it up! Sorry we had that stupid quarrel. May I come round and see you this evening?"

Rennick nodded and gave him again the very friendly smile. He did not speak, but the nod and the smile quite plainly said: "All right, old man, come round by all means, but we won't talk about it now." This was all Dorby wanted. Packham, he gathered, was in a hurry. He turned and trotted back to the car.

"Sorry to hurry you," Packham said. "Thought you wanted to buy something, not only just go and look in the window. But I promised to be home sharp at half-past four, and it's that now."

*

Five minutes later, having shaken the loose snow off his coat, Dorby entered his small dining-room, where Mrs Dorby was hugging an economical fire. She rose immediately and began to prepare his high tea.

Mrs Dorby was a depressed little woman who believed that it was healthy and economical to feed her family on stuff that came out of tins. There was no waste, she would say; and there wasn't, because all scraps were eaten, even after they had been kept a perilous length of time. Still, none of them had yet suffered from ptomaine poisoning, and had Dorby been one of those men who aspire to breaking records he might have claimed to have eaten more tinned salmon that any other living man. It was tinned salmon this evening.

While he ate and drank, Dorby shared his new grievance with his life partner. Mrs Dorby was herself, and not without cause, a painstaking and highly efficient grumbler, and Dorby lost few opportunities of letting her know that *his* life wasn't all honey.

"A ghost story!" he exclaimed, disgust on his face and in his voice. "Who believes in ghosts nowadays! It's childish. It's against nature and it's against religion. And I could have written something to make people feel that there's still some goodness in human nature. But, no—a ghost story!"

"Need it be about a real ghost, dear?" Mrs Dorby asked. "I mean to say, I read a pretty little story in a ladies' paper once. It was about a young lady who was put into a haunted room. The room wasn't really haunted, of course, but supposed to be. And in the middle of the night the ghost came in and frightened her. But it wasn't a real ghost, it was a man dressed up in a sheet. So," Mrs Dorby concluded simply, "she married him."

"Pah!" said Dorby.

"Couldn't you write something like that, dear?"

"No, I couldn't. I suppose if Marvell says he wants a ghost story he means a real ghost story. Why couldn't he let me write about something that I believe in? I believe in humanity, I believe in Christmas, I believe in Charles Dickens. But ghosts!"

"You're always saying that a good journalist ought to be able to write about anything," commented Mrs Dorby.

"Oh, so I could, I suppose," he answered moodily, "but it doesn't say I want to. I suppose I shall get hold of some silly local legend and twist something out of it. At six o'clock I'm going to step round to see old Rennick—"

"Rennick? But I thought—"

"Pooh," said Dorby, "that's all over now. I met him in the High Street about half-past four, and he was quite friendly. I don't bear any malice. He knew he was in the wrong and he apologized."

Dorby believed in maintaining his dignity in the home even at the expense of truth. It was his dignity which had caused him to select six o'clock as the hour of his call. Very soon his boys would be home from school, and the elder, Sidney—yes, I am afraid they called him Sid—was involved in the mysteries of quadratic equations. Dorby, who had lived most of his life under the delusion that algebra was an Oriental language, did not know what a quadratic equation was, but he was not going to expose his ignorance to a younger and critical generation. By six o'clock the boys would have had their tea and would start discussing their home-work; and that was the time for Dorby to go.

Events proved that he had timed his departure almost to the minute. At the first glance of a Hall and Knight and an exercise book Dorby rose and prepared to go out.

It was a wretched evening. It had stopped snowing, but the wind had veered east and cut through his thin overcoat like a cold knife. As he walked he huddled himself in his clothes.

What a life it was! An editor who wanted to make him write about something he didn't believe in, a son who wanted to be told about quadratic equations, and now this brutal east wind! Still, he was going to make friends again with old Rennick, and that was something. Dorby estimated that Rennick's home was ten minutes' walking distance from his own, but on this occasion, spurred by the desire to keep warm, he covered the ground in eight.

The house was very dark and silent. Not a light anywhere. Dorby pressed the electric bell three or four times without attracting attention from within, and shivered on the doorstep for four or five minutes before coming to the conclusion that the Rennicks were all out. He was in the act of turning when he heard flat and heavy footfalls approach the door from the other side, and a faint and muffled voice—Mrs Rennick's voice—called out: "Yes? Who is it?" Dorby answered, and the door was hesitatingly opened. Mrs Rennick stared at him across the threshold. She showed him a face which was very white save for the eyes, and these were red-rimmed and swollen.

Like so many small men, Rennick had taken himself a wife of noble proportions who had grown mountainous in middle age. Dorby had now only to look at her to see that there was something wrong. The long channels running down her flaccid cheeks were now watercourses for tears.

"Mrs Rennick," he exclaimed. "What's the matter?"

"Haven't you heard?" she faltered. "I thought that was perhaps why—"

"I haven't heard anything. Tell me."

"My husband. My dear husband. He took to his bed three weeks ago. He thought it was only a chill. He wouldn't let me send for a doctor. I d-didn't until—until it was too late. It was pneumonia."

Dorby stared and then reeled forward. A kind of sickness seized him. All that he had believed was shattered and came toppling around him like the ruins of a falling tower. He buried his face in the wet sleeve of his coat and leaned against the doorpost, whimpering. He knew instinctively what he was going to hear. The voice of Mrs Rennick came to him like something heard in a dream:

"He died... at half past four... this afternoon."

THE WRONG STATION

W<small>E</small> had been together in the miserable waiting-room at Ixtable Junction nearly a quarter of an hour, and had not spoken for no better reason, perhaps, than that we were Englishmen. The fire was nearly out, and the light of the gas lamp showed signs of following its bad example. A dense fog had thrown the train service into utter confusion. It was not at all a cheerful kind of night.

My companion was a man of fifty, of medium height, rather grey, and certainly not handsome. He was dressed comfortably but not well. His long black overcoat and bowler hat, neither of which was shabby, seemed to make him appear more commonplace than he need have looked. He had big, fishy-looking eyes, and a large, untidy moustache with a pathetic droop to its ends. He had with him a heavy valise. He looked what I afterwards found him to be—a commercial traveller of the not too prosperous kind.

For a long while he sat fidgeting, staring down at his bag, which rested beside him on the floor. Then suddenly he sprang up and crossed the room to examine a map of the line hanging on the opposite wall. He frowned over it for a full minute, his eyes following a moving thumbnail. Then he turned to me.

"It was somewhere between Reading and Plymouth," he said.

"I beg your pardon?"

"It was somewhere between Reading and Plymouth. Do you know that part well, sir?"

"Pretty well. Why?"

His big, fishy eyes were fixed on me in a stare of pathetic appeal.

"If I could only remember the name of that station! If I saw it any-where, if somebody said it, I should know it at once. A beautiful name it is. It's always just on the edge of my memory, but I can never quite get it."

"That's rather awkward," I said, "if you want to go there."

"I do, sir, I do! I was a fool ever to leave. I ought to have stood up for myself and refused to go. But she persuaded me. And now I don't suppose I shall ever find that little town again."

"If there's a station there," I said, puzzled and amused, "it must be on the map. But perhaps it's on the Southern Railway."

"No, the Great Western it was—a train that gets you into Plymouth in about four and a half hours, and lands you there in the small hours of the morning. I know most of the towns along that route, too—Newbury, Westbury, Taunton, Exeter, but it wasn't any of them. I wonder if you know the place I want?" He laughed a little shamefacedly. "Everybody thinks I'm mad when I tell them."

"It all sounds very mysterious," I said. "I gather that you've been to some place that took your fancy very much, and that you want to go there again, only you don't happen to remember the name of it?"

"That's it," he said, eagerly. "I tell you I'd know that name at once directly I saw it or heard it. But it's not on any map. Every time I see a map I go and have a look. It happened about two years ago, and I've been worrying about it all this time."

My curiosity was by then sufficiently aroused to make me want to hear the whole story. There was nothing of the madman or the romancer about this commonplace little man with his big bag and his air of petty commerce.

"What was your town like?" I asked.

He turned his eyes away from me and seemed to think.

"Well—I only saw a bit of it, but I'd like to have seen all. There's not such another place in England—in the whole world, for that matter. I don't mean only because it was pretty, but there was something in the air—I can't very well explain. If you like, I'll tell you just how everything happened. Perhaps you'll laugh. Most people do."

I promised not to.

"Oh, I don't mind. Nineteen people in twenty say there's no such place, tell me I dreamt it all, but I know I didn't. I do have dreams, of course, but they're never clear like that, and anybody knows the difference between a dream and a fact."

"I always do," said I, to give him confidence.

"Of course, of course!" He sat down on the yellow bench under the map he had been studying, and looked away from me into the grey embers of the dying fire. "There's one or two things I ought to explain first of all," he said. "I'm not a bit an imaginative sort of man, and I'm not what you'd call poetical. I've been in business ever since I was thirteen, and if I didn't begin with a pretty hard head, I've got one now, I give you my word. Very well! Another thing is I'm a married man with four kids. We've got a nice little home at Willesden. I'm a good father and a good husband, though I say it who shouldn't. The missus and me have been married eighteen years, and we're still pretty fond of each other. Not quite like we were at first, mind you, but only fools 'ud expect that. Still, I'd cut off my hand for her if need be. You take me, sir?"

"Perfectly."

"Well, I travel for a big firm of comb manufacturers, and at that time, two years ago, I was taken off my usual round to work up what we call the Western circuit. That's the whole county of Cornwall and about half Devonshire, beginning with Plymouth. The man on there had been making rather a mess of things—young man without much go and less experience. So they put me on there to buck things up a bit.

"I caught the night express from Paddington, and had the good luck to get a compartment to myself. Plymouth was the first stop, and I tipped the guard to wake me up there if I went to sleep, for I didn't want to find myself at Penzance or Falmouth next morning.

"I read for the best part of an hour, and then began to feel sleepy. We whizzed through a big station, and I looked out and saw that it was Reading. I leaned back and put my feet on the opposite seat. I didn't feel very well. I had a sort of feeling—I can't describe it—that I generally get before a heart attack. I've got a bad heart. It may last me for years yet, or it may carry me off tonight. You can't really tell with these things. I've got to be careful of myself.

"Well, that night I was sure it was going to give me a doing, within an hour or two. However, I'd got some stuff the doctor gave me, and I took the bottle out of my breast-pocket and had a pull at it. Then I dropped off to sleep, which rather surprised me afterwards, for generally I keep awake when I'm feeling queer. And when I woke up I felt better than I'd ever felt before."

He paused and looked at me. His great ugly eyes were shining with a light that made them almost beautiful.

"I don't mean only better in health. I felt as I used to feel when I was a nipper—a kind of lightness—I'd never felt it since. I swear I could have danced without music, or run, or jumped—that kind of feeling. The train had stopped. 'Halloa!' I thought, 'this is Plymouth. That guard ought to have called me.'

"Just as those words were going through my mind the door opened and a railway man put his head into the compartment. He wasn't my guard, but some other, or, perhaps, a porter—I didn't look to see what he was. But he was extraordinary to look at—extraordinary! I've never used the word before when speaking of a man, but he was beautiful. Yes, sir, there's not another word in the language to describe his looks. I'd never seen a man's face like his before. There's one or two pictures of angels in the National Gallery a bit like him, but that's the nearest I've come to seeing his like. And what does he do, but call me by my Christian name.

"'This is your station, Harry,' he said, as gravely as you please.

"I wasn't a bit offended, only a little surprised.

"'What, Plymouth?' says I.

"'No, not Plymouth.'

"I looked out, and there was the name of the station on a board, the lovely name I can't remember. And when I saw it I knew that I must get out. It didn't matter if I missed all my appointments the next day. I had to get out there. And yet—and yet, somehow I didn't want to.

"The porter took hold of me by the arm. 'Come on, Harry,' he said. 'It's a beautiful town, the most beautiful town in all the world.'

"'But I've got to go on to Plymouth,' I said, making a kind of struggle. 'I'll come here later on; I will, really. I don't want to get out here now. Let me go on to Plymouth.'

"The man put his mouth close to my ear. His voice was very soft and wheedling, just like a woman's.

"'It's such a lovely town, Harry,' he whispered. 'Don't be afraid.'

"Well, I let him lead me out on to the platform, and then I turned round for my bag. 'We don't take luggage here,' he said, and it seemed to me at the time perfectly reasonable. I know this sounds just like a dream to you, but it was real—real!

"The porter left me. I don't know if he got on to the train or not, but presently I was all alone on the platform. I lingered for a moment, and then started out to see the town.

"It must have been somewhere round two in the morning, and quite dark. But it wasn't an ordinary darkness, it was a kind of deep blue. And there was a smell of flowers in the air, faint but very refreshing. I don't know where it came from, for I saw no gardens. I walked down a kind of alley, just as you find at the entrance of any ordinary station, into one of the streets of that town."

He fixed me with his great eyes, held his speech for a moment, and then burst out:—

"Oh, my God! That wonderful town!"

He relapsed into silence, as if a little ashamed of his emotion. After a pause he went on:—

"It doesn't sound so much to describe—not the place itself. The street was wide, and on each side was a row of large old houses, with diamond panes to the windows, and top storeys projecting out over the ground floors. There were lights in several of the windows, and they reflected on the pavements so that the diamond panes looked like lattice work of light and shadow. And in most of the houses there was music and singing—wonderful music.

"I said the road was very wide. At one side a stream, lined with poplars, ran between two stone embankments. And little bridges of old red brick spanned the stream every few yards, one bridge to the front door of every house on that side. And the stream tinkled as it ran, for all the world as if somebody was playing the harp. Oh, I can't make you feel what it was like—the old houses, the stream, the bridges, the blue darkness, the scents, the music.

"I saw nobody about but children. Yes, there were children playing in the road at that hour of the morning! They played hide-and-seek behind the bridges and danced and laughed and sang. Such children, believe me! I never cared much for kids, except my own, but I didn't mind them playing around me, and instead of growling at those who caught hold of the skirt of my coat, I turned and patted their heads, and laughed because they were laughing.

"I had not gone far when I came to a house I seemed to know. At least, if I didn't know it, I seemed to know that I ought to go there—that I was expected. I didn't stop to ask questions of myself; I just went up to the door and knocked. And presently a young girl opened it to me."

He stopped again.

"That is the queerest thing of all. This is where everybody laughs, and you'll laugh too. I was an ugly old devil then, just the same as I am now. No girl had looked at me twice in the last twenty years. I'd got my wife, I'd settled down; it was a long time since I'd thought of girls. But at the sight of her my heart beat like a boy's, and I knew that I knew her, that we had loved each other for God knows how many years.

"And I remembered her just as I should remember the name of that town if somebody told it to me, only it was a long memory. It seemed to go back hundreds and hundreds of years. And I loved her with a kind of love I had never felt before—and I knew that she loved me. At the sight of her, something in me changed. I wasn't any longer an ugly, common little man, beginning to grow old. I was young again, and as fine a gentleman as any in the land. I could feel it in my very blood.

"She uttered a little cry, and called me by a name that I knew had once belonged to me, only I'd forgotten it. I've forgotten it again since. I can only remember her look and the tone of her voice. She ran right into my arms and kissed me, and laughed and cried over me, and my brain reeled and reeled with happiness, for I had been waiting for such a long while for that moment to come.

"My wife seemed a long way away, and it didn't seem as if I was being the least unfaithful to her. It seemed as if, in marrying her, I'd done this girl who was clinging to me some little wrong. She had been first, she had come hundreds and hundreds of years before the other woman who lay asleep in our little house at Willesden.

"'Let me come in,' I remember saying to the girl who clung to me; and when I said that she began to cry. It was all a mistake, she said, and I would have to go back to the station and catch the next train. I mustn't stop; and she had been waiting for me so long! We must both wait a little longer, and it was such a pity, because now I had had a peep at that town, and seen her, and I shouldn't be happy or contented any more until I came back.

"I said I wasn't going back to catch the next train or any other train, but she said I must. She said the time had not yet come and that some-body had made a mistake. She said that the porter ought to have let me go on to Plymouth—and somehow the word Plymouth sounded queer coming from her.

"I stood there, suddenly very miserable. I didn't want to go. I wanted to stay with her and live in that old house beside the stream, and play with the children, and go on feeling young. And I began to beg of her to let me stop.

"But she wouldn't hear me. She said they'd called me out at the wrong station, and that I must go on to Plymouth, but one day I would come back. And somehow I couldn't argue with her much. I seemed to have no will.

"I wish I'd stood up for myself now. I'd found my way there and it didn't seem fair to send me away. But she took me by the hand, and together in silence we went back the way I had come through the bluish night. And those wonderful children played around us as we walked.

"There was a train waiting at the station, and we stood on the platform for a moment and kissed good-bye. She said I must be patient and I would soon come back. She had been patient, too, and she had been waiting for me so long, she whispered. So I got into the train and it started off, and then—then I tried to remember the name of that station, and couldn't.

"After a while I dropped asleep, and when I woke up there was a doctor and two railway men in the compartment, and they were pouring brandy down my throat, and seemed rather surprised to find I was alive. We were at Plymouth now, and it seemed I'd nearly died in my sleep, and only the brandy had pulled me through.

"The doctor said he quite thought I was dead when they fetched him to look at me, and I must say I've never had quite such a bad turn as that before or since. I never travel without something in my pocket now, in case of accidents."

He paused and in the ensuing silence we heard the sound of an approaching train.

"Mine," he said. "I'm going on to Charr. Well, that's the story, and whatever you say won't convince me that it was a dream. What do you make of it?"

But I could not tell him what I made of it.

THE ACQUITTAL

THEY kept Frenchal waiting below-stairs a long time—a very long time. Evidently the jury was not finding it easy to make up its individual minds. It must have been three hours before the ten men and the two women were brought back, closely guarded by those ridiculous javelin men, and ranged in neat rows in the little tiered box on the right of the judge's throne.

It had been a long trial, interesting enough to the newspaper students of such matters, who have only the tit-bits served up for their delectation by expert journalists; but those compelled to be in court, and the sensation-seekers, who had come for entertainment, had found long periods barren of drama and even of interest.

It was a poison trial. John Frenchal stood indicted for the wilful murder of his wife by administering arsenic. The evidence was all circumstantial and almost entirely technical. Two pathologists with conflicting opinions had each spent hours in the witness-box and given evidence which counsel, jury, and probably even the judge, had failed wholly to understand. The summing-up had been neither for nor against the prisoner, and the scales were evenly balanced when the judge said his last words to the jury. Only the newspaper men, highly experienced in such matters, knew during those long three hours what the verdict must eventually be. "Oh, of course, he did it. But they haven't quite brought it home. The jury are bound to funk it. They'll have to let him off."

Frenchal sat and sweated. He had no means of telling whether this long deliberation of the jury was in his favour or against him. He had borne himself all through the long trial with a calmness and dignity which had compelled a certain amount of admiration. Now, when at last they tapped him on the shoulder, he wondered if he would be able to walk.

Yet, once he was upon his legs, strength and the power of emotion returned to him, and he walked firmly up the wooden stairs between the two warders. He had scarcely reached the rail of the dock when a door opened on the other side of the court, and all around him sounded the rustling and scuffling of people rising from their seats. Through a mist he saw the judge in scarlet and ermine seating himself on the throne under the Royal arms; very far away, it seemed, he heard voices. The members of the jury were answering to their names. Well, one way or another, it would all be over in a few seconds now.

"Members of the jury, are you agreed? Do you find the prisoner at the bar Guilty of wilful murder or Not Guilty?"

"Not Guilty."

He wondered for one aching moment if he had heard aright, if that short first word had really been uttered. Then one or two sentimental women, high up in the gallery on his left, began to clap and were sharply reprimanded.

What was happening now? The judge was speaking to him. He saw a faintly cynical smile on the thin, hard lips. Then a finger touched his arm and a voice whispered: "Come along, sir. Better come downstairs and wait a bit."

Inherent courtesy made him bow to the judge. Then he turned and walked downstairs in almost a state of trance. He did not need the supporting hands on his arms. He was strong enough, but nothing just then seemed real.

The warders, who had been sternly respectful, were now more friendly. But there was something cynical and restrained in their manner, as if they thought him a lucky man, as if they *knew*! They brought him brandy which brought new life to him and gave his surroundings more of the deeper colours of reality. He lit a cigarette and handed his case to the two men in blue, each of whom selected a cigarette and put it in his pocket. His counsel came down to congratulate him and receive his thanks, so did his solicitor, who had worked wondrously hard. But on the faces of each of them he remarked that smile, a little like the judge's, a little like the warders'—as if they thought him undeservedly fortunate.

Presently he remembered that now, after long weeks of confinement, he was free. He got up and spoke of going. His solicitor bade him wait a moment, and went to confer with a policeman standing near the door.

"Better wait a little while. You're not in a hurry. There's a crowd out-side. Presently there'll be a rumour that you've been smuggled out, and then they'll go."

A crowd! That meant a crowd which might possibly be hostile. So they thought he did it, did they? Well, confound them, they were right. Everybody knew, except those twelve fools who, faced with a responsibil-ity beyond their powers of endurance, had given him the benefit of the doubt. The prosecution had bungled its work badly; *he* could have told that harsh-voiced, eminent K.C. where he had got the poison and how it had been administered.

The policeman came forward.

"Your car's just been round to the back, sir. I sent it away and told the man to come back in about twenty minutes."

"My car?"

"A taxi, sir. He said it'd been ordered."

Frenchal turned to his solicitor.

"Did you order me a car?"

"No. I was going to, of course."

Then who had? Some friend of his who was present in court, he supposed. But he had seen no friends. Even Edith—but, of course, it would have been too much for Edith. And the train of thought, starting on a new trail, ran on. Did Edith know? Thank heaven that *something* hadn't come out at the trial. If the fools who, as the defence triumphantly proclaimed, could find no adequate motive, had known about Edith and put her in the witness-box, the trial might have come to a different end. Edith's circumspection, the secrecy on which she had insisted through their intrigue, her slavish worship of the conventions, and the outward show of respectability which had helped bring about the crime, had at least saved him from the consequences. This handsome young widow, his neighbour and his wife's friend, had not been mentioned at the trial.

The tale was as old as passion and crime, the yearning for romance of an unscrupulous man, who, tied to a wife who bored and irritated him, felt the sands of his youth already beginning to slip away. If Edith Longley, who came to live in the grey house across the common, had loved him a little more and her own reputation a little less, the affair might have ended less tragically in some other court.

Frenchal was in the forties, and he had been married for nearly twenty years to a woman who had begun to bore him on their honeymoon. He was not capable of giving a love which outlived passion. His wife was; and she was sentimental and clinging rather than ardent. He soon came to hate her. He had hated her for years, and it was her relentlessly continuing to love him which had lit an ugly red fire in the ashes of boredom and indifference. If she'd only been indifferent, too, if she'd only left him alone instead of fawning around him and making his flesh creep with her caresses and endearments! Like a great ugly cat, she was, he thought, purring and nudging against him for caresses! Her little attentions to his comfort, and she was forever warming his slippers and filling his pipe, sickened him because they spoke of her unwanted love. He had borne it wonderfully, he told himself, and might have gone on bearing it indefinitely if the whisper had not come that life—as he counted it—with its ardours and capacities, was draining away. And then had come Edith

Longley, young and warm-blooded and widowed, to bring him once more the thing he called love.

Oh, yes, she loved him—in her fashion. But she would not burn her boats. She did not like to think of certain houses being closed against her, and of having to find new friends among people who were not quite—you know! If he were free as she was it would, of course, have been so different! No more of the simple and ugly story need be told.

The court-house stood among narrow streets in the older part of a cathedral city. It was at a few minutes to six on a damp, dark autumn evening when Frenchal stepped out quickly and quietly through an arched doorway and into the taxi-cab which awaited him. He had trouble in fastening the door, and the driver, perhaps because he was anxious to get a view of his fare, left his seat and came round to help him.

"Farnham House, Benford Common," said Frenchal.

"Yes, I know, sir." As if everybody in the county didn't know his address by now!

"Wait a moment. Who ordered you?"

"A lady, sir."

"Oh, really! I wonder who. Tall, dark lady with black hair—?"

He was describing Edith Longley. The man shook his head.

"No, sir. She was fairly tall for a lady, but from what I could see of 'er 'air it was fair and goin' a bit grey. I didn't notice what her clothes was like. They wasn't any particular colour."

"Thank you. All right."

Who could it have been? Not Edith, certainly. It was more like—hang it all, it might have served for a description of Mary—Mary dead and in her last resting place. What a strange spark that fellow's words had struck, half ghastly and half humorous. If one believed in ghosts! Faithful and affectionate wife arranges for the comfort of her husband after his trial for having murdered her. Just what Mary might be expected to do if she

73

could! She had always tried to live up to copybook maxims on the subject of forgiveness and returning good for evil.

It was a whimsical thought, but it began to give him discomfort, and he tossed it away. Not that he believed in anything of that sort. He held that dead men and women were as dead as dead dogs. Nor had his conscience given him the least trouble. All he had endured since his arrest was an agony of anxiety regarding his own fate. That anxiety was past now, and into its vacant place came crowding a host of other and smaller cares. His financial condition was a worry. He had been compelled to spend on his defence much more than he could afford. And Edith? How would Edith feel towards him now, when he came back with the stigma of his trial. For he was well aware that he had no more proved his innocence than had the prosecution succeeded in proving his guilt. And—hang it!— who was that woman who'd ordered the car for him immediately after the trial? Hair beginning to turn grey, clothes not any particular colour... Just like Mary; you never noticed her clothes. Why couldn't he get that silly bizarre thought out of his head? He began to sweat again and felt weak.

The car swung out into a broad, lighted thoroughfare and turned south. Frenchal tapped at the glass in front of him and spoke through the tube.

"Drive straight on until six o'clock," he said, "and then stop at the first inn. I want a drink."

Six o'clock found them on a lonely stretch of road, but within a minute or two the lights of Carncross village shone mistily at them out of a hollow, and the driver slowed down and pulled up before an inn which stood a little way back from the road on the outskirts of the hamlet.

Frenchal got out and took a step or two towards the door, only to discover suddenly that he had a shrinking fear of being recognized, and needed the moral support of the driver.

"You'd better come in and have something," he said.

The driver followed him. They entered a brightly-lit tap-room where some half a dozen rustic workers were already assembled. One or two of them made way for Frenchal before the narrow counter, on the other side of which a fat, florid landlord stood polishing glasses.

"A large Three Star brandy," Frenchal muttered, "and—what's yours?—oh, and a pint."

The landlord brought the drinks, and stood for a moment trying to look over the heads of his customers and then craning his neck to right and left.

"Well, that's a rum 'un," he said. "Wasn't there a lady come in with you?"

Frenchal started and spilled some of the spirit.

"No," he said, and almost snarled the word.

"Well, I could have sworn I see a lady follow you in."

"I thought I see one, too," remarked an aged farm-labourer from a far corner. "Must have been shadders."

The landlord laughed uneasily, and delivered himself of the inevitable joke.

"Well, you and I had better take more worter with it, George, 'adn't us? You ain't got an evenin' paper on you, I s'pose, sir?" he added, addressing Frenchal.

"No."

"Ah! I wanted to know 'ow the trial of that there Frenchal's gettin' on. You don't happen to know if it's over?"

"Yes, it's all over." Frenchal tried to speak indifferently. "He got off."

There was a low, growling chorus and then a laugh.

"There, 'Arry!" said a voice. "Wot did I tell yer?"

"I don't care wot you told me," the landlord retorted hotly. "I reckon they didn't ought to 'ang nobody after that!"

"You'd 'ave liked the job of 'anging 'im yerself, 'Arry," chuckled the old labourer in the corner.

"'Anging 'im! I'd like to burn 'im!' Ires this 'ere Sir James Champion to defend 'im. Bin a pore man, 'e'd have swung all right. All I've got to say is, if 'e didn't do it, nobody did."

Frenchal had the wit to perceive that he had not been recognized. His identity was known only to the embarrassed driver, who shuffled beside him awkwardly, sipping his beer. So this was how the Man in the Street regarded him. Well, it was more or less what he had expected. He braced himself, knowing that the driver would have a tale to tell before closing-time that night.

"Possibly," he said coldly, "if you'd attended the trial you might have come to another decision, the same as the jury. After all, my friend, you've only read bits of it in the newspapers."

"I've read quite enough, sir, and nothing won't alter my opinions. You mark my words, there was a lady in that case which nobody knows nothing about. 'Ushed up, somehow, that was. Bin a pore man, now—"

In spite of himself, Frenchal was put out of countenance. A lady in the case! Strange how a stupid, vulgar mind, which did not know how to begin to reason, had stumbled upon the truth! He turned to the driver, trying to smile.

"You ready?" he asked. "Good-night, landlord."

He wanted to snarl an insult at that fool of a publican, and yet felt that he might be grateful for the warning. How closely the eyes of his little village world would watch him now! If he married again too soon, if he saw too much of Edith, the self-appointed critics would draw their own conclusions. He cursed them in thought as he clambered into the car. Let them think and say what they liked; prove what they liked now. Not again could he be tried for his life because of Mary. And yet he knew in his heart that popular opinion mattered much to him, that he could not bear social ostracism. During his time of waiting he had dreamed of a popular acquittal, of people coming out to cheer him as he drove back to his home. He knew already how this dream was to be fulfilled. People knew! He was returning to them, not stainless, but having the benefit of a shadowy doubt.

If only he could get away! But financial ruin already stared him in the face. He had been living beyond his income for years: and the price of his defence had added very materially to the encumbrance on his small property. To sell now would leave him poor indeed. He saw himself tied fast to his little house, the "gentleman's farm," with its memories of Mary and its circle of hostile neighbours.

Nobody except the driver saw his arrival home. The car purred up the short drive, turned in the circle of gravel, and stopped outside his door. He saw a light in the dining-room and the flicker of a fire on the blind. They expected him then!

He got out and tipped the man, handsomely. The man thanked him hoarsely, and shamefacedly wished him luck. "He don't look like a murderer," the driver thought, forgetting that no murderer ever did.

His indoor servants, a married couple named Townsend, both came to welcome him. The door opened as he set foot on the steps, and revealed them standing in the lighted hall. They were both obviously embarrassed, and had spent long hours in discussing how they should receive him if, and when, he returned. They were agreed that it was unnecessary to make any speech of congratulation, and yet they could scarcely behave as if nothing had happened. Their both being in the hall to receive him was a tacit vote of confidence, for they were both loyal believers in his innocence. How could he be a murderer when they had been with him so long and knew him so well?

Frenchal was a little cheered and reassured by the sight of them standing there, with the shy, tremulous smiles on their old faces. Like them, he found it unnecessary to refer to the ordeal through which he had just passed, but he shook hands with them in turn.

"Well, Townsend, how are things?" he asked, trying to assume a bluff heartiness of manner.

"Pretty much as usual, sir. Dick Baines is comin' up early tomorrow mornin' to see you about the stock. Dinner's all ready for you, sir, and Mrs T. have done the chops the way you like 'em."

"Dinner ready! How did you know—"

"We was rung up, sir, just before six, and told as you'd be home about seven."

Frenchal frowned, and, because he was bewildered, his overstrained nerves snapped the thin thread of his temper.

"But hang it, I didn't know that myself, then. The—the—*it* wasn't over until after five. Who rang you up?"

"A lady, sir. She just said that you'd be in for dinner at about seven. Nothing more than that. And then, of course, sir, we knew—"

"What lady was it?"

"I don't know, sir," Townsend faltered. "It gave me rather a turn. I thought it sounded like—"

"Hush, T!" his wife interposed sharply.

She might have added that she, too, had received a "turn," when her husband had rushed to her white-faced and said that the voice he had just heard on the 'phone was so like the old Missus's that he didn't know how to hold the receiver to his ear.

A chill struck Frenchal, accompanied by a sudden spell of giddiness. He knew exactly what Townsend had been about to say, and found himself not daring to ask the man to end the interrupted sentence.

"Oh, somebody who knew me, I expect," he said, with a quaver in his voice. "We shall find out tomorrow, I dare say. Did you say dinner was ready, Mrs Townsend? All right, I shall be ready, too, in a couple of minutes. I'm just going up to wash."

He went upstairs to his dressing-room, where a fire, blazing in the little grate, gave him a welcome with which he would have gladly dispensed. The sight of that fire burning there reminded him of Mary. A fire in his dressing-room was one of Mary's little "attentions," which used to irritate him because they proclaimed her unwanted love. For such he was expected to kiss her and say, "Thank you, darling!" A wave of anger swept over him. What right had Mrs Townsend to light fires without orders? He was a very poor man now; he must make sweeping economies.

He was half-way to the linen cupboard in search of a towel when he glanced back at the hearth and uttered an ugly little choked cry. Just inside the fender were his slippers and pyjamas, and nobody but Mary had ever dreamed of laying them there. Seeing them there made him think that after all she couldn't be dead, that she was in the next room on the other side of that half-open door, preparing for dinner. He who believed in nothing but the plain creed of materialism glanced stealthily and uneasily at that door, and involuntarily his ears listened for once familiar sounds—footfalls, the rhythmic sound of long hair being brushed, the tinkle of hairpins in a china tray.

He went downstairs again, stumbling and cursing. In the kitchen he found Mrs Townsend and rated her wildly. What the devil had she meant by lighting that fire? He couldn't afford fires in his dressing-room. And what the devil did she mean by putting out his pyjamas and slippers like that? When he wanted a valet he'd engage one, he told her.

Mrs Townsend looked startled and abashed.

"I lit the fire because I thought you'd like it, sir," she said. "You often used to have a fire. And I'm sure I didn't touch your pyjamas and slippers, sir! No, that I didn't!"

He turned to Townsend, who had come in in time to overhear.

"Then it was you," he said.

"No, sir. I haven't been upstairs all this evening!"

Frenchal included the pair in a snarl.

"Well, one of you must have done. One of you is lying. I found them there!"

He turned away muttering, trying to shut out from his mind the dreadful thought which now clamoured all the more insistently. Suppose neither of them had put his shoes and pyjamas there to warm? Suppose they had been put there by the same woman who had rung the Townsends up on the telephone and sent the taxi round to the Court House at Hanchester. Suppose it were true, after all, that people had souls which survived their bodies? Suppose Mary still hovered about him, unseen by him as yet, forgiving him for what he had done, still anxious for his comfort, still loving him and angling for his love in the ways which had irritated and nauseated him while she lived?

He grappled with the thought and flung it away. It was too fantastic, too utterly appalling. He told himself that his brain must have been affected to create a fancy so hideous, so utterly unfit for any man's mind. But thoughts, once begotten, bred quickly, and their dreadful freakish offspring over-ran him.

He found himself unwilling to go up to the dressing-room again, and dispensed with washing. Instead, he passed through the gloomy hall into the dining-room. The hall was only dimly lighted, and for him the great, shapeless blots of shadow were the lurking places of other shadows. Now that he had begun to imagine things he could feel Mary's presence. She was watching him sorrowfully, hungrily, always somewhere behind him, and cunningly eluding his gaze whenever he gave way to his sick fancy and swung about, staring this way and that.

The dining-room was more cheerful. It was brightly lit up, and a fire burned cheerfully in a wide, old-fashioned grate. A place was laid for him at the end of the table where he had always sat. Here there was little at first to remind him of Mary, but he noticed, as he was about to sit down, the empty chair at the opposite end. He got up and pushed it back against the wall. He was a sick man, he told himself, his nervous system had been deranged by what he had already endured, and his fancy was likely to play him tricks. Suppose he looked up suddenly at table and saw in that opposite chair—No, he dared not think of it!

With Mary's chair out of its accustomed place he was satisfied for a moment or two. Then, with a curse, he realized that this slight rearrangement of the furniture would not escape the notice of the Townsends. They might even divine the motive which had made him move it, and begin to suspect, and whisper that the master was haunted by his conscience. So he returned the chair to its old place, found himself weak and perspiring, and went to the sideboard for brandy. As he helped himself liberally he was conscious of a Presence which was aware of his misery—although, perhaps, not comprehending the cause—and was nauseatingly sympathetic and trying to caress him.

He thought, quite reasonably, that he was going mad. Never in his cell had he been tormented like this. There he had faced another terror in single combat. He made a supreme effort to reason with himself as he drank the spirit and felt a little of his courage ebbing back. Very soon he would find out who had ordered that taxi for him and rung up the Townsends. All these sick fancies had sprung from the fact that some good-natured busybody had tried to befriend him. And, of course, one of the Townsends had put his slippers and pyjamas in front of the fire upstairs, and afterwards forgotten all about it. They were a pair of fools, and the sooner he got rid of them, the better.

He began to be angry with that perverse imagination of his. If it had to whisper to him that Mary was near him, why couldn't it have been logical and told him that she hated him and wished him dead. He could have endured the imagined presence of a vengeful spirit, but not the spirit of Mary, forgiving and smarmily loving as she had always been. And suppose his imagination went further, learned new tricks? There was no knowing where it was going to stop.

Sooner or later he would have to go to bed, to sleep in that dressing-room which led into another room where, lying in the double-bed, she used to come in and say good-night, bending over him and brushing his face with her long, loose hair. She had never plaited it, and sometimes, after she had washed it, it was dank and sticky. Suppose he were to fancy—Ugh! It did not bear thinking about!

Mrs Townsend brought him in soup, and then a brace of chops. He ate little, and was careful never to raise his eyes to that chair at the other end of the table. He drank unsparingly, keeping to brandy, but it seemed to have no more effect on him than water. Only when one of the Townsends was in the room did he look straight and calmly at that chair at the far end of the table.

Townsend came in after the plates had been removed.

"Some letters for you, sir," he said apologetically. "I'm sorry. I forgot them."

He took the little bundle and turned the envelopes one by one until he came to one addressed to him in a thick, round, feminine hand. As the door closed he tore it open feverishly, and stared out of hot, dry, feverish eyes at Edith's unsigned note.

"In the event of your being acquitted, please do not make any attempt to see me. I wish neither to see you nor speak to you again."

So Edith knew! He realized now that all the time she, of all people, must have known. And this was how she now felt towards him—she for whose sake he had risked everything. He stared at the written words in an agony of frustration, of foiled desire. His heart seemed to rise and swell as if it would choke him. Then terror had him by the throat and he stood rigid in an agony of fear.

High up near the right shoulder he felt on his arm the sympathetic pressure of slim fingers. Somebody, some woman standing behind him, was touching him, fondling him, being sorry for him. It seemed to his stricken senses that the air close to his ear was faintly stirred by a fluttering warmth of breath. This—*this* was no fancy. *She* had touched him like this a score of times when he was angry, when things had gone wrong, when he was disappointed and unhappy.

He could not move nor cry out. He knew that she was there, that, could he turn his head, he would endure the culminating horror of seeing the presence which he already felt. She was being sorry for him, "smarming" him, because his poor heart had been bruised by her rival! He suffered physical besides mental nausea. He stood there in indescribable agony of mind, while his life and reason rocked and reeled on the edge of some fathomless abyss.

At last the hand on his arm relaxed its pressure. He felt himself being softly patted twice. Then he reeled to the sideboard, clutched it, buried his face in his arms and crouched there, moaning.

He had at last to face the dreadful prospect of going to bed, and although he drugged himself with all that was left of the brandy, he walked upstairs as sober as any living man.

The fire in the dressing-room was nearly out, but there was still a glow in the ashes, and he thought of trying to revive it. But a fire sets shadows in motion all about the room, and he could not face the prospect of a wakeful night in such a company. He undressed, with his gaze for ever turning sidelong to the door which led into the room which had once been Mary's.

The electric light switch was by the door, and he kept the light burning when he got into bed. Then it seemed to him, as his courage revived a little, that he might have some chance of sleeping if he turned it out. Besides, in the dark, one might feel and hear; but at least one could not see, and all the man's five senses had become his enemies.

In the dark he returned to bed, thankful for the closed door between him and that other room. But he was hardly in bed for the second time when it opened with the click of a slipping latch, setting his heart jumping and his nerves tingling.

He remembered that this was an old trick of that particular door, and wished that he had remembered to find the key and lock it. He could hardly endure the thought of it standing a few inches ajar, but to get up and close it—no, he could not quite do that. He began to sweat again at the thought of all manner of hideous possibilities which began to jostle like gamins to attract his attention.

For a full hour he lay tossing and turning, hearing the bed creak under him at every turn. It was a noisy spring mattress, and when Mary was alive she always knew when he was wakeful and often came in to ask why he could not sleep. That thought instantly begot another which was unspeakably hideous. He wished he hadn't remembered. He plunged over from his left to his right side, as if to shake himself free of it. The bed creaked—and an answering creak from the bed in the next room brought the sweat from every pore in his body.

He had heard that sound before when Mary was awake. He used to lie still then, lest she should come in to him with her tender inquiries and her irritating nerve-destroying solicitude; but never did he lie as still as he lay now.

Frenchal, rigid as a corpse, scarcely dared to breathe. His pyjamas, sodden with perspiration, clung to him and irritated his skin. He found himself in an attitude quite unendurable, but dared not stir. When at last he moved, it was as if his tortured nerves had rebelled and shifted a leg and elbow. The tell-tale bed creaked, and sharp upon the sound he heard an answering creak from the bed on the other side of the wall.

He was quickly losing control now, and a low moan escaped him, and it was answered by a familiar sound in the next room—the soft, shuddery sound of somebody turning over in bed. Sparks of light now began to dance before the man's eyes, keeping time with the galloping of his heart. He stuffed bedclothes into his mouth and bit into sheet and blanket. He writhed this way and that, and the tell-tale mattress creaked and tinkled.

In the next room a pair of feet thudded softly on the carpet beside the double-bed. Footfalls came softly to the door. The hinges creaked, and the footfalls crossed the threshold. The window fronting Frenchal's bed was a dimly luminous rectangle. For a moment it framed part of a human shape which moved, looming nearer. He closed his eyes. He was far gone now, and capable of no other movement. He heard the sound of breathing drawing nearer, and then, close above him, the soft, dreadful voice he knew so well.

"Can't my darling sleep? Oh, what's the matter with my darling?"

And there fell upon his upturned grimacing face a soft rain of cold, damp tresses.

When Mrs Townsend brought Frenchal's morning tea at eight o'clock, she knocked without being able to make him hear. Presently she walked in and pulled up the blind. Then she turned, looked at the bed, and uttered scream after scream, which brought her husband to her side.

It was a doctor who, speaking in low tones to others in the room, presently drew down the blind again.

THE RUNNING TIDE

WHEN my cousin Anstice was left a widow she had securities to the value of about two thousand pounds and the pension to which her husband's calling entitled her. I don't know how much goes to the widow of an Army captain who has met his death through an illness to which his military duties in no way contributed; but I know it isn't very much. As soon as her affairs had been put in order and explained to her, with great pains and at no small cost, by poor John's lawyers, Anstice began to see the necessity of doing something for herself.

Her intention of going into business was warmly applauded by all the wealthier members of the family who might otherwise have felt morally compelled to "do something." If one has money and poor relations it's very gratifying, I suppose, to see the latter develop a spirit of independence and get down to a job of work. But the difficulty was to find out what she could do and get her started on it, for Anstice, while being a woman of average common sense, had no special aptitude for anything, and knew nothing much about anything except lawn tennis, curry, and some of the Indian stations.

I suppose in the circumstances it was quite natural that she should decide to run a private hotel or boarding-house. Women, when they go into business, love some kind of job in which they can be perpetually turning over ready money. It's a survival of that instinct which, as children, set them playing at keeping shops. Besides, Anstice liked company, and she confided in me her intention of charging such high terms that none but the nicest people would want to come and stay with her.

Most people were doubtful when they heard of her intention to pitch her camp in Lostormel. It was "so far from London, my dear." But I for one was able to perceive the common sense behind the intention.

I dare say most of you know Lostormel, on the south coast of Cornwall? In those days, four years ago, it had just been discovered as a holiday resort, through the faithful who visited it year after year not being able to keep their find to themselves. Anstice had visited the place with John in the August before his last illness, and had fallen in love with it, in spite of having found it overcrowded. There was very little hotel accommodation, every lodging in the town could have been let three times over, and she remembered having said at the time that anybody might make a small fortune by building and running another hotel. There was no doubt that she would have very little difficulty in keeping a full house throughout the summer. And, as she very pertinently said, the farther you got people to travel the longer they stayed.

Having decided on Lostormel, the next thing was to find a suitable house and get settled in it, and here Anstice confessed herself at a loss. She could run her boarding-house once it had got a start, but the preliminaries baffled her. She could drive the engine but didn't know how to get up steam. Somebody must be with her to help and advise her until she was properly settled.

I don't know why everybody at once decided that I was the very person who ought to go and help poor, dear Anstice. I dare say my being a bachelor and having a year's leave at home may have had something to do with it. I was supposed to have no ties, you see, and have nothing to do but indulge a selfish inclination to treat a well-earned holiday as a holiday. However that may be, every uncle and aunt, and every cousin within range of a three-ha'penny letter, seemed suddenly to regard me as a potential authority on boarding-houses.

Anyhow, I took the line of least resistance and went. There were certain uncles and aunts whom it wouldn't have been politic to offend, and, besides, I knew and liked Lostormel. There's some bass fishing there that has to be tried to be believed, although nowadays it isn't what it was. So Anstice and I went down together in the early spring and put up at the "Ship."

For the sake of those who don't know Lostormel, I'd better say at once that it's a typical small Cornish coast town of normally about four thousand inhabitants, cut in two by a river, up and down which the tides pass twice daily with the speed of racing greyhounds. It's a tricky river for visitors who like paddling about in small boats. They're liable to be left suddenly stranded on the mud until the tide turns, or shot out to sea like a pea out of a shooter, according to which way it happens to be flowing; and neither experience is worth having.

The town itself is very nearly as old as the hills which hem it in on all sides except the sea front. It's just like any other small Cornish seaside town—narrow streets, small and crazy-looking lime-washed houses, cobbles, stone steps going up precipitous slopes between one tier of houses and the next, and around everything a kind of atmosphere which gets into your head and is in itself a kind of tonic.

In Lostormel you suddenly realize that England isn't, after all, one huge stinking industrial town, seething with class-hatred and discontent. This *is* England, the real England, you think. For you find big, healthy men who haven't forgotten how to laugh, and all classes of people seem to mix together as naturally and happily as if we were already half-way through the millennium. As you thread your way through the streets you half expect to meet sailors with stocking caps and tarred pig-tails, men from Nelson's fleet, privateersmen, sly-faced smugglers, and even a stray pirate masquerading as Honest Jack.

For Lostormel was once a port of some consequence, but steam brought ruin to the town nearly a hundred years before petrol began to bring summer visitors. In the old days of the Wooden Walls men-of-war had rested in Lostormel harbour and merchantmen from all over the world had unshipped their cargoes on the quay. But with steam came the giant ships, and the little harbour—shallow enough when the tide was in, and mud when it was out—was given over to the fishing fleet.

Anstice and I spent long hours every day on house-hunting, which I soon regarded as a boring and unprofitable sport. Land values were going up and house values with them. All the houses on the market were too big or too small, or in an unsuitable position. Anstice was not easy to please. She wanted what she described as "a darling old-world house with about fourteen rooms, facing the sea," and she wanted it at a price which put lines between the eyebrows of the local estate agents.

When you've given up hunting for a thing you often stumble across it accidentally. Every morning towards midday I used to sneak away from Anstice if I could and go and explore the wonderful old inns which you find in all the elbow-wide streets all over the town. There's a pub to every four adult inhabitants of Lostormel, and every one you go into is more curious than the last. And in the course of my explorations I found the "Queen of India," the interior of which looked like the deserted cuddy of a condemned hulk.

The bar, with its smoke-grimed match-boarding, was deserted on both sides of the counter when I entered it, or so I thought, and I was rapping with some money in the hope of attracting attention, when I was startled to hear a loud and sinister laugh behind me and a sudden rush of words.

"Joe Fox is a dirty old crimp! Yah-hah-hah! Joe Fox is a dirty old crimp!"

There is a fine old seafaring flavour about the word "crimp." I believe it means in the best technical sense a kind of boarding-house keeper who made a practice of doping and selling sailors to masters of ships about to embark. But I believe the term has been applied to other sorts of land-sharks. I started and turned to discover, of course, that the information about Joe Fox had been volunteered by a parrot.

He was a wicked old grey bird whose cage stood on a shelf just above a settle, and as I looked at him he chuckled hugely and began to mark time on his perch. I went over to him, of course, and as I approached he lowered his head to be scratched—and just missed my fingers with a vicious snap. I'd hardly started to curse him when I heard somebody stump into the room and a moment later a red-visaged, wooden-legged landlord, with a face which might have been carved out of teak, was standing beside me and thrusting his fingers through the bars.

"*Gkk*, Nero," he said, and the parrot rubbed its beak against his stubby finger with every evidence of affection.

"What do you think of Joe Fox, Nero?" asked mine host.

"*Joe Fox is a dirty old crimp!*" screamed the parrot. "*Yah-hah-hah! Joe Fox is a dirty old crimp!*"

"And what does Joe Fox live on?" Nero's master inquired.

"*Sailors' blood, blast him, sailors' blood!*"

I laughed.

"How on earth did you teach him that trick?" I asked.

"Me teach him, sir? I've taught him naught. He knew them words in answer to them same questions afore I was born. I've only kep' 'im up to it. I don't know how old Nero is, but he belonged to my grandfather who died in 'fifty-six. I've heard as Nero caught them sayin's off another bird my grandfather used to have what was old when this 'un was young. The two birds used to hang up side by side, and people 'ud come up and ask the old one what he thought of Joe Fox until this 'un got it off as pat as t'other."

"That's interesting," I said. "Who was Mr Joe Fox, and how did he like it?"

Mine host winked at me.

"I reckon Joe Fox was dead before any parrot dared talk about him," he said. "I dunno when he lived, if he ever lived at all, but if he did he left a name behind him which don't smell very sweet to this day. When I was a lad old people used to tell tales about him that they'd heard from their grannies. They say he kept a pub here called 'The Running Tide', back along in the days when he was fighting the French in the daytime and doin' a bit of free-trading with 'em after dark. If all's true, more sailors was seen goin' into his house than was ever seen comin' out. But what with the press-gang comin' ashore here, and little quarrels between smugglers and Customs officers, and accidents bein' always likely to happen, sailor chaps was always disappearin' like."

There it was again—that atmosphere of Nelson's time, and that rather jolly feeling one was always getting in Lostormel that the remote and picturesque past had crept up on to the very heels of yesterday. Mine host himself—I learned that his name was Jack Moggs—might have been a survivor of those splendid but doubtless uncomfortable days.

Well, finding that Jack Moggs was a good talker, and delighting in his society, I helped him to drink some of his own excellent beer; and after a while I asked him where I could find "The Running Tide," for I liked the name of the inn and thought it might be worth a visit.

"Oh, bless your heart," said Moggs, "it ain't a pub now, and ain't been one since I can remember! It stands round the corner on the quay, and they just stores things in it now. Maybe they got the licence transferred to another house, maybe not. But the place 'ad a bad name through Joe Fox, and when the ships from foreign parts stopped comin' in there wasn't much trade for a house standin' there. I'll step along and show you where it is, if you like."

I readily accepted his offer, and he stepped along—or, rather, stumped along—with me. I don't know why, but without seeing the place I had immediately got the impression that it might do for Anstice, but when I saw it the impression gained in strength. It was quite a good-sized house, and although thoroughly dilapidated it stood in an ideal position and had that air of antiquity which most visitors to Cornwall expect and require.

Inside I found a queer assortment of lumber, such as crab-pots, fishing-nets, anchors, small masts, and broken oars. Everything was in an abominable mess, and it would obviously cost a great deal to put the house into a habitable state; but to counterbalance that the price of it was likely to be proportionately low.

I told Anstice about it, and brought her along to see it in the afternoon. She came, saw, and was conquered. She loved its name—she intended continuing to call it "The Running Tide" in the event of her coming to occupy it—and she loved the bit of tradition about Joe Fox. She loved the old oak and teak inside, and she loved her vision of the house when her imagination showed her flattering pictures of what the decorators might be able to do with it. She was sure that it could be transformed into just the place which people would love to come and stay in, and as for Joe Fox—she asked me if it would be untruthful to boast that the house had once belonged to a smuggler or a pirate.

The next step was to find out who was the owner and how much he wanted for it. I managed both for her that very day. The price asked was even less than I had estimated, and a deposit was paid over within the week. I had then to make careful notes of everything Anstice wanted done to the exterior, and to the interior of every room, and to endure long interviews with Mr Ephraim Barbell, the head of a local firm of builders and decorators.

Getting the house habitable was, as I had warned her, a costly job. Anstice was not short of ready money, for one of our uncles had stood guarantor for a pretty long overdraft, and it wasn't easy to get her to listen to any advice about economy. It was such a love of a house, she said, that it deserved to be made perfect. Besides, her contention was that if you intend rooking people for five or six guineas a week, you must give them a nice house to live in. It was a pretty dear place by the time she'd done with it, but I must say that the result almost justified the expenditure.

By the time the summer season had started the furniture was in. She'd given a London firm carte blanche, and they filled it with imitation antique stuff, and the house was ready to receive guests. Two of Anstice's women friends had booked rooms and were due to come on the last week in June.

I thought then that I might safely say my *Nunc dimittis*, so far as Anstice was concerned, but she wouldn't hear of it. I'd been so sweet about everything, and now I must see her venture safely launched, and stay with her for the first few days after Mrs Ianson and Mrs Strode had arrived. We four were to hold a sort of housewarming. And she didn't want me to leave her until we were all sure that everything was running *quite* smoothly.

While the decorators were at work I'd been in and out the house two or three times a day, and I could not help noticing that our activities were creating a good deal of local interest. People came and stood around the house and watched what was going on with the half curious, half sympathetic look of people who have gathered after a street accident. The fishermen seemed specially interested, but they said very little except perhaps among themselves. The Cornish are not famed for being communicative to strangers.

One man, however, with whom I had got into conversation, told me that he didn't think the London lady would like the house. He said under pressure of questions that it was likely to be too noisy for her. Further questions elicited a fact of which I was already aware, namely, that the fishing fleet, which could only enter or leave the harbour when the tide was in, had sometimes to put out and return in the dead of night, and their comings and goings were not attended by deathly silences. But I thought that a minor inconvenience, and one from which other waterside hotels and boarding-houses had to suffer.

On the night before we were due to occupy the house, I went on an errand from Anstice to see that everything was in order. The servants were already installed, and were supposed to be preparing the house for our reception. We had just had the water laid on, and Anstice was fidgety in case it shouldn't be working properly. Besides which, I think she was anxious to find out how the servants were behaving.

We hadn't been able to get local servants, but that hadn't given us to think, for Lostormel shared in the pretty general scarcity. Anstice had engaged four, two girls from Plymouth, and a married couple named Hockley, who were to act as butler and cook respectively, and who had lately been in service in a big house near Liskeard.

The quay was deserted, for the tide was about half out, and the fishing fleet had gone to sea some hours since. It was a dark night, and it must have been after ten o'clock, so that I half expected to find that the servants had gone to bed. However, the way by which I came took me past the kitchen, and I saw both the windows lit up, and heard voices from within. And when I got round to the front of the house I saw that the dining-room window was dimly illumined and that some-body was standing just behind the glass. I went close to look and see who it was.

I'd seen the Hockleys before, and liked them well enough, but I hadn't encountered either of the two maids. Thus, when I stared at the woman who stood looking out of the window, I naturally supposed her to be one of them, and was momentarily staggered by Anstice's choice of servants.

I needn't particularize too much. The woman who stood in the window leering out upon the empty quay was obviously of the coarsest type which abounds everywhere where there are seafaring men. She was dark, and handsome enough after a bold and sullen-seeming fashion, and I saw her plainly enough to remember that she had heavy but plain rings bored through her ears. Seeing me, she gave me a brazen grin and jerked her head back a little, as if inviting me to enter.

This was a little too much. Angry, and yet half laughing at the ghastly mistake for which I imagined Anstice's innocence was responsible, I made quickly for the front door. Enter I did, and quickly, having a key, and I made straight for the dining-room to interview the lady who, it seemed, had been so unfortunate as to try her siren attractions on her mistress's cousin. Rather to my surprise I found the dining-room in darkness, and when I had switched on the electric light, I saw that it was empty. At the same moment, almost, the kitchen door opened, and a gruff voice asked who was there. This was Hockley's, and I called out to reassure him. He came through the passage from the kitchen to meet me in the hall.

"It's all right, Hockley," I said. "I've just come in to have a look round. One of the maids was in here just now—"

He interrupted me quickly, and I noticed that his eyes dilated a little as he spoke.

"No, sir. Not one of the maids. We're all together in the kitchen."

"Then it must have been a friend of one of you. There's no harm in your having friends here so long as they behave—"

Once more he cut me short.

"Was she a big, dark woman with ear-rings, sir?"

"That's right. Who is she! I'm glad to know it isn't one of the maids. Whoever she is, I'm quite sure your mistress wouldn't approve of her being here."

The man eyed me doubtfully.

"She looks like—" he began, and stopped abruptly.

"What our grandmothers would have called a painted hussy," I said with half a laugh.

"Just so, sir. I've seen her myself. But I don't know who she is, or how she got into the house, or how she got out again. We'll go all over the house if you like, sir, but we shan't find her."

I stared hard at him.

"I don't understand you. Somebody must know something about her. Haven't you questioned Mrs Hockley and the maids?"

He dropped his voice almost to a whisper.

"I haven't, sir. They wouldn't stay if they thought what I think. I was meaning to tell you, sir, but for the mistress's sake I daren't tell the others.

We've all had one turn already which I've been trying to explain away. But the house is haunted, sir—I'm sure of that."

You can imagine how annoyed I was. I could foresee poor Anstice's troubles being multiplied by an insoluble servant problem if such a tale were allowed to circulate.

"Oh, nonsense, nonsense, nonsense!" I exclaimed impatiently.

"Very well, sir. Just listen to this. Two or three hours ago, about an hour after high tide, when it was still quite light, we were sitting at supper in the kitchen, and we all of us heard a sort of screaming which sounded in the distance and yet seemed to come from upstairs. We thought a cat might have got into the house and couldn't get out, and I went out into the hall intending to go upstairs and see what it was. However, it wasn't necessary to do that, as I could hear heavy footfalls coming down and the sound of something heavy being dragged across the floor of the landing. They reached the stairs—the footsteps and the dragging noise—and I looked up, and there was nothing there.

"I couldn't believe my eyes, but there it was. I thought I'd gone mad and just stood staring. The sounds came slowly downstairs, passed me where I stood in the hall, and then the door slammed without opening or shutting. I ran to it and opened it. There was nobody on the quay just in front, and yet after a moment came the sound of a big splash as if something heavy had been dropped into the water. It's my belief there's been murder done here, sir."

It was my belief that somebody had been telling him about that possibly mythical character, Joe Fox.

"Well," I said non-committally, "it all sounds very extraordinary. Meanwhile, I think I'll satisfy myself that that woman isn't in the house. I know the front door is locked. Take me round to the back and I'll make sure of that. Then I'll have a look round."

To cut that bit of a long story short, I searched the house thoroughly, but found no trace of that very unpleasant woman I had seen through the window. Hockley, it transpired, had seen her standing in the same place on the previous night. I swore him to secrecy. He was a good chap, as I was soon to discover, with a nerve of iron.

Anstice and I visited the house at about ten on the following morning with the intention of installing ourselves. The two paying guests were due to arrive by the afternoon train. Anstice made straight for the kitchen, and a moment or two afterwards I heard muffled sounds of surprise and lamentation. Then she came hurrying out to me.

"Isn't it a nuisance?" she exclaimed. "Those two wretched girls from Plymouth have run away. They went out early this morning. What are we going to do now?"

I daren't look her in the face.

"Oh," I said, "I expect the Hockleys can carry on for a day or so until you get someone else. I suppose they didn't say why they went?"

"The Hockleys don't seem to know," said Anstice.

Afterwards I interviewed Hockley. He said that they'd had trouble in the night after I'd gone, and that although his wife hadn't seen anything she was getting scared. The two girls had called him up in the night in a state of panic. All he could get out of them was something about "the one-eyed sailor and the man with the knife." They'd caught the first train back to Plymouth.

I didn't believe in ghosts, but I was on the way to conversion. There certainly seemed to be something radically wrong with the house. But still, from a mistaken sense of consideration, I kept my thoughts from Anstice. Mrs Ianson and Mrs Strode duly arrived and we passed quite a happy and peaceful evening. At about half-past eleven I went to bed and slept.

I don't know what time it was when I woke, for I confess that I dared not reach out for my watch on my bedside table. I woke in an extremity of terror, drenched with perspiration, and not in the least knowing the cause of my mental torment. I found myself lying still and listening to the sound of the sea, and it must have been a minute or so before I became aware of another sound which mingled with it—a sound from close at hand and inside the house.

It was really a series of sounds, each one sharp and distinct, but running in a slow rhythm. Of course, one may translate nocturnal sounds to mean all sorts of unpleasant things. These seemed to me as if somebody, quite close at hand, were whetting a large knife with an expert and unpleasant air of thoughtful deliberation. And because I dared not believe *that*, I told myself it couldn't be. With one tremendous effort I got my head under the bedclothes and shut out those unpleasant noises. And after a while I fell asleep again.

It was on the following night that the worst happened. I went out fishing in the latter part of the day and returned in time to dress for early dinner. It was quite light. Anstice came out to meet me in the hall.

"We've had rather a scare," she said. "Some man's been into the house and taken something out. We were all sitting in the drawing-room just now when we distinctly heard a man dragging something downstairs and across the hall. Then the front door banged. I naturally thought it was Hockley who'd gone to throw some rubbish over the quay, and went out in the hall to waylay him when he came back and tell him he must use the back door for that sort of thing. But it seems he was in the kitchen all the time. Whom do you think it could have been?"

I could only shrug my shoulders.

"If nobody's lost anything I shouldn't worry," I said. "I dare say it *was* Hockley, and he remembered himself and returned by way of the back door."

I was still hoping for the best, you see, and trying to keep things from the three women. I don't need to be told now that I was wrong to have done it.

That night I didn't go to sleep at all. At about midnight, when I was just beginning to doze, I was jerked into full consciousness by a terrible and bloodcurdling scream. It was followed by the banging of a door and a rush of feet on the landing. Then came Mrs Ianson's voice, high-pitched and cracking with terror:

"*There's a man with a knife in my room! There's a man with a knife in my room!*"

I sprang out of bed, just as I was, in my pyjamas, and ran out on to the landing. Mrs Ianson stood there in her nightdress, her face a mask of terror, and modesty flung to the four winds of heaven.

"He's looking for someone—a man with a knife!"

Before I could move another scream rang out, this time from Mrs Strode's room.

"*Help, help, help! He's in here! He's in here!*"

I made a rush for Mrs Strode's room, and Mrs Ianson dived into mine. There was nothing in Mrs Strode's room except Mrs Strode herself. She was sitting up in bed gripping handfuls of bedclothes and staring straight before her out of dilated eyes.

"Where is he?" she cried. "Where is he?"

"The man with a knife?" I made myself ask.

"No, no. A sailor. A sailor with a patch over one of his eyes. He was crawling about on the floor in an agony of terror, looking as if he were trying to hide... Oh, don't go! Don't leave me alone! Take me with you!"

That was enough for all of us. We camped out in the drawing-room for the rest of the night, and presently the Hockleys joined us. What had really happened to them I don't know, except that Hockley afterwards told me they'd seen murder done, and Mrs Hockley sobbed and shivered and whimpered all night.

Fortunately it was a very short night, and when light came Anstice and I returned to the hotel at which we had been staying, taking Mrs Ianson and Mrs Strode with us. And later in the day I dismissed the Hockleys, paying them something above their month's wages, which they well deserved. Anstice, who had come off lightest of any of us, wisely decided never to spend another night in that house. Nor did she, and nor did I.

I suppose the explanation's simple enough if one accepts the hypothesis that such things *can* happen. I haven't the least doubt that it was a house to which sailors were once decoyed and afterwards robbed and murdered and their bodies given to the outgoing tide. At least, one of these evil deeds has left an ineradicable impression upon the house. Thus I am sure that I saw the decoy, that Mrs Ianson saw the murderer, and Mrs Strode saw the victim.

Anstice sold the house at only a small loss to a retired naval man, who said he didn't believe in ghosts. She was perfectly frank with him, but he insisted that phenomena of that sort—in which he protested that he didn't believe—would be an additional attraction.

However, I think he believes in ghosts now, for he did not stay very long, nor has the house been inhabited since. It stands empty to this day, save for the crab-pots and nets and masts which have found their way back, and already it is half in ruins again.

THE LITTLE BLUE FLAMES

FERRERS had been looking at the brass candlesticks for some time. Presently he rose, took them from my sitting-room mantelpiece, and held them in his hands appraisingly as if he were trying to guess their weight. He closed his eyes for a moment and frowned.

"Where did you get these?" he asked.

"Oh, I came by them honestly!" I laughed. "I bought them at a second-hand shop. Why?"

"You don't know anything about their history?"

"One doesn't ask for the pedigree of almost worthless second-hand articles. They're of no intrinsic value, a bit battered, and not old enough to be called antiques. But I'm fond of brass, and I happened to like their shape. You apparently don't."

"I don't object to their shape," said Ferrers, "but I don't like them. To me there's something repellent in the sight of them, much more in the touch. They've been connected with something ghastly."

He put them back with a theatrical air of haste and wiped his perfectly clean fingers on his coat.

Ferrers was a very good fellow, but a bit of a crank and, I was sure, more than a bit of a charlatan. We were office mates. Like most cranks he played chess rather well, and although I believed myself to be fairly normal, I, too, played a pretty good game. Thus we often came to visit each other's rooms of an evening.

Ferrers was of the type much beloved of middle-aged, superstitious women. You know those dear ladies who have outgrown a faith which has supported millions during the past two thousand years, but can still believe that their futures can be ascertained by shaking up the dregs in a teacup.

"Dear Mr Ferrers is so clever! He is ever so psychic and susceptible to 'atmospheres,' but not *quite* a clairvoyant, my dear, because he will not develop his wonderful *gift*." Ferrers was taken about and exhibited at quite a lot of tea-parties.

When he was taken to a house three or four hundred years old he generally had some shuddersome things to say about it. A tragedy had happened there. He couldn't say what it was, but there was a sinister atmosphere in one of the rooms. And since nobody could contradict him everybody accepted his word, and was impressed by his remarkable gift.

If on the other hand he went to a house which he knew had been specially built by the happy young married couple who still inhabited it he looked just as wise and discoursed on the benevolence of the atmosphere. Nothing tragic had ever happened there! Clever Mr Ferrers! For those who care to try it this is the simplest way in the world of getting kudos and free meals.

Please note the simplicity of his methods. He had first noticed that my candlesticks were fairly old and rather battered. After that he had ascertained from my own lips that I knew nothing of their history. All then was plain sailing. He "sensed" something sinister about them, and although I might laugh at him I could not disprove his statement.

I did laugh at him.

"I've been lying to you," I said. "Those candlesticks were standing on a table in the room at Holyrood when Rizzio was murdered. Afterwards they came south to England, and provided the light by which Sir Edmondbury Godfrey was murdered. Afterwards they passed into the possession of Thurtell, the murderer of Weir. I forget how many other murders they've been connected with. They seem to *cause* murder. Very likely they will make me murder you. Have a drink, Ferrers."

He smiled at me as a man will when he dismisses a weak joke.

"If I were you," he said, "I should get rid of them—sell them, or give them away, and get another pair."

"What'll you give me for them? They're only worth a shilling or two."

"Oh, I don't want them! I wouldn't live with them for anything!"

"Come off it!" I laughed. "You're not in good psychic form tonight otherwise you wouldn't have lost the game, when you had it well in hand, by letting me take your queen."

"It was those darned things," Ferrers said, pointing to the mantelpiece. "I couldn't keep my mind off them."

"You've met them before," I said mildly. "They've been here for months, but they haven't worried you until tonight."

"I know," he answered. "I don't pretend to understand it. There are no discovered laws about these things. Perhaps it is only at certain seasons of the year that they become repulsive to a sensitive like myself. Probably you're quite safe with them. If you've got a brick instead of a head you can't expect to feel much."

I swallowed the jibe. I could always get my own back on Ferrers, the deluder of old maids who were always having their fortunes told, and were not in the least deterred by the fact that they came out different every time. I mixed him a drink, sat on chatting with him for another quarter of an hour, and then verbally turfed him out by telling him that I was jolly well going to bed.

But quite unconsciously I was affected by Ferrers' words. You know how it is when you meet a man and like him, and then somebody comes and warns you against him, whispering in your ear a word or two of unpleasant scandal. You may not believe it, but you haven't quite the same ease in his company afterwards. So it was with me and my candlesticks. Ferrers had uttered the poisoned word, and for two or three days afterwards I found myself disliking them and nearly following his advice. Then I forgot all about it.

It happened that about three weeks later I shuffled my household goods. Those who live, or have lived, in two rooms understand the deadly monotony of that sort of existence. You get sick of the sight of your small possessions. The best way to overcome that is to move them about—shift the bookcase from one wall to another, turn the table so that its long ends are where its flanks used to be, find new places for the pictures and ornaments.

Thus it happened that the battered, old brass candlesticks came to occupy positions on either side of my bedroom mantelpiece.

My bedroom was on the second floor and the one large window looked out across a street in Bloomsbury on the sooty facade of another house similar to the one in which I lodged. The window was flanked by the inevitable dirty "lace" curtains, looped towards the lower ends and bearing the design of a shepherd boy surrounded by impossible flowers piping to invisible sheep.

My bed pointed straight at this window, the head of it lying flush with the opposite wall. There was a space on either side. The door was at my right hand when I lay on my back. The fireplace and mantelpiece were in the middle of the left-hand wall. Here my candlesticks rested, and on those mornings when the sun happened to be shining I could see the gleam of their brass by looking slightly to my left across the foot of the bed. These details of my bedroom are as necessary as they may be tiresome.

I never had candles in the sticks. I had both gas and electric light, obtainable through little boxes clamped to the floor which were always hungry for shillings at inconvenient moments. The candlesticks were merely articles of decoration and not of utility.

Most nights I went to bed early, but occasionally I went to a theatre and had a late meal afterwards. Late suppers never agreed with me and it was on those nights that I slept worst. It was on the occasion when I had been to see "Journey's End" and taken a hurried meal afterwards—including lobster—that the first and lesser of my two unpleasant experiences befell me.

I want to be quite impartial, stating all the facts, and that is why I confess to the lobster.

I got into bed at about half-past twelve, having first turned out the electric light. The switch was by the door and out of reach from the bed. It was a black night, and while I undressed I heard the steady *whirr* of the expected rain on the road outside and a gurgling and choking of water running into gutters. The window was just a pale rectangle and I could hardly discern any of the bedroom furniture.

The lobster has his own way of taking revenge on mankind. The poor devil is plunged alive into boiling water. He therefore gets his own back on those who eat him. Mine arranged for me many sleepless hours. I kept my eyes resolutely closed, lay on my right side, and waited for sleep in vain. I heard the London clocks striking every quarter of an hour, the sonorous voice of Big Ben deepening or softening his tone at the wind's will. And still the rain droned and pattered outside, and still I could not sleep.

After a long while I turned over and opened my eyes. The best thing, it seemed to me, was to jump out, turn on the light and go and fetch a book. But when I opened my eyes I was astonished to see that a dim light already pervaded the room.

It was not moonlight. Besides, there could be no moon with that drenching downpour still going on. Nor could the light have come from the opposite window across the street, for my own window looked darker than ever.

I was idly curious at first. There was no smell of burning, nothing at which to take alarm. The light was very dim and bluish. Although the window was dark it must surely, I thought, be reflected into the room from outside.

And then I looked straight over at the mantelpiece and gasped.

Flickering just over the tops of my two brass candlesticks were two little blue flames. There were no candles in the sticks: indeed, so far as I knew there was not a candle in the house. These small flames seemed to be feeding on nothing, to have independent lives, to be hovering in the air like little phosphorescent moths. You know when sometimes you light a new candle and it seems uncertain for a few moments if the candle will burn. The little weak flame you see then is just like the flames I stared at from my bed.

To me—since I knew they could not be candle-flames—the oddest thing was that they were poised just above the candlesticks. Of course, it was a reflection, some sort of optical illusion, and the obvious step to take was to jump out of bed and walk across to take a closer view. It was only when I moved a leg, preparatory to doing so, that I found myself powerless. Fear leaped upon me like a wild beast out of a thicket. It was an inexplicable panic terror of which I was afterwards thoroughly ashamed, but which at the time I was powerless to combat.

In the midst of this sudden wild and galloping brain-storm I remembered what Ferrers had said about the candlesticks. There was something sinister and uncanny about them. And I knew with a certainty—which had grown, like my dread, out of nothing—that if I lay and watched I should see something unbearable. I did what I had so often done as a little frightened child when I woke in the night and thought I heard some strange noise in the dark. I plunged down into the bed and drew the clothes right over me.

I lay in mental torture for a period which threatened eternity. Once I thought I heard a scuffling in the room close to the foot of my bed. Then I suppose I must have fallen asleep, for I returned to consciousness when I heard a teacup rattling in its saucer close to my ear and the familiar friendly sound of my landlady's voice.

"Oh, Mr Roberts! Fancy! It's a wonder you didn't die of suffocation."

It was a man with a headache and very little pride who got out of bed a few minutes later. What was I to think? Had any other man told me the experience which I have just described I should have laughed at him. I should have said: "This charlatan Ferrers tells you some rot about those candlesticks, and eventually you get a bad dream about them after a lobster supper." It was the feasible and only reasonable explanation, but such explanations, while they're always applicable to the other fellow, are no good to ourselves. Because it had happened to me, I couldn't convince myself that it was a dream.

I carried the memory of it all day like a burden, but the burden lightened as the day drew on. My work in the office lightened it, for one cannot concentrate one's mind on two things at once. By the evening I had decided that my last night's experience was just "queer," but capable of some absurdly simple explanation. My sudden terror was induced by the memory of what Ferrers had said.

That evening I went round to Ferrers' rooms to play chess, but I said nothing to him about the previous night. It would have been a score for him, and also it might have tempted him to enlarge on the subject to such an extent as to give me another beastly dream. I returned to my rooms at about midnight, entered my bedroom, and, walking about while I took off my collar and tie, I suddenly found myself confronting the two brass candlesticks.

The obvious thing to do, to insure against a recurrence of what had happened last night, was to dump them in the sitting-room. I had almost seized one of them, when I drew back. That would be cowardly. I had not yet recovered from the shame of my last night's fear, and I knew that the way to breed terror was to make concessions to it. What I had seen last night was capable of some simple explanation, and my fear had bubbled out of my subconscious mind for reasons already stated. Here was I, sane and sound and healthy, and what had I to fear from a pair of brass candlesticks?

Put them back in my sitting-room? Certainly not! They must stay in my bedroom and I must teach myself that what I dreamed or imagined last night was nonsense. It was that idiot Ferrers who dropped the germ into my mind. Let all his bogies come and do their worst—if they existed.

Eventually I switched off the electric light, jumped into bed, and was soon asleep.

I don't know what woke me, but when I did wake the room was once more illumined. I did not at once think about the candlesticks, for I had all the hazy feelings of one who becomes half-awake in a strange room. I began to ask myself where on earth I could be.

To begin with, the door was in the wrong place. It should have been at the end of the wall close to my right hand. Now it was diagonally opposite, set in the far corner of the left-hand wall and close to the window. It was standing wide open, so wide that it formed an acute angle with the wall. This was very odd!

Another odd thing was a change which had taken place in the window. It used to be high and narrow, now it was long and low. It used to be flanked by not too clean lace curtains. Now it wore a veil of pink-muslin, hanging down from brass rings along a curtain pole at the top.

Between my bed-rail and the window there was a table, laid for a meal. A woman stood with her back to me and seemed to be preparing food. She was poorly dressed and after a fashion which died before I was born. She wore a blouse, and a belt around her waist, and the hem of the blouse lay around her hips like a soldier's tunic.

My gaze travelled to the fireplace. It had become an open hearth with a log fire burning on it and a kettle stood suspended from a chain. On the high mantel stood several tawdry cottage ornaments—and my two brass candlesticks. There were candles in them now, burning faint and blue, but they brightened even as I watched, and these, together with the firelight, illumined the room.

*

I stirred, mystified, but as yet not fully awake. How had I got to bed in some country cottage? Where was I, anyhow? Yet the bed was familiar, indeed the bed was mine. And those candlesticks—

Then I began to remember. I had certainly gone to bed in my own room. Had I not been playing chess with Ferrers? Then what had happened, and who was this woman, and how had the room beyond my bedrail become so changed.

I knew that I was not dreaming. In dreams one loses all one's critical faculty. The most impossible and incredible things happen without causing the least surprise. But my critical faculty was not lost. It was arguing passionately against the evidence of my senses. Still, I must own that when I tried to speak I found that I had no voice.

And then fear leaped upon me again. I knew that something unspeakable was about to happen. Some remorseless Power had decreed that this time I was to endure the whole horror of it, and my gaze was forced in the direction of the open door.

The door had thrown a black shadow on the wall, and in this dark angle I was aware of something crouching. I saw the gleam of a long knife, and once more I tried to cry out, to move, to do something to warn that woman whose back was towards me; but only a convulsion seized me, and the sweat poured from me.

I seemed to know already what must happen. The woman was not preparing the meal for herself. When all was ready she would blow out those candles, preparatory to retiring for the night. And then—oh, I knew what was going to happen then.

There was something particularly ghastly to me in the leisured movements of the woman. I wanted to shriek out to her, like a yokel at a melodrama who sees the villain about to pounce on the heroine. But could I have shrieked I knew that it would make no difference, for the tragedy I was watching did not belong to the present. It had all happened so very long ago.

Presently she stood upright and, still half turned from me, moved across to the fireplace. I never saw her face. She picked up each candle in turn and out it went, and now the room was lit only by the flickering blood-red glow of the fire.

I heard the door swing and close with a crash. Something leaped from behind it into the firelight. There was a scream and a snarl and a mad mingling and leaping of shadows. Then I fainted.

When I awoke in the morning my room was normal, and the brass candlesticks beamed innocently at me in the pallid sunlight of a half-hearted dawn.

Of course, I told Ferrers about it. He affected to understand these things, and I began to think that he was not such a charlatan after all. He began by making that particularly irritating remark:

"I told you so."

"But what do you make of it?" I asked.

"I know as much as you do," he replied, "and I doubt if either of us will ever know any more. You're not likely to find out much about a cottage tragedy of the 'seventies or 'eighties. Such things were common enough and always will be.

"Influences sometimes cling to rooms, houses, country lanes, areas of open space; sometimes they cling to inanimate objects. I told you I didn't like your candlesticks. I should get rid of them if I were you."

"I have," I told him promptly.

"What have you done with them?" he asked.

"Chucked them into the dust-bin, and I didn't like even carrying them downstairs in broad daylight."

"You should have slung them into the river," Ferrers said.

Well, they've gone now, and I hope they were destroyed. But if the dustmen picked them out and sold them, I am afraid that there is a chance that somebody else may have a very uncomfortable time.

PLAYMATES

ALTHOUGH everybody who knew Stephen Everton agreed that he was the last man under Heaven who ought to have been allowed to bring up a child, it was fortunate for Monica that she fell into his hands; else she had probably starved or drifted into some refuge for waifs and strays. True her father, Sebastian Threlfall the poet, had plenty of casual friends. Almost everybody knew him slightly, and right up to the time of his final attack of *delirium tremens* he contrived to look one of the most interesting of the regular frequenters of the Café Royal. But people are generally not hasty to bring up the children of casual acquaintances, particularly when such children may be suspected of having inherited more than a fair share of human weaknesses.

Of Monica's mother literally nothing was known. Nobody seemed able to say if she were dead or alive. Probably she had long since deserted Threlfall for some consort able and willing to provide regular meals.

Everton knew Threlfall no better than a hundred others knew him, and was ignorant of the daughter's existence until the father's death was a new topic of conversation in literary and artistic circles. People vaguely wondered what would become of "the kid"; and while they were still wondering, Everton quietly took possession of her.

Who's Who will tell you the year of Everton's birth, the names of his *Almæ Matres* (Winchester and Magdalen College, Oxford), the titles of his books and of his predilections for skating and mountaineering; but it is necessary to know the man a little less superficially. He was then a year or two short of fifty and looked ten years older. He was a tall, lean man, with a delicate pink complexion, an oval head, a Roman nose, blue eyes which looked out mildly through strong glasses, and thin straight lips drawn tightly over slightly protruding teeth. His high forehead was bare, for he was bald to the base of his skull. What remained of his hair was a neutral tint between black and grey, and was kept closely cropped. He contrived to look at once prim and irascible, scholarly and acute; Sherlock Holmes, perhaps, with a touch of old-maidishness.

The world knew him for a writer of books on historical crises. They were cumbersome books with cumbersome titles, written by a scholar for scholars. They brought him fame and not a little money. The money he could have afforded to be without, since he was modestly wealthy by inheritance. He was essentially a cold-blooded animal, a bachelor, a man of regular and temperate habits, fastidious, and fond of quietude and simple comforts.

Nobody is ever likely to know why Everton adopted the orphan daughter of a man whom he knew but slightly and neither liked nor respected. He was no lover of children, and his humours were sardonic rather than sentimental. I am only hazarding a guess when I suggest that, like so many childless men, he had theories of his own concerning the upbringing of children, which he wanted to see tested. Certain it is that Monica's childhood, which had been extraordinary enough before, passed from the tragic to the grotesque.

Everton took Monica from the Bloomsbury "apartments" house, where the landlady, already nursing a bad debt, was wondering how to dispose of the child. Monica was then eight years old, and a woman of the world in her small way. She had lived with drink and poverty and squalor; had never played a game nor had a playmate; had seen nothing but the seamy side of life; and had learned skill in practising her father's petty shifts and mean contrivances. She was grave and sullen and plain and pale, this child who had never known childhood. When she spoke, which was as seldom as possible, her voice was hard and gruff. She was, poor little thing, as unattractive as her life could have made her.

She went with Everton without question or demur. She would no more have questioned anybody's ownership than if she had been an inanimate piece of luggage left in a cloak-room. She had belonged to her father. Now that he was gone to his own place she was the property of whomsoever chose to claim her. Everton took her with a cold kindness in which was neither love nor pity; in return she gave him neither love nor gratitude, but did as she was desired after the manner of a paid servant.

Everton disliked modern children, and for what he disliked in them he blamed modern schools. It may have been on this account that he did not send Monica to one; or perhaps he wanted to see how a child would contrive its own education. Monica could already read and write and, thus equipped, she had the run of his large library, in which was almost every conceivable kind of book from heavy tomes on abstruse subjects to trashy modern novels bought and left there by Miss Gribbin. Everton barred nothing, recommended nothing, but watched the tree grow naturally, untended and unpruned.

Miss Gribbin was Everton's secretary. She was the kind of hatchet-faced, flat-chested, middle-aged sexless woman who could safely share the home of a bachelor without either of them being troubled by the tongue of Scandal. To her duties was now added the instruction of Monica in certain elementary subjects. Thus Monica learned that a man named William the Conqueror arrived in England in 1066; but to find out what manner of man this William was, she had to go to the library and read the conflicting accounts of him as given by the several historians. From Miss Gribbin she learned bare irrefutable facts; for the rest she was left to fend for herself. In the library she found herself surrounded by all the realms of reality and fancy, each with its door invitingly ajar.

Monica was fond of reading. It was, indeed, almost her only recreation, for Everton knew no other children of her age, and treated her as a grown-up member of the household. Thus she read everything from translations of the *Iliad* to Hans Andersen, from the Bible to the love-gush of the modern female fiction-mongers.

Everton, although he watched her closely, and plied her with innocent-sounding questions, was never allowed a peep into her mind. What muddled dreams she may have had of a strange world surrounding the Hampstead house—a world of gods and fairies and demons, and strong silent men making love to sloppy-minded young women—she kept to herself. Reticence was all that she had in common with normal childhood, and Everton noticed that she never played.

Unlike most young animals, she did not take naturally to playing. Perhaps the instinct had been beaten out of her by the realities of life while her father was alive. Most lonely children improvise their own games and provide themselves with a vast store of make-believe. But Monica, as sullen-seeming as a caged animal, devoid alike of the naughtiness and the charms of childhood, rarely crying and still more rarely laughing, moved about the house sedate to the verge of being wooden. Occasionally Everton, the experimentalist, had twinges of conscience and grew half afraid...

II

When Monica was twelve Everton moved his establishment from Hampstead to a house remotely situated in the middle of Suffolk, which was part of a recent legacy. It was a tall, rectangular, Queen Anne house standing on a knoll above marshy fields and wind-bowed beech woods. Once it had been the manor house, but now little land went with it. A short drive passed between rank evergreens from the heavy wrought-iron gate to a circle of grass and flower beds in front of the house. Behind was an acre and a half of rank garden, given over to weeds and marigolds. The rooms were high and well lighted, but the house wore an air of depression as if it were a live thing unable to shake off some ancient fit of melancholy.

Everton went to live in the house for a variety of reasons. For the most part of a year he had been trying in vain to let or sell it, and it was when he found that he would have no difficulty in disposing of his house at Hampstead that he made up his mind. The old house, a mile distant from a remote Suffolk village, would give him all the solitude he required. Moreover he was anxious about his health—his nervous system had never been strong—and his doctor had recommended the bracing air of East Anglia.

He was not in the least concerned to find that the house was too big for him. His furniture filled the same number of rooms as it had filled at Hampstead, and the others he left empty. Nor did he increase his staff of three indoor servants and a gardener. Miss Gribbin, now less dispensable than ever, accompanied him; and with them came Monica to see another aspect of life, with the same wooden stoicism which Everton had remarked in her on the occasion of their first meeting.

As regarded Monica, Miss Gribbin's duties were then becoming more and more a sinecure. "Lessons" now occupied no more than half-an-hour a day. The older Monica grew, the better she was able to grub for her education in the great library. Between Monica and Miss Gribbin there was neither love nor sympathy, nor was there any affectation of either. In their common duty to Everton they owed and paid certain duties to each other. Their intercourse began and ended there.

Everton and Miss Gribbin both liked the house at first. It suited the two temperaments which were alike in their lack of festivity. Asked if she too liked it, Monica said simply "Yes," in a tone which implied stolid and complete indifference.

All three in their several ways led much the same lives as they had led at Hampstead. But a slow change began to work in Monica, a change so slight and subtle that weeks passed before Everton or Miss Gribbin noticed it. It was late on an afternoon in early spring when Everton first became aware of something unusual in Monica's demeanour.

He had been searching in the library for one of his own books—*The Fall of the Commonwealth in England*—and having failed to find it went in search of Miss Gribbin and met Monica instead at the foot of the long oak staircase. Of her he casually inquired about the book, and she jerked her head up brightly, to answer him with an unwonted smile:

"Yes, I've been reading it. I expect I left it in the schoolroom. I'll go and see."

It was a long speech for her to have uttered, but Everton scarcely noticed that at the time. His attention was directed elsewhere.

"*Where* did you leave it?" he demanded.

"In the schoolroom," she repeated.

"I know of no schoolroom," said Everton coldly. He hated to hear anything mis-called, even were it only a room. "Miss Gribbin generally takes you for your lessons in either the library or the dining-room. If it is one of those rooms, kindly call it by its proper name."

Monica shook her head.

"No, I mean the schoolroom—the big empty room next to the library. That's what it's called." Everton knew the room. It faced north, and seemed darker and more dismal than any other room in the house. He had wondered idly why Monica chose to spend so much of her time in a room bare of furniture, with nothing better to sit on than uncovered boards or a cushionless window-seat; and put it down to her genius for being unlike anybody else.

"Who calls it that?" he demanded.

"It's its *name*," said Monica, smiling.

She ran upstairs and presently returned with the book, which she handed to him with another smile. He was already wondering at her.

It was surprising and pleasant to see her run, instead of the heavy and clumsy walk which generally moved her when she went to obey a behest. And she had smiled two or three times in the short space of a minute. Then he realized that for some little while she had been a brighter, happier creature than ever she had been at Hampstead.

"How did you come to call that room the schoolroom?" he asked, as he took the book from her hand.

"It *is* the schoolroom," she insisted, seeking to cover her evasion by laying stress on the verb.

That was all he could get out of her. As he questioned further the smiles ceased and the pale, plain little face became devoid of any expression. He knew then that it was useless to press her, but his curiosity was aroused. He inquired of Miss Gribbin and the servants, and learned that nobody was in the habit of calling the long, empty apartment the schoolroom.

Clearly Monica had given it its name. But why? She was so altogether remote from schools and schoolrooms. Some germ of imagination was active in her small mind. Everton's interest was stimulated. He was like a doctor who remarks in a patient some abnormal symptom.

"Monica seems a lot brighter and more alert than she used to be," he remarked to Miss Gribbin.

"Yes," agreed the secretary, "I have noticed that. She is learning to play."

"To play what? The piano?"

"No, no. To play childish games. Haven't you heard her dancing about and singing?" Everton shook his head and looked interested.

"I have not," he said. "Possibly my presence acts as a check upon her—er—exuberance."

"I hear her in that empty room which she insists upon calling the schoolroom. She stops when she hears my step. Of course, I have not interfered with her in any way, but I could wish that she would not talk to herself. I don't like people who do that. It is somehow—uncomfortable."

"I didn't know she did," said Everton slowly.

"Oh, yes, quite long conversations. I haven't actually heard what she talks about, but sometimes you would think that she was in the midst of a circle of friends."

"In that same room?"

"Generally," said Miss Gribbin, with a nod.

Everton regarded his secretary with a slow, thoughtful smile.

"Development," he said, "is always extremely interesting. I am glad the place seems to suit Monica. I think it suits all of us."

There was a doubtful note in his voice as he uttered the last words, and Miss Gribbin agreed with him with the same lack of conviction in her tone. As a fact, Everton had been doubtful of late if his health had been benefited by the move from Hampstead. For the first week or two his nerves had been the better for the change of air; but now he was conscious of the beginning of a relapse. His imagination was beginning to play him tricks, filling his mind with vague, distorted fancies. Sometimes when he sat up late, writing—he was given to working at night on strong coffee—he became a victim of the most distressing nervous symptoms, hard to analyse and impossible to combat, which invariably drove him to bed with a sense of defeat.

That same night he suffered one of the variations of this common experience.

It was close upon midnight when he felt stealing over him a sense of discomfort which he was compelled to classify as fear. He was working in a small room leading out of the drawing-room which he had selected for his study. At first he was scarcely aware of the sensation. The effect was always cumulative; the burden was laid upon him straw by straw.

It began with his being oppressed by the silence of the house. He became more and more acutely conscious of it, until it became like a thing tangible, a prison of solid walls growing around him.

The scratching of his pen at first relieved the tension. He wrote words and erased them again for the sake of that comfortable sound. But presently that comfort was denied him, for it seemed to him that this minute and busy noise was attracting attention to himself. Yes, that was it. He was being watched.

Everton sat quite still, the pen poised an inch above the half-covered sheet of paper. This had become a familiar sensation. He was being watched. And by what? And from what corner of the room?

He forced a tremulous smile to his lips. One moment he called himself ridiculous; the next, he asked himself hopelessly how a man could argue with his nerves. Experience had taught him that the only cure—and that a temporary one—was to go to bed. Yet he sat on, anxious to learn more about himself, to coax his vague imaginings into some definite shape.

Imagination told him that he was being watched, and although he called it imagination he was afraid. That rapid beating against his ribs was his heart, warning him of fear. But he sat rigid, anxious to learn in what part of the room his fancy would place these imaginary "watchers"—for he was conscious of the gaze of more than one pair of eyes being bent upon him.

At first the experiment failed. The rigidity of his pose, the hold he was keeping upon himself, acted as a brake upon his mind. Presently he realized this and relaxed the tension, striving to give his mind that perfect freedom which might have been demanded by a hypnotist or one experimenting in telepathy.

Almost at once he thought of the door. The eyes of his mind veered around in that direction as the needle of a compass veers to the magnetic north. With these eyes of his imagination he saw the door. It was standing half open, and the aperture was thronged with faces. What kind of faces he could not tell. They were just faces; imagination left it at that. But he was aware that these spies were timid; that they were in some wise as fearful of him as he was of them; that to scatter them he had but to turn his head and gaze at them with the eyes of his body.

The door was at his shoulder. He turned his head suddenly and gave it one swift glance out of the tail of his eye.

However imagination deceived him, it had not played him false about the door. It was standing half open although he could have sworn that he had closed it on entering the room. The aperture was empty. Only darkness, solid as a pillar, filled the space between floor and lintel. But although he saw nothing as he turned his head, he was dimly conscious of something vanishing, a scurrying noiseless and incredibly swift, like the flitting of trout in clear, shallow water.

Everton stood up, stretched himself, and brought his knuckles up to his strained eyes. He told himself that he must go to bed. It was bad enough that he must suffer these nervous attacks; to encourage them was madness.

But as he mounted the stairs he was still conscious of not being alone. Shy, timorous, ready to melt into the shadows of the walls if he turned his head, *They* were following him, whispering noiselessly, linking hands and arms, watching him with the fearful, awed curiosity of—Children.

III

The Vicar had called upon Everton. His name was Parslow, and he was a typical country parson of the poorer sort, a tall, rugged, shabby, worried man in the middle forties, obviously embarrassed by the eternal problem of making ends meet on an inadequate stipend.

Everton received him courteously enough, but with a certain coldness which implied that he had nothing in common with his visitor. Parslow was evidently disappointed because "the new people" were not church-goers nor likely to take much interest in the parish. The two men made half-hearted and vain attempts to find common ground. It was not until he was on the point of leaving that the Vicar mentioned Monica.

"You have, I believe, a little girl?" he said.

"Yes. My small ward."

"Ah! I expect she finds it lonely here. I have a little girl of the same age. She is at present away at school, but she will be home soon for the Easter holidays. I know she would be delighted if your little—er—ward would come down to the Vicarage and play with her sometimes."

The suggestion was not particularly welcome to Everton, and his thanks were perfunctory. This other small girl, although she was a vicar's daughter, might carry the contagion of other modern children and infect Monica with the pertness and slanginess which he so detested. Altogether he was determined to have as little to do with the Vicarage as possible.

Meanwhile the child was becoming to him a study of more and more absorbing interest. The change in her was almost as marked as if she had just returned after having spent a term at school. She astonished and mystified him by using expressions which she could scarcely have learned from any member of the household. It was not the jargon of the smart young people of the day which slipped easily from her lips, but the polite family slang of his own youth. For instance, she remarked one morning that Mead, the gardener, was a whale at pruning vines.

A whale! The expression took Everton back a very long way down the level road of the spent years; took him, indeed, to a nursery in a solid respectable house in a Belgravian square, where he had heard the word used in that same sense for the first time. His sister Gertrude, aged ten, notorious in those days for picking up loose expressions, announced that she was getting to be a whale at French. Yes, in those days an expert was a "whale" or a "don"; not, as he is today, a "stout fellow." But who was a "whale" nowadays? It was years since he had heard the term.

"Where did you learn to say that?" he demanded in so strange a tone that Monica stared at him anxiously.

"Isn't it right?" she asked eagerly. She might have been a child at a new school, fearful of not having acquired the fashionable phraseology of the place.

"It is a slang expression," said the purist coldly. "It used to mean a person who was proficient in something. How did you come to hear it?"

She smiled without answering, and her smile was mysterious, even coquettish after a childish fashion. Silence had always been her refuge, but it was no longer a sullen silence. She was changing rapidly, and in a manner to bewilder her guardian. He failed in an effort to cross-examine her, and, later in the day, consulted Miss Gribbin.

"That child," he said, "is reading something that we know nothing about."

"Just at present," said Miss Gribbin, "she is glued to Dickens and Stevenson."

"Then where on earth does she get her expressions?"

"I don't know," the secretary retorted testily, "any more than I know how she learned to play Cat's Cradle."

"What? That game with string? Does she play that?"

"I found her doing something quite complicated and elaborate the other day. She wouldn't tell me how she learned to do it. I took the trouble to question the servants, but none of them had shown her."

Everton frowned.

"And I know of no book in the library which tells how to perform tricks with string. Do you think she has made a clandestine friendship with any of the village children?"

Miss Gribbin shook her head.

"She is too fastidious for that. Besides, she seldom goes into the village alone."

There, for the time, the discussion ended. Everton, with all the curiosity of the student, watched the child as carefully and closely as he was able without at the same time arousing her suspicions. She was developing fast. He had known that she must develop, but the manner of her doing so amazed and mystified him, and, likely as not, denied some preconceived theory. The untended plant was not only growing but showed signs of pruning. It was as if there were outside influences at work on Monica which could have come neither from him nor from any other member of the household.

Winter was dying hard, and dark days of rain kept Miss Gribbin, Monica and Everton within doors. He lacked no opportunities of keeping the child under observation, and once, on a gloomy afternoon, passing the room which she had named the schoolroom, he paused and listened until he became suddenly aware that his conduct bore an unpleasant resemblance to eavesdropping. The psychologist and the gentleman engaged in a brief struggle in which the gentleman temporarily got the upper hand. Everton approached the door with a heavy step and flung it open.

The sensation he received, as he pushed open the door, was vague but slightly disturbing, and it was by no means new to him. Several times of late, but generally after dark, he had entered an empty room with the impression that it had been occupied by others until the very moment of his crossing the threshold. His coming disturbed not merely one or two, but a crowd. He felt rather than heard them scattering, flying swiftly and silently as shadows to incredible hiding-places, where they held breath and watched and waited for him to go. Into the same atmosphere of tension he now walked, and looked about him as if expecting to see more than only the child who held the floor in the middle of the room, or some tell-tale trace of other children in hiding. Had the room been furnished he must have looked involuntarily for shoes protruding from under tables or settees, for ends of garments unconsciously left exposed.

The long room, however, was empty save for Monica from wainscot to wainscot and from floor to ceiling. Fronting him were the long high windows starred by fine rain. With her back to the white filtered light Monica faced him, looking up to him as he entered. He was just in time to see a smile fading from her lips. He also saw by a slight convulsive movement of her shoulders that she was hiding something from him in the hands clasped behind her back.

"Hullo," he said, with a kind of forced geniality, "what are you up to?"

She said: "Nothing," but not as sullenly as she would once have said it.

"Come," said Everton, "that is impossible. You were talking to yourself, Monica. You should not do that. It is an idle and a very, very foolish habit. You will go mad if you continue to do that."

She let her head droop a little.

"I wasn't talking to myself," she said in a low, half playful but very deliberate tone.

"That's nonsense. I heard you."

"I wasn't talking to myself."

"But you must have been. There is nobody else here."

"There isn't—now."

"What do you mean? Now?"

"They've gone. You frightened them, I expect."

"What do you mean?" he repeated, advancing a step or two towards her. "And whom do you call 'they'?"

Next moment he was angry with himself. His tone was so heavy and serious and the child was half laughing at him. It was as if she were triumphant at having inveigled him into taking a serious part in her own game of make-believe.

"You wouldn't understand," she said.

"I understand this—that you are wasting your time and being a very silly little girl. What's that you're hiding behind your back?"

She held out her right hand at once, unclenched her fingers and disclosed a thimble. He looked at it and then into her face.

"Why did you hide that from me?" he asked. "There was no need."

She gave him her faint secretive smile—that new smile of hers—before replying.

"We were playing with it. I didn't want you to know."

"*You* were playing with it, you mean. And why didn't you want me to know?"

"About them. Because I thought you wouldn't understand. You *don't* understand."

He saw that it was useless to affect anger or show impatience. He spoke to her gently, even with an attempt at displaying sympathy.

"Who are 'they'?" he asked.

"They're just them. Other girls."

"I see. And they come and play with you, do they? And they run away whenever I'm about, because they don't like me. Is that it?"

She shook her head.

"It isn't that they don't like you. I think they like everybody. But they're so shy. They were shy of me for a long, long time. I knew they were there, but it was weeks and weeks before they'd come and play with me. It was weeks before I even saw them."

"Yes? Well, what are they like?"

"Oh, they're just girls. And they're awfully, awfully nice. Some are a bit older than me and some are a bit younger. And they don't dress like other girls you see today. They're in white with longer skirts and they wear sashes."

Everton inclined his head gravely. "She got that out of the illustrations of books in the library," he reflected.

"You don't happen to know their names, I suppose?" he asked, hoping that no quizzical note in his voice rang through the casual but sincere tone which he intended.

"Oh, yes. There's Mary Hewitt—I think I love her best of all—and Elsie Power, and—"

"How many of them altogether?"

"Seven. It's just a nice number. And this is the schoolroom where we play games. I love games. I wish I'd learned to play games before."

"And you've been playing with the thimble?"

"Yes. Hunt-the-thimble they call it. One of us hides it, and then the rest of us try to find it, and the one who finds it hides it again."

"You mean you hide it yourself, and then go and find it."

The smile left her face at once, and the look in her eyes warned him that she was done with confidences.

"Ah!" she exclaimed. "You don't understand after all. I somehow knew you wouldn't."

Everton, however, thought he did. His face wore a sudden smile of relief.

"Well, never mind," he said. "But I shouldn't play too much if I were you."

With that he left her. But curiosity tempted him, not in vain, to linger and listen for a moment on the other side of the door which he had closed behind him. He heard Monica whisper:

"Mary! Elsie! Come on. It's all right. He's gone now."

At an answering whisper, very unlike Monica's, he started violently and then found himself grinning at his own discomfiture. It was natural that Monica playing many parts, should try to change her voice with every character. He went downstairs sunk in a brown study which brought him to certain interesting conclusions. A little later he communicated these to Miss Gribbin.

"I've discovered the cause of the change in Monica. She's invented for herself some imaginary friends—other little girls, of course."

Miss Gribbin started slightly and looked up from the newspaper which she had been reading.

"Really?" she exclaimed. "Isn't that rather an unhealthy sign?"

"No, I should say not. Having imaginary friends is quite a common symptom of childhood, especially among young girls. I remember my sister used to have one, and was very angry when none of the rest of us would take the matter seriously. In Monica's case I should say it was perfectly normal—normal, but interesting. She must have inherited an imagination from that father of hers, with the result that she has seven imaginary friends, all properly named, if you please. You see, being lonely, and having no friends of her own age, she would naturally invent more than one 'friend'. They are all nicely and primly dressed, I must tell you, out of Victorian books which she has found in the library."

"It can't be healthy," said Miss Gribbin, pursing her lips. "And I can't understand how she has learned certain expressions and a certain style of talking and games—"

"All out of books. And pretends to herself that 'they' have taught her. But the most interesting part of the affair is this: it's given me my first practical experience of telepathy, of the existence of which I had hitherto been rather sceptical. Since Monica invented this new game, and before I was aware that she had done so, I have had at different times distinct impressions of there being a lot of little girls about the house."

Miss Gribbin started and stared. Her lips parted as if she were about to speak, but it was as if she had changed her mind while framing the first word she had been about to utter.

"Monica," he continued smiling, "invented these 'friends', and has been making me telepathically aware of them, too. I have lately been most concerned about the state of my nerves."

Miss Gribbin jumped up as if in anger, but her brow was smooth and her mouth dropped at the corners.

"Mr Everton," she said, "I wish you had not told me all this." Her lips worked. "You see," she added unsteadily, "I don't believe in telepathy."

IV

Easter, which fell early that year, brought little Gladys Parslow home for the holidays to the Vicarage. The event was shortly afterwards signalized by a note from the vicar to Everton, inviting him to send Monica down to have tea and play games with his little daughter on the following Wednesday.

The invitation was an annoyance and an embarrassment to Everton. Here was the disturbing factor, the outside influence, which might possibly thwart his experiment in the upbringing of Monica. He was free, of course, simply to decline the invitation so coldly and briefly as to make sure that it would not be repeated; but the man was not strong enough to stand on his own feet impervious to the winds of criticism. He was sensitive and had little wish to seem churlish, still less to appear ridiculous. Taking the line of least resistance he began to reason that one child, herself no older than Monica, and in the atmosphere of her own home, could make little impression. It ended in his allowing Monica to go.

Monica herself seemed pleased at the prospect of going but expressed her pleasure in a discreet, restrained, grown-up way. Miss Gribbin accompanied her as far as the Vicarage doorstep, arriving with her punctually at half-past three on a sullen and muggy afternoon, and handed her over to the woman-of-all-work who answered the summons at the door.

Miss Gribbin reported to Everton on her return. An idea which she conceived to be humorous had possession of her mind, and in talking to Everton she uttered one of her infrequent laughs.

"I only left her at the door," she said, "so I didn't see her meet the other little girl. I wish I'd stayed to see that. It must have been funny."

She irritated Everton by speaking exactly as if Monica were a captive animal which had just been shown, for the first time in its life, another of its own kind. The analogy thus conveyed to Everton was close enough to make him wince. He felt something like a twinge of conscience, and it may have been then that he asked himself for the first time if he were being fair to Monica.

It had never once occurred to him to ask himself if she were happy. The truth was that he understood children so little as to suppose that physical cruelty was the one kind of cruelty from which they were capable of suffering. Had he ever before troubled to ask himself if Monica were happy, he had probably given the question a curt dismissal with the thought that she had no right to be otherwise. He had given her a good home, even luxuries, together with every opportunity to develop her mind. For companions she had himself, Miss Gribbin, and, to a limited extent, the servants…

Ah, but that picture, conjured up by Miss Gribbin's words with their accompaniment of unreasonable laughter! The little creature meeting for the first time another little creature of its own kind and looking bewildered, knowing neither what to do nor what to say. There was pathos in that—uncomfortable pathos for Everton. Those imaginary friends—did they really mean that Monica had needs of which he knew nothing, of which he had never troubled to learn?

He was not an unkind man, and it hurt him to suspect that he might have committed an unkindness. The modern children whose behaviour and manners he disliked, were perhaps only obeying some inexorable law of evolution. Suppose in keeping Monica from their companionship he were actually flying in the face of Nature? Suppose, after all, if Monica were to be natural, she must go unhindered on the tide of her generation?

He compromised with himself, pacing the little study. He would watch Monica much more closely, question her when he had the chance. Then, if he found she was not happy, and really needed the companionship of other children, he would see what could be done.

But when Monica returned home from the Vicarage it was quite plain that she had not enjoyed herself. She was subdued, and said very little about her experience. Quite obviously the two little girls had not made very good friends. Questioned, Monica confessed that she did not like Gladys—much. She said this very thoughtfully with a little pause before the adverb.

"Why don't you like her?" Everton demanded bluntly.

"I don't know. She's so funny. Not like other girls."

"And what do you know about other girls?" he demanded, faintly amused.

"Well, she's not a bit like—"

Monica paused suddenly and lowered her gaze.

"Not like your 'friends,' you mean?" Everton asked.

She gave him a quick, penetrating little glance and then lowered her gaze once more.

"No," she said, "not a bit."

She wouldn't be, of course. Everton teased the child with no more questions for the time being, and let her go. She ran off at once to the great empty room, there to seek that uncanny companionship which had come to suffice her.

For the moment Everton was satisfied. Monica was perfectly happy as she was, and had no need of Gladys, or, probably, any other child friends. His experiment with her was shaping successfully. She had invented her own young friends, and had gone off eagerly to play with the creations of her own fancy.

This seemed very well at first. Everton reflected that it was just what he would have wished, until he realized suddenly with a little shock of discomfort that it was not normal and it was not healthy.

v

Although Monica plainly had no great desire to see any more of Gladys Parslow, common civility made it necessary for the vicar's little daughter to be asked to pay a return visit. Most likely Gladys Parslow was as unwilling to come as was Monica to entertain her. Stern discipline, however, presented her at the appointed time on an afternoon pre-arranged by correspondence, when Monica received her coldly and with dignity, tempered by a sort of grown-up graciousness.

Monica bore her guest away to the big empty room, and that was the last of Gladys Parslow seen by Everton or Miss Gribbin that afternoon. Monica appeared alone when the gong sounded for tea, and announced in a subdued tone that Gladys had already gone home.

"Did you quarrel with her?" Miss Gribbin asked quickly.

"No—o."

"Then why has she gone like this?"

"She was stupid," said Monica, simply. "That's all."

"Perhaps it was you who was stupid. Why did she go?"

"She got frightened."

"Frightened!"

"She didn't like my friends."

Miss Gribbin exchanged glances with Everton.

"She didn't like a silly little girl who talks to herself and imagines things. No wonder she was frightened."

"She didn't think they were real at first, and laughed at me," said Monica, sitting down.

"Naturally!"

"And then when she saw them—"

Miss Gribbin and Everton interrupted her simultaneously, repeating in unison and with well-matched astonishment, her two last words.

"And then when she saw them," Monica continued, unperturbed, "she didn't like it. I think she was frightened. Anyhow, she said she wouldn't stay and went straight off home. I think she's a stupid girl. We all had a good laugh about her after she was gone."

She spoke in her ordinary matter-of-fact tones, and if she were secretly pleased at the state of perturbation into which her words had obviously thrown Miss Gribbin she gave no sign of it. Miss Gribbin immediately exhibited outward signs of anger.

"You are a very naughty child to tell such untruths. You know perfectly well that Gladys couldn't have *seen* your 'friends.' You have simply frightened her by pretending to talk to people who weren't there, and it will serve you right if she never comes to play with you again."

"She won't," said Monica. "And she *did* see them, Miss Gribbin."

"How do you know?" Everton asked.

"By her face. And she spoke to them too, when she ran to the door. They were very shy at first because Gladys was there. They wouldn't come for a long time, but I begged them, and at last they did."

Everton checked another outburst from Miss Gribbin with a look. He wanted to learn more, and to that end he applied some show of patience and gentleness.

"Where did they come from?" he asked. "From outside the door?"

"Oh, no. From where they always come."

"And where's that?"

"I don't know. They don't seem to know themselves. It's always from some direction where I'm not looking. Isn't it strange?"

"Very! And do they disappear in the same way?"

Monica frowned very seriously and thoughtfully.

"It's so quick you can't tell where they go. When you or Miss Gribbin come in—"

"They always fly on our approach, of course. But why?"

"Because they're dreadfully, dreadfully shy. But not so shy as they were. Perhaps soon they'll get used to you and not mind at all."

"That's a comforting thought!" said Everton with a dry laugh.

When Monica had taken her tea and departed, Everton turned to his secretary.

"You are wrong to blame the child. These creations of her fancy are perfectly real to her. Her powers of suggestion have been strong enough to force them to some extent on me. The little Parslow girl, being younger and more receptive, actually *sees* them. It is a clear case of telepathy and auto-suggestion. I have never studied such matters, but I should say that these instances are of some scientific interest."

Miss Gribbin's lips tightened and he saw her shiver slightly.

"Mr Parslow will be angry," was all she said.

"I really cannot help that. Perhaps it is all for the best. If Monica does not like his little daughter they had better not be brought together again."

For all that, Everton was a little embarrassed when on the following morning he met the vicar out walking. If the Rev. Parslow knew that his little daughter had left the house so unceremoniously on the preceding day, he would either wish to make an apology or perhaps require one, according to his view of the situation. Everton did not wish to deal in apologies one way or the other, he did not care to discuss the vagaries of children, and altogether he wanted to have as little to do with Mr Parslow as was conveniently possible. He would have passed with a brief acknowledgement of the vicar's existence, but, as he had feared, the vicar stopped him.

"I had been meaning to come and see you," said the Rev. Parslow.

Everton halted and sighed inaudibly, thinking that perhaps this casual meeting out of doors might after all have saved him something.

"Yes?" he said.

"I will walk in your direction if I may." The vicar eyed him anxiously. "There is something you must certainly be told. I don't know if you guess, or if you already know. If not, I don't know how you will take it. I really don't."

Everton looked puzzled. Whichever child the vicar might blame for the hurried departure of Gladys, there seemed no cause for such a portentous face and manner.

"Really?" he asked. "Is it something serious?"

"I think so, Mr Everton. You are aware, of course, that my little girl left your house yesterday afternoon with some lack of ceremony."

"Yes, Monica told us she had gone. If they could not agree it was surely the best thing she could have done, although it may sound inhospitable of me to say it. Excuse me, Mr Parslow, but I hope you are not trying to embroil me in a quarrel between children?"

The vicar stared in his turn.

"I am not," he said, "and I am unaware that there was any quarrel. I was going to ask you to forgive Gladys. There was some excuse for her lack of ceremony. She was badly frightened, poor child."

"Then it is my turn to express regret. I had Monica's version of what happened. Monica has been left a great deal to her own resources, and, having no playmates of her own age, she seems to have invented some."

"Ah!" said the Rev. Parslow, drawing a deep breath.

"Unfortunately," Everton continued, "Monica has an uncomfortable gift for impressing her fancies on other people. I have often thought I felt the presence of children about the house, and so, I am almost sure, has Miss Gribbin. I am afraid that when your little girl came to play with her yesterday afternoon, Monica scared her by introducing her invisible 'friends' and by talking to imaginary and therefore invisible little girls."

The vicar laid a hand on Everton's arm.

"There is something more in it than that. Gladys is not an imaginative child; she is, indeed, a practical little person. I have never yet known her to tell me a lie. What would you say, Mr Everton, if I were to tell you that Gladys positively asserts that she *saw* those other children?"

Something like a cold draught went through Everton. An ugly suspicion, vague and almost shapeless, began to move in dim recesses of his mind. He tried to shake himself free of it, to smile and to speak lightly.

"I shouldn't be in the least surprised. Nobody knows the limits of telepathy and auto-suggestion. If I can feel the presence of children whom Monica has created out of her own imagination, why shouldn't your daughter, who is probably more receptive and impressionable than I am, be able to see them?"

The Rev. Parslow shook his head.

"Do you really mean that?" he asked. "Doesn't it seem to you a little far-fetched?"

"Everything we don't understand must seem far-fetched. If one had dared to talk of wireless thirty years ago—"

"Mr Everton, do you know that your house was once a girls' school?"

Once more Everton experienced that vague feeling of discomfiture.

"I didn't know," he said, still indifferently.

"My aunt, whom I never saw, was there. Indeed she died there. There were seven who died. Diphtheria broke out there many years ago. It ruined the school which was shortly afterwards closed. Did you know that, Mr Everton? My aunt's name was Mary Hewitt—"

"Good God!" Everton cried out sharply. "Good God!"

"Ah!" said Parslow. "Now do you begin to see?"

Everton, suddenly a little giddy, passed a hand across his forehead.

"That is—one of the names Monica told me," he faltered. "How could she know?"

"How indeed? Mary Hewitt's great friend was Elsie Power. They died within a few hours of each other."

"That name too… she told me… and there were seven. How could she have known? Even the people around here wouldn't have remembered names after all these years."

"Gladys knew them. But that was only partly why she was afraid. Yet I think she was more awed than afraid, because she knew instinctively that the children who came to play with little Monica, although they were not of this world, were good children, blessed children."

"What are you telling me?" Everton burst out.

"Don't be afraid, Mr Everton. You are not afraid, are you? If those whom we call dead still remain close to us, what more natural than these children should come back to play with a lonely little girl who lacked human playmates? It may seem inconceivable, but how else explain it?

How could little Monica have invented those two names? How could she have learned that seven little girls once died in your house? Only the very old people about here remember it, and even they could not tell you how many died or the name of any one of the little victims. Haven't you noticed a change in your ward since first she began to—imagine them, as you thought?"

Everton nodded heavily.

"Yes," he said, almost unwittingly, "she learned all sorts of tricks of speech, childish gestures which she never had before, and games... I couldn't understand. Mr Parslow, what in God's name am I to do?"

The Rev. Parslow still kept a hand on Everton's arm.

"If I were you I should send her off to school. It may not be very good for her."

"Not good for her! But the children, you say—"

"Children? I might have said angels. They will never harm her. But Monica is developing a gift of seeing and conversing with—with beings that are invisible and inaudible to others. It is not a gift to be encouraged. She may in time see and converse with others—wretched souls who are not God's children. She may lose the faculty if she mixes with others of her age. Out of her need I am sure, these came to her."

"I must think," said Everton.

He walked on dazedly. In a moment or two the whole aspect of life had changed, had grown clearer, as if he had been blind from birth and was now given the first glimmerings of light. He looked forward no longer into the face of a blank and featureless wall, but through a curtain beyond which life manifested itself vaguely but at least perceptibly. His footfalls on the ground beat out the words: "There is no death. There is no death."

VI

That evening after dinner he sent for Monica and spoke to her in an unaccustomed way. He was strangely shy of her, and his hand, which he rested on one of her slim shoulders, lay there awkwardly.

"Do you know what I'm going to do with you, young woman?" he said. "I'm going to pack you off to school."

"O—oh!" she stared at him, half smiling. "Are you really?"

"Do you want to go?"

She considered the matter, frowning and staring at the tips of her fingers.

"I don't know. I don't want to leave *them*."

"Who?" he asked.

"Oh, you know!" she said, and turned her head half shyly.

"What? Your—friends, Monica?"

"Yes."

"Wouldn't you like other playmates?"

"I don't know. I love *them*, you see. But they said—they said I ought to go to school if you ever sent me. They might be angry with me if I was to ask you to let me stay. They wanted me to play with other girls who aren't—who aren't like they are. Because you know, they are *different* from children that everybody can see. And Mary told me not to—not to encourage anybody else who was different, like them."

Everton drew a deep breath.

"We'll have a talk tomorrow about finding a school for you, Monica," he said. "Run off to bed, now. Good-night, my dear."

He hesitated, then touched her forehead with his lips. She ran from him, nearly as shy as Everton himself, tossing back her long hair, but from the door she gave him the strangest little brimming glance, and there was that in her eyes which he had never seen before.

Late that night Everton entered the great empty room which Monica had named the schoolroom. A flag of moonlight from the window lay across the floor, and it was empty to the gaze. But the deep shadows hid little shy presences of which some unnamed and undeveloped sense in the man was acutely aware.

"Children!" he whispered. "Children!"

He closed his eyes and stretched out his hands. Still they were shy and held aloof, but he fancied that they came a little nearer.

"Don't be afraid," he whispered. "I'm only a very lonely man. Be near me after Monica is gone."

He paused, waiting. Then as he turned away he was aware of little caressing hands upon his arm. He looked around at once, but the time had not yet come for him to see. He saw only the barred window, the shadows on either wall and the flag of moonlight.

ONE WHO SAW

THERE are certain people, often well enough liked, genial souls whom one is always glad to meet, who yet have the faculty of disappearing without being missed. Crutchley must have been one of them. It wasn't until his name was casually mentioned that evening at the Storgates' that most of us remembered that we hadn't seen him about for the last year or two. It was Mrs Storgate's effort at remembering, with the help of those nearest her at table, the guests at a certain birthday party of four years since that was the cause of Crutchley's name being mentioned. And no sooner had it been mentioned than we were all laughing, because most of us had asked one another in the same breath what had become of him.

It was Jack Price who was able to supply the information.

"For the last year or two," he said, "he's been living very quietly with his people in Norfolk. I heard from him only the other day."

Mrs Storgate was interested.

"I wonder why he's chosen to efface himself," she asked of nobody in particular. "He was rather a lamb in his way. I used to adore that shiny black hair of his which always made me think of patent leather. I believe he owed half his invitations to his hair. I told him once that he dined out on it four nights a week."

"It's as white as the ceiling now," Price remarked.

Having spoken he seemed to regret it, and Mrs Storgate exclaimed:

"Oh, no! We're speaking of *Simon* Crutchley."

"I mean Simon," said Price unwillingly.

There was a faint stir of consternation, and then a woman's voice rose above the rustle and murmur.

"Oh, but it seems impossible. That sleek, blue-black hair of his! And he can't be more than thirty-five."

Somebody said that he'd heard of people's hair going suddenly white like that after an illness. Price was asked if Simon Crutchley had been ill. The answer was Yes. A nervous breakdown? Well, it was something very like that.

A lady who turned night into day all the year round and was suspected of drinking at least as much as was good for her, sighed and remarked that everybody nowadays suffered from nerves. Mrs Storgate said that Simon Crutchley's breakdown and the change in his appearance doubtless accounted for his having dropped out and hidden himself away in Norfolk. And then another conversational hare was started.

Instead of joining in the hunt I found myself in a brown study, playing with breadcrumbs. I had rather liked Crutchley, although he wasn't exactly one of my own kind. He was one of those quiet fellows who are said colloquially to require a lot of knowing. In social life he had always been a detached figure, standing a little aloof from his fellow men and seeming to study them with an air of faint and inoffensive cynicism. He was a writing man, which may have accounted for his slight mannerisms, but he didn't belong to the precious, superior and rather detestable school. Everybody agreed that he was quite a good scout, and nobody troubled to read his books which consisted mainly of historical essays.

I tried to imagine Simon Crutchley with white hair, and then I caught myself speculating on the cause of his illness or "breakdown." He was the last sort of fellow whom one would have expected to be knocked to pieces like that. So far from indulging in excesses he had always been something of an *æsthete*. He had a comfortable private income and he certainly didn't overwork. Indeed I remembered his once telling me that he took a comfortable two years over a book.

It would be hard for me to say now whether it was by accident or design that I left at the same time as Price. Our ways lay in the same direction, and while we were lingering in the hall, waiting for our hats and coats, we agreed to share a taxi. I lived in the Temple, he in John Street, Adelphi. "I'll tell the man to drive down Villiers Street," I said, "and up into the Strand again by the Tivoli, and I can drop you on the way."

In the taxi we talked about Crutchley. I began it, and I asked leading questions. Price, you see, was the only man who seemed to have heard anything of him lately, and he was now sufficiently evasive to pique my curiosity.

"It's a queer and rather terrible story," he said at last. "There's no secret about it, at least I'm not pledged in any way, but I don't think poor old Simon would have liked me to tell it publicly over the dinner-table. For one thing, nobody would believe it, and, for another, it's rather long. Besides, he didn't tell me quite all. There's one bit he couldn't— or wouldn't—tell. There was just one bit he couldn't bring himself to describe to me, and I don't suppose he'll ever manage to describe it to anybody, so nobody but himself will ever have an idea of the actual *sight* which sent him off his head for six months and turned his hair as white as a table-cloth."

"Oh," said I, "then it was all through something he *saw?*"

Price nodded.

"So he says. I admit it's a pretty incredible sort of story—yet somehow Simon Crutchley isn't the sort to imagine things. And after all, something obviously did happen to him. I'll tell you his story if you like. The night's young. Come into my place and have a drink, if you will."

I thanked him and said that I would. He turned towards me and let a hand fall on my knee.

"Mind you," he said, "this is Crutchley's own story. If you don't believe it I don't want you to go about thinking that I'm a liar. I'm not responsible for the truth of it; I'm only just passing it on. In a way I hope it isn't true. It isn't comfortable to think that such things may happen—*do* happen."

Twenty minutes later, when we were sitting in the snug little library in Price's flat he told me his story, or, rather, Crutchley's. This is it.

You know the sort of work Crutchley used to do? If you don't, you at least know Stevenson's "Memories and Portraits," and Crutchley worked with that sort of material. His study of Margaret of Anjou, by the way, is considered a classic in certain highbrow circles.

You will remember that Joan of Arc was very much in the air two or three years back. It was before Bernard Shaw's play was produced, but her recent canonization had just reminded the world that she was perhaps the greatest woman in history. It may have been this revival of interest in her which decided Crutchley to make her the subject of one of his historical portraits. He'd already treated Villon and Abelard and Heloise, and as soon as he'd decided on St Joan he went over to France to work, so to say, on the spot.

Crutchley always did his job conscientiously, using his own deductive faculties only for bridging the gaps in straight history. He went first to Domrémy, where the Maid was born, followed the old trail of that fifteenth century campaign across France, and of course his journey ended inevitably at Rouen, where English spite and French cowardice burned her in the marketplace.

I don't know if you know Rouen? Tourists don't stay there very much. They visit, but they don't stay. They come and hurry round the cathedral, gape at the statue of Joan of Arc in the Place de la Pucelle, throw a victorious smile at Napoleon Buonaparte galloping his bronze horse on a pedestal in the Square, and rush on to Paris or back to one of the Channel ports. Rouen being half-way between Paris and the coast the typical English tourist finds that he can "do" the place without sleeping in it.

Crutchley liked Rouen. It suited him. It is much more sober and austere than most of the French towns. It goes to bed early, and you don't have sex flaunted before you wherever you look. You find there an atmosphere like that of our own cathedral cities, and there is a great deal more to see than ever the one-day tourist imagines. Crutchley decided to stay on in the town and finish there his paper on Joan of Arc.

He found an hotel practically undiscovered by English and Americans—l'Hôtel d'Avignon. It stands half-way down one of those narrow old-world streets, quite near the Gare de la Rue Jeanne d'Arc. A single tramline runs through the narrow street in front of its unpretentious façade, and to enter you must pass a narrow archway, and through a winter garden littered with tables and chairs to a somewhat impressive main entrance with statuary on either side of the great glass-panelled doors.

Crutchley found the place by accident on his first day and took *déjeuner* in the great tapestried salle à manger. The food was good, and he found that the chef had a gift for Sole Normand. Out of curiosity he asked to see some of the bedrooms.

It was a hotel where many ate but few slept. At that time of the year many rooms were vacant on the first floor. He followed a chambermaid up the first flight of stairs and looked out through a door which he found open at the top. To his surprise he found that it gave entrance to a garden on the same level. The hotel, parts of which were hundreds of years old, had been built on the face of a steep hill, and the little garden thus stood a storey above the level of the street in front.

This garden was sunk deep in a hollow square, with the walls of the hotel rising high all around it. Three rows of shuttered windows looked out upon an open space which never saw the sun. For that obvious reason there had been no attempt to grow flowers, but one or two ferns had sprung up and a few small tenacious plants had attached themselves to a rockery. The soil was covered with loose gravel, and in the middle there grew a great plane tree which thrust its crest above the roof-tops so that, as seen by the birds, it must have looked as if it were growing in a great lidless box. To imagine the complete quietude of the spot one has only to remember how an enclosed square in one of the Inns of Court shuts out the noise of traffic from some of the busiest streets in the world. It did not occur to Crutchley that there may be something unhealthy about an open space shut out entirely from the sun. Some decrepit garden seats were ranged around the borders, and the plane tree hid most of the sky, sheltering the little enclosure like a great umbrella. Crutchley told me that he mistook silence and deathly stillness for peace, and decided that here was the very spot for him to write his version of the story of Jeanne d'Arc.

He took a bedroom on the same level, whose high, shuttered windows looked out on to the still garden square; and next day he took a writing-pad and a fountain-pen to one of the faded green seats and tried to start work.

From what he told me it wasn't a very successful attempt. The unnatural silence of the place bred in him an indefinable restlessness. It seemed to him that he sat more in twilight than in shade. He knew that a fresh wind was blowing, but it won not the least responsive whisper from the garden. The ferns might have been water-plants in an aquarium, so still they were. Sunlight, which burnished the blue sky, struck through the leaves of the plane tree, but it painted only the top of one of the walls high above his head. Crutchley frankly admitted that the place got on his nerves, and that it was a relief to go out and hear the friendly noise of the trams, and see the people drinking outside cafés and the little boys fishing for roach among the barges on the banks of the Seine.

He made several attempts to work in the garden, but they were all fruitless, and he took to working in his bedroom. He confessed to me that, even in the afternoon, he felt that there was something uncanny about the place. There's nothing in that. Many people would have felt the same; and Crutchley, although he had no definite belief in the supernatural, had had one or two minor experiences in his lifetime—too trifling, he said, to be worth recording—but teasing enough in their way, and of great interest to himself. Yet he had always smiled politely when ardent spiritualists had told him that he was "susceptible." He began by feeling vaguely that there was something "wrong," in the psychical sense, with the garden. It was like a faint, unseizable, but disagreeable odour. He told me that he did not let it trouble him greatly. He wanted to work, and when he found that "it" would not let him work in the garden, he removed himself and his writing materials to his room.

Crutchley had been five days at the hotel when something strange happened. It was his custom to undress in the dark, because his windows were overlooked by a dozen others and, by first of all turning off the light, he was saved from drawing the great shutters. That night he was smoking while he undressed, and when he was in his pyjamas he went to one of the open windows to throw out the stub of his cigarette. Having done so he lingered, looking out.

The usual unnatural stillness brooded over the garden square, intensified now by the spell of the night. Somewhere in the sky the moon was shining, and a few stray silver beams dappled the top of the north wall. The plane tree stood like a living thing entranced. Not one of its lower branches stirred, and its leaves might have been carved out of jade. Just enough light filtered from the sky to make the features of the garden faintly visible. Crutchley looked where his cigarette had fallen and now lay like a glow-worm, and raised his eyes to one of the long green decrepit seats. With a faint unreasonable thrill and a cold tingling of the nostrils he realized that somebody was sitting there.

As his eyes grew more used to the darkness the huddled form took the shape of a woman. She sat with her head turned away, one arm thrown along the sloping back of the seat, and her face resting against it. He said that her attitude was one of extreme dejection, of abject and complete despair.

Crutchley, you must understand, couldn't see her at all clearly, although she was not a dozen yards distant. Her dress was dark, but he could make out none of its details save that something like a flimsy scarf or thick veil trailed over the shoulder nearest him. He stood watching her, pricked by a vague sense of pity and conscious that, if she looked up, he would hardly be visible to her beyond the window, and that, in any event, the still glowing stub of cigarette would explain his presence.

But she did not look up, she did not move at all while Crutchley stood watching. So still she was that it was hard for him to realize that she breathed. She seemed to have fallen completely under the spell of the garden in which nothing ever stirred, and the scene before Crutchley's eyes might have been a nocturnal picture painted in oils.

Of course he made a guess or two about her. At the sight of anything unusual one's subconscious mind immediately begins to speculate and to suggest theories. Here, thought Crutchley, was a woman with some great sorrow, who, before retiring to her room had come to sit in this quiet garden, and there, under the stars, had given way to her despair.

I don't know how long Crutchley stood there, but probably it wasn't for many seconds. Thought is swift and time is slow when one stands still watching a motionless scene. He owned that his curiosity was deeply intrigued, and it was intrigued in a somewhat unusual way. He found himself desiring less to know the reason of her despair than to see her face. He had a definite and urgent temptation to go out and look at her, to use force if necessary in turning her face so that he might look into her eyes.

If you knew Crutchley at all well you must know that he was something more than ordinarily conventional. He concerned himself not only with what a gentleman ought to do but with what a gentleman ought to think. Thus when he came to realize that he was not only spying upon a strange woman's grief, but actually feeling tempted to force himself upon her and stare into eyes which he guessed were blinded by tears, it was sufficient to tear him away from the window and send him padding across the floor to the high bed at the far end of the room.

But he made no effort to sleep. He lay listening, waiting for a sound from the other side of those windows. In that silence he knew he must hear the least sound outside. But for ten minutes he listened in vain, picturing to himself the woman still rigid in the same posture of despair.

Presently he could bear it no longer. He jumped out of bed and went once more to the window. He told himself that it was human pity which drove him there. He walked heavily on his bare feet and he coughed. He made as much noise as he was reasonably able to make, hoping that she would hear and bestir herself. But when he reached the open window and looked out the seat was empty.

Crutchley stared at the empty seat, not quite crediting the evidence of his eyes. You see, according to his account, she couldn't have touched that loose gravel with her foot without making a distinct sound and to re-enter the hotel she must have opened a door with creaking hinges and a noisy latch. Yet he had heard nothing, and the garden was empty. Next morning he even tried the experiment of walking on tiptoe across the garden to see if it could be done in utter silence, and he was satisfied that it could not. Even an old grey cat, which he found blinking on a window ledge, made the gravel clink under its pads when he called it to him to be stroked.

Well, he slept indifferently that night, and in the morning, when the chambermaid came in, he asked her who was the sad-looking lady whom he had seen sitting at night in the garden.

The chambermaid turned towards the window, and he saw a rapid movement of her right hand. It was done very quickly and surreptitiously, just the touch of a forefinger on her brow and a rapid fumbling of fingers at her breast, but he knew that she had made the Sign of the Cross.

"There is no lady staying in the house," she said with her back towards him. "Monsieur has been mistaken. Will Monsieur take coffee or the English tea?"

Crutchley knew very well what the girl's gesture meant. He had mentioned something which she held to be unholy, and the look on her face when she turned it once more in his direction warned him that it would be useless to question her. He had a pretty restless day, doing little or no work. You mustn't think that he already regarded the experience as a supernatural one, although he was quite well aware of what was in the mind of the chambermaid; but it was macabre, it belonged to the realm of the seemingly inexplicable which was no satisfaction to him to dismiss as merely "queer."

Crutchley spoke the French of the average educated Englishman, and the only other person in the house who spoke English was the head waiter, who had spent some years in London. His English was probably at least as good as Crutchley's French, and he enjoyed the opportunity of airing it. He was in appearance a true Norman, tall, dark, and distinguished-looking. One sees his type in certain English families which can truthfully boast of Norman ancestry. It was at *déjeuner* when he approached Crutchley, and, having handed him the wine list, bent over him confidentially.

"Are you quite comfortable in your room sir?" he ventured.

"Oh, quite, thank you," Crutchley answered briefly.

"There is a very nice room in the front, sir. Quite so big, and then there is the sun. Perhaps you like it better, sir?"

"No, thanks," said Crutchley, "I shouldn't get a wink of sleep. You see, none of your motor traffic seems to be equipped with silencers, and with trams, motor-horns, and market carts bumping over the cobbles I should never have any peace."

The waiter said no more, merely bowing, but he looked disappointed. He managed to convey by a look that he had Monsieur's welfare at heart, but that Monsieur doubtless knew best and must please himself.

"I believe I'm on the trail of something queer," Crutchley thought. "That chambermaid's been talking to Pierre. I wonder what's wrong or what they think is wrong."

He re-opened the subject when the waiter returned to him with a half-bottle of white wine.

"Why do you wish me to change my room, Pierre?"

"I do not wish Monsieur to change his room if he is satisfied."

"When I am not satisfied I say so. Why did you think I might not be?"

"I wish Monsieur to be more comfortable. There is no sun behind the house. It is better to be where the sun come som'times. Besides, I think Monsieur is one who sees."

This seemed cryptic, but Crutchley let it go. Pierre had duties to attend to, and, besides, Crutchley did not feel inclined to discuss with the waiter the lady he had seen in the garden on the preceding night.

During the afternoon and evening he tried to work, but he fought only a series of losing battles against distraction. He was as incapable of concentration as a boy in love. He knew—and he was angry with himself because he knew—that he was ekeing out his patience until night came, in the hope of seeing once more that still figure of despair in the garden.

Of course, I don't pretend to understand the nature of the attraction, nor was Crutchley able to explain it to me. But he told me that he couldn't keep his thoughts off the face which had been turned away from him. Imagination drew for him a succession of pictures, all of an unearthly beauty, such pictures as he had never before conceived. His mind, over which he now seemed to have only an imperfect control, exercised its new creative faculty all that afternoon and evening. Long before the hour of dinner he had decided that if she came to the garden he must see her face and thus end this long torment of speculation.

He went to his room that night at eleven o'clock, and he did not undress, but sat and smoked in an armchair beside his bed. From that position he could only see through the window the lighted windows of other rooms across the square of garden shining through the leaves of the plane tree. Towards midnight the last lights died out and the last distant murmur of voices died away. Then he got up and went softly across the room.

Before he reached the window he knew instinctively that he would see her sitting in the same place and in the same attitude of woe, and his eagerness was mingled with an indescribable fear. He seemed to hear a cry of warning from the honest workaday world into which he had been born—a world which he now seemed strangely to be leaving. He said that it was like starting on a voyage, feeling no motion from the ship, and then being suddenly aware of a spreading space of water between the vessel and the quay.

That night the invisible moon threw stronger beams upon the top of the north wall, and the stars burned brighter in a clearer sky. There was a little more light in the well of the garden than there had been on the preceding night, and on the seat that figure of tragic desolation was limned more clearly. The pose, the arrangement of the woman's garments, were the same in every detail, from the least fold to the wisp of veil which fell over her right shoulder. For he now saw that it was a veil, and guessed that it covered the face which was still turned from him. He was shaken, dragged in opposite directions by unreasonable dread and still more unreasonable curiosity. And while he stood looking, the palms of his hands grew wet and his mouth grew dry.

He was well nigh helpless. His spirit struggled within him like a caged bird, longing to fly to her. That still figure was magnetic in some mighty sense which he had never realized before. It was hypnotic without needing to use its eyes. And presently Crutchley spoke to it for the first time, whispering through the open window across the intervening space of gloom.

"Madame," he pleaded, "look at me."

The figure did not move. It might have been cast in bronze or carved out of stone.

"Oh, Madame," he whispered, "let me see your face!"

Still there was no sound nor movement, but in his heart he heard the answer.

"So, then, I must come to you," he heard himself say softly; and he groped for the door of his room.

Outside, a little way down the corridor, was one of the doors leading into the enclosed garden. Crutchley had taken but a step or two when a figure loomed up before him, his nerves were jerked like a hooked fish, and he uttered an involuntary cry of fear. Then came the click of an electric light switch, a globe overhead sprang alight, and he found himself confronted by Pierre the head waiter. Pierre barred the way and he spoke sternly, almost menacingly.

"Where are you going, sir?"

"What the devil has that got to do with you?" Crutchley demanded fiercely.

"The devil, eh? *Bien*, Monsieur, I think perhaps he have something to do with it. You will have the goodness, please, to return to your room. No, not the room which you have left, sir—that is not a good room—but come with me and I shall show you another."

The waiter was keeping him from her. Crutchley turned upon him with a gesture of ferocity.

"What do you mean by interfering with me? This is not a prison or an asylum. I am going into the garden for a breath of air before I go to sleep."

"That, sir, is impossible," the waiter answered him. "The air of the garden is not good at night. Besides, the doors are locked and the patron have the keys."

Crutchley stared at him for a moment in silent fury.

"You are insolent," he said. "Tomorrow I shall report you. Do you take me for a thief because I leave my room at midnight? Never mind! I can reach the garden from my window."

In an instant the waiter had him by the arm, holding him powerless in a grip known to wrestlers.

"Monsieur," he said in a voice grown softer and more respectful, "the *bon Dieu* has sent me to save you. I have wait tonight because I know you must try to enter the garden. Have I your permission to enter your room with you and speak with you a little while?"

Crutchley laughed out in angry impotence.

"This is Bedlam," he said. "Oh, come, if you must."

Back in his room, with the waiter treading close upon his heels, Crutchley went straight to the window and looked out. The seat was empty.

"I do not think that she is there," said the waiter softly, "because I am here and I do not see. Monsieur is one who sees, as I tell him this morning, but he will not see her when he is with one who does not see."

Crutchley turned upon the man impatiently.

"What are you talking about?" he demanded. "Who is she?"

"Who she is, I cannot say." The waiter blessed himself with quick, nervous fingers. "But who she *was* I can perhaps tell Monsieur."

Crutchley understood, almost without surprise, but with a sudden clamouring of fear.

"Do you mean," he asked, "that she is what we call a ghost, an apparition—"

"It matters not what one calls her, monsieur. She is here sometimes for certain who are able to see her. Monsieur wishes very much to see her face. Monsieur must not see it. There was one who look five years ago, and another perhaps seven, eight. The first he make die after two, three days; the other, he is still mad. That is why I come to save you, Monsieur."

Crutchley was now entirely back in his own world. That hidden face had lost its fascination for him, and he felt only that primeval dread which has its roots deep down in every one of us. He sat down on the bed, trying to keep his lips from twitching, and let the waiter talk.

"You asked Yvonne this morning, sir, who is the lady in the garden. And Yvonne guess, and she come and tell me, for all of us know of her. Monsieur it all happened a long time ago—perhaps fifty—sixty years. There was in this town a notary of the name Lebrun. And in a village half-way from here to Dieppe is a grand château in which there live a lady, *une jeune fille*, with her father and her mother. And the lady was very beautiful but not very good, Monsieur.

"Well, M. Lebrun, he fall in love with her. I think she love him, too—better as all the others. So he make application for her hand, but she was aristocrat and he was bourgeois, and besides he had not very much money, so the application was refused! And they find her another husband whom she love not, and she find herself someone else, and there is divorce. And she have many lovers, for she was very beautiful, but not good. For ten years—more, perhaps—she use her beauty to make slaves of men. And one, he made kill himself because of her, but she did not mind. And all the time M. Lebrun stayed single, because he could not love another woman.

"But at last this lady, she have a dreadful accident. It is a lamp which blow up and hurt her face. In those days the surgeons did not know how to make new features. It was dreadful, Monsieur. She had been so lovely, and now she have nothing left except just the eyes. And she go about wearing a long thick veil, because she have become terrible to see. And her lovers, they no longer love, and she have no husband because she have been divorce.

"So M. Lebrun, he write to her father, and once more he make offer for her hand. And her father, he is willing, because now she is no longer very young, and she is terrible to see. But her father, he was a man of honour, and he insist that M. Lebrun must see her face before he decide if he still wish her in marriage. So a meeting is arrange and her father and her mother bring her to this hotel, and M. Lebrun he come to see them here.

"The lady come with them wearing her thick veil. She insist to see M. Lebrun alone, so she wait out there in the garden, and when he come they bring him to her.

"Monsieur, I do not know what her face was like, and nobody know what pass between him and her in that garden there. Love is not always what we think it. Perhaps M. Lebrun think all the time that his love go deeper than her beauty, and when he see her dreadful changed face he find out the truth. Perhaps when she put aside the veil she see that he flinch. I only say perhaps, because nobody know. But M. Lebrun he walk out alone, and the lady stay sitting on the seat. And presently her parents come but she does not speak or move. And they find in her hand a little empty bottle, Monsieur...

"All her life she have live for love, for admiration, and M. Lebrun, he is the last of her lovers, and when he no longer love it is for her the end of everything. She have bring the bottle with her in case her last lover love her no more. That is all, monsieur. It happen many years ago, and if there is more of the story one does not remember it today. And now perhaps Monsieur understands why it would be best for him to sleep tonight in a front room, and change his hotel tomorrow."

Crutchley sat listening and staring. He felt faint and sick.

"But why does she—come back?" he managed to ask.

The head waiter shrugged his shoulders.

"How should we know, Monsieur? She is a thing of evil. When her face was lovely, while she live, she use it to destroy men. Now she still use it to destroy—but otherwise. She have some great evil power which draw those who can see her. They feel they must not rest until they have looked upon her face. And, Monsieur, that face is not good to look upon."

I had listened all this while to Price's version of Crutchley's story without making any comment, but now he paused for so long that at last I said:

"Well, that can't be all."

Price was filling a pipe with an air of preoccupation.

"No," he said, "it isn't quite all. I wish it were. Crutchley was scared, and he had the sense to change to a room in the front of the house, and to clear out altogether next day. He paid his bill, and made Pierre a good-sized present in money. Having done that, he found that he hadn't quite enough money to get home with, and he'd used his last letter of credit. So he telegraphed for more, meaning to catch the night boat from Havre.

"Well, you can guess what happened. The wired money order didn't arrive in time, and he was compelled to stay another night in Rouen. He went to another hotel.

"All that day he could think of nothing else but that immobile figure of despair which he had seen on the seat. I imagine that if you or I had seen something which we believed to be a ghost we should find difficulty in concentrating our minds on anything else for some while afterwards.

"The horror of the thing had a fascination for Crutchley, and when night fell he began to ask himself if she were still there, hiding her face in that dark and silent garden. And he began to ask himself: 'Why shouldn't I go and see? It could not harm me just to look once, and quickly, and from a distance.'

"He didn't realize that she was calling him, drawing him to her through the lighted streets. Well, he walked round to the Hotel d'Avignon. People were still sitting at the little tables under the glass roof, but he did not see Pierre. He walked straight on and through the swing doors, as if he were still staying in the house, and nobody noticed him. He climbed the stairs and went to one of the doors which opened out into the high enclosed garden behind. He found it on the latch, opened it softly and looked out. Then he stood, staring in horror and fascination at that which was on the seat.

"He was lost then, and he knew it. The power was too strong for him. He went to her step by step, as powerless to hold himself back as a needle before a magnet or a moth before a flame. And he bent over her...

"And here is the part that Crutchley can't really describe. It was painful to see him straining and groping after words, as if he were trying to speak in some strange language. There aren't really any words, I suppose. But he told me that it wasn't just that—that there weren't any features left. It was something much worse and much more subtle than that. And—oh, something happened, I know, before his senses left him. Poor devil, he couldn't tell me. He's getting better, as I told you, but his nerves are still in shreds and he's got one or two peculiar aversions."

"What are they?" I asked.

"He can't bear to be touched, or to hear anybody laugh."

THE RECURRING TRAGEDY

POST-WAR business brought William E. Fitchett to England, and pleasure lured him from the great northern manufacturing city down to Arborhaven, there to renew a friendship which had been broken off at the end of his last term at Yale.

Standring was a specialist in nerves and mental diseases. Before the war he had achieved a reputation. During the war his successful treatment of cases roughly diagnosed as shell-shock had brought him worldwide fame. He was still a youngish man, round-faced and kindly-looking, with big searching grey eyes and a full head of dark hair flecked here and there with white.

To Fitchett the Tudor mansion, designed in the shape of an E by an architect anxious to do honour to the Virgin Queen, was a place made out of dreams. The first sight one has of it, the gabled pile of mellowed red bricks, standing at the top of long terraces across the water meadows, is something not to be forgotten. The interior is a wonder of crooked floors, oak panelling and beams, great stately rooms, rooms absurdly small, with mysterious little passages and staircases leading to unexpected parts of the house. Here it would seem that Time had stood still, had not the men and women who trod the hollow floors changed the fashion of their clothes and the manner of their speech through the three centuries.

"They built real houses in those days," Fitchett said. "I don't remember your telling me in the old days that you had a family mansion."

They were sitting alone in the long dining-room after dinner. The table was an island of light set in a sea of shadows. The gleaming white cloth, the shirt-fronts of the two men, the flowers and silver, the red wine in the glasses, all stood out in shining contrast to the darkness around them. Only an occasional reflection from the fire went questing into the mysterious dimness, and little focusses of light gleamed on the polished surface of furniture or panels.

"I hadn't," Standring answered. "I bought this place only six months ago. It used to belong to General Sir Thomas Shiel."

"General Shiel." Fitchett repeated the name as if he were trying to wake a memory. "Now what did I hear about him? He's dead, isn't he?"

"Yes. Before he died he was one of my patients. I came down here to attend to him. I knew him slightly before. While I was here I fell in love with the house. After his death it came onto the market and I bought it."

"Yes, yes." Fitchett's brows were gathered up into a frown. "But what did I hear about General Shiel? I know there was something."

"He commanded one of our divisions over in France."

"Yes, that's right. And didn't he get sent back for making a mess of things—losing a lot of men or something? Wasn't that it?"

"There were questions asked about him in Parliament, certainly."

"Ah, I thought so."

"Actually, though, he was invalided home with shell-shock."

Fitchett laughed and turned a quizzical eye upon his friend.

"Well, that's just your British way of doing things," he said. "No general was ever sent back for being incompetent. He was always sick. It sounds so much better."

The specialist smiled and sipped his wine.

"I can tell you," he said, "that the General was in a pretty bad way."

"Oh, yes: I forgot. He died. And you couldn't cure him. So you're not infallible after all, Standring?"

"I haven't pretended to be. And, mind you, there were several forms of what was popularly known as shell-shock. There was the kind experienced by the poor devil who was blown up, or lay for hours under the wreck of a dug-out. There was another kind which was a polite name for funk. There was also, as you have remarked, the kind which afflicted generals who never went near the line, but about whom questions were asked in the House of Commons."

"And he had that kind and yet—he died. You should have found him all the easier to cure, Standring."

"You don't understand. Suppose you came to me and told me you suffered from delusions, and suppose when I inquired their nature you told me that all the grass you saw looked green—what then? Your delusion would consist in your thinking that it ought to be some other colour, and you would be much more difficult to cure. Even if I succeeded in making you think that grass looked red you would be very far from cured."

Fitchett smiled and broke the long ash from his cigar into a little silver tray at his elbow.

"I see. And if a man tells you he's been seeing ghosts you can only cure him if he's been seeing imaginary ghosts—not real ones. Was that the General's trouble? Did he see ghosts?"

"He did not. At least he didn't say so. But in a sense I suppose he was a haunted man."

He came to an abrupt pause. Fitchett regarded him with eyebrows slightly raised.

"Well?" he asked. "I'm not going to pretend that I'm not curious."

Standring lowered his gaze.

"I'm sorry," he said. "I can't tell you. There's such a thing as professional—"

"Professional secrecy. Professional humbug! Do you remember when we were at Yale, and bitten with the literary bug? I remember one evening we were talking about novels and short stories and the old gag about truth being stranger than fiction. We both agreed that every man, no matter how humdrum his life, had at least one experience which, if he cared to tell it, would make a tremendous story. You may also remember that we agreed to tell each other when the great story in real life came to each of us. Mine hasn't come yet. I rather think yours has."

"Perhaps it has," Standring agreed. "I'm sorry, though, but I can't tell it to you."

"All right." Fitchett was plainly disappointed. "If you can't, you can't. But listen. Years ago when we made that compact you knew me for a man who could keep his head shut. That was before you joined a profession which made you pigeon-hole your memories and label half of them 'secret.' I heard some sort of queer story about General Shiel in New York. Who brought it over I can't say. You tell me the truth, and I'll pass it along if that is your wish. If it isn't—next week I leave Liverpool for New York, and I won't say a single word in this country or mine."

For a little while Standring seemed to consider.

"You can say," he replied at last, "that whatever were General Sir Thomas Shiel's faults he suffered for them."

Fitchett inclined his head.

"I'll say that. And what are you going to tell *me*?"

"The whole thing if you're really so anxious to hear it and willing to swear to say not a word about it. The General is dead now, and his story— I don't know if that deserves quite to die. At least it's a queer story and there's certainly a moral in it."

He sat silent a moment, the fingers of one hand on the stem of his half-empty glass, which he rocked slowly to and fro.

"I'd known the General slightly for some time. I knew him when he was a lieutenant-colonel in command of the first battalion of one of the county regiments. He had then the reputation of a martinet, nobody liking him except perhaps one or two of the senior officers. He gained promotion before the war and went out as a brigadier. Afterwards he was given the command of a division. I believe he was pretty thoroughly hated by the men. Every petty annoyance which he could devise to make their lives more miserable he inflicted at a time when life for them was little better than hell. His men all died with their buttons in a high state of polish, their equipment and shrapnel helmets shining. If it sounds splendid it seems at least purposeless. Too much of that sort of thing only harassed them, made them irritable and injured their *morale*. His orders about prisoners, care of wounded and so on were monumentally brutal. He was a specimen of our own home-grown kind of Prussian, of which there were, fortunately, few. On courts-martial he was extraordinarily severe. He thought only of himself and his own glory. Were it not for another picture which I shall always carry in my mind, I should think of him as a serio-comic goose-stepping figure, with a big sword and a mouthful of oaths. Well, as you know, he ended by losing nine-tenths of the *personnel* of his division and being sent home—"

"With shell-shock," Fitchett interpolated drily.

"At least he came home a broken man. Lady Shiel came to see me after a time. She could not get him to put himself into professional hands. She did not tell me much. How much she actually knew I can't say. We made an arrangement. I was to come down to Arborhaven apparently as a guest, actually as a physician. I was to try to win the General's confidence and do what I could for him. In the end I agreed, mostly for the sake of acquaintance, which she was pleased to call friendship.

"I arrived here on a Friday, and Lady Shiel met me at the door. She took me into her husband's study—that small room across the hall—but he was not there at the time, and she went to look for him. While I was there alone I picked up an open book which evidently the General had been reading. The books a patient reads often afford a guide, or at least a finger-post, to his mental state. The book was Eugene Sue's *The Wandering Jew*.

"When Lady Shiel returned with the General his appearance had a great and very disagreeable effect on me. I will not say that I was shocked, for that is no word for a doctor to use, and yet I do not know of any other word capable of conveying what I mean. To begin with he had aged terribly. From a red-blooded, middle-aged man typical of the Army he had grown old and haggard. Somehow he seemed to have shrunk inside his great frame, like a punctured football. His voice, when he greeted me, had lost its depth of tone. It was as if old age had come upon him in a night.

"Strangest of all he did not impress me as a sick man. His eyes certainly told their tale of suffering, but it was not physical nor yet of that mental kind which any physician may heal. Mind you, in describing this to one of my own profession I should have to consider my words and pick them carefully. To you I tell frankly exactly how I felt about him without stopping to consider any niceties of phraseology. Tell me, have you ever seen a man suffering terribly from remorse, from consciousness of sin? I don't use the phrase in a necessarily pietistic sense."

Fitchett inclined his head. It was the first movement he had made for some minutes.

"I once saw a man who had been acquitted of murder," he said. "Nobody had much doubt about it, although the jury wouldn't convict. I know what you mean."

"I think you've only a dim idea for all that. It was as if the General bore upon his soul ten thousand crimes, each one ten thousand times worse than murder. I never had much faith in God or devil, heaven or hell until that moment, when I knew that I looked into the eyes of a damned soul. I tell you, Fitchett, my own nerves are pretty sound, and I am not a man whom most would describe as 'sensitive', but something like nausea overtook me as I made some kind of pretence to shake his hand.

"I will pass over the early part of the evening and the dreary dinner which followed in this room. There were no other guests, and the Shiels were a childless couple. I found myself dreading the departure of Lady Shiel to the drawing-room. I was almost childishly averse to being left alone with her husband.

"When she had gone, however, I resigned myself to the inevitable, and, at the General's invitation, mixed myself a stiff whisky and soda. I sat where you are sitting now. The General sat here in my place at the head of the table. The low shade of a lamp cut off the light from the upper part of his face, and, thank Heaven, I could scarcely see those dreadful eyes of his.

"He came very abruptly to the point before Lady Shiel had been absent a full minute. 'I know exactly why my wife has asked you here,' he said, with a kind of weary indifference. 'If you cannot see it for yourself I suppose it is hopeless for me to tell you that I am no material for your skill. You will, of course, persist in trying to cure me?'

"'As you have guessed, that is why I am here,' I answered.

"He poured himself out a stiff tot of whisky, and regarded me with a mirthless smile.

"'Of course,' he said, 'this is the first thing I am to give up?'

"'That and morbid books,' I answered.

"'Oh, you mean *The Wandering Jew*? Do you know the story?'

"'I haven't read Eugene Sue's book, but I know the legend. He passes from life to life, doesn't he? And cannot die until Christ's second coming? I have heard various accounts of the legend. Christ on His way to Calvary had fallen under the weight of His Cross. One of the crowd struck Him and urged Him to go faster. Christ replied: "I go on, but you shall linger until I return." Some accounts have it that the Wandering Jew was Pilate's porter, others that he was one of the Pharisees, a shoemaker.'

"'He was neither,' said the General, as if he were stating an item of authentic news. 'He was Judas Iscariot.'

"'That is quite new to me,' I said.

"'He was Judas Iscariot,' he repeated. 'He stood jeering with the crowd, and Christ fell at his feet—the Cross was so heavy—and Judas—Judas was so eager to show that he had renounced his Master. He kicked Him as He lay fainting and said: "What are you feigning, Man?" And Christ, presently rising up, gazed at him and—and spoke that dreadful sentence.'

"The General's voice shook terribly, and the words ended in a whisper.

"'Who told you that version?' I asked as lightly as I could.

"'Who told me?' he repeated. 'Who told me?' He let his face fall between his hands and groaned aloud. 'Oh, my God, if somebody had only *told* me!' He raised his face once more. 'Do you know why Judas betrayed his Master? I can tell you that, too. It was pride. His some-time friends had jeered at him for a follower of the charlatan who pretended to be the Messiah, the King of the Jews. It wasn't for the thirty silver coins—it was all pride!'

"He spoke with an uncanny air of certainty and ended with a deep shuddering groan. Rather belatedly, perhaps, I thought it best to change the topic of conversation.

"'Come, General,' I said. 'I don't think too much theorizing about Scriptural matters is good for you. I am here to try to do something for you. If you don't mind my asking a few questions so soon after dinner—'

"He cut me short with a motion of his hand.

"'My dear doctor,' he said, 'I will tell you the whole truth about myself, as far as I know it. If, after having heard what I am going to tell you, you still think that my malady comes within the scope of science, then—I was going to say for the sake of peace—I will submit myself to your hands. You will probably regard me as an interesting case, but you will not have much time in which to experiment upon me. First, I know, you require perfect frankness. You shall have it. And I had better begin by stating that just as a few rare men have never been able to understand the meaning of the word fear, so I have never understood the meaning of the word sympathy. I know it to be a sensation which makes people shrink from hurting others, but I never experienced it.

"'I have had the reputation of a hard, proud, ambitious man. I have earned it. The men under my command hated and feared me, not without cause. I wanted them to. I had my head full of the hard great men of old times: Moor, who lashed men for breaking step on the march; the swearing, steel-hearted Iron Duke. I wanted my name to go down to history coupled with names like these. My great aim was to win battles, to take ground, not for the sake of my country, but for the reputation of General Sir Thomas Shiel.

"'He had no heart, no feeling. He was an automaton, but what an automaton! What a soldier! Almost I could see the printed word.

"'To that end my men had to be the smartest in France. I caused them to be continually harried while they were resting. While they were in the line my brigade staffs continually went round to see that their buttons, boots, and equipment were as brilliantly polished as if they were parading on the barrack square. It mattered nothing to me what rest and sleep I deprived them of. Those last letters home, which might have been written and were not, troubled me not at all. I was the Iron General; they were my soldiers, my pawns. When men were sniped at night because of the moonlight shining on a polished shrapnel helmet it mattered nothing to me. Men were cheap enough. England was full of them; the bases were full of them; long processions of drafts thronged all the lines of commu-nication. One asked for men and got them, as if one were indenting for quantities of soap or rifle oil. I did not mind sacrificing lives to enhance my reputation. I wanted to command an army; I might even rise to be Commander-in-Chief if the war lasted long enough. There was no end to my ambition.

"'I had orders at last to move my division on to the Somme, to take part in one of those attacks which proved so disastrous. My division had a certain objective. I gave my brigades orders that they had to take it. There must be no flinching or bungling. I warned them. If a unit failed to take its objective, whatever the cause, it must attack and attack again so long as there was one man left. I said it, I meant it, and I stuck to it. I was the Iron General until the end.

"'I had my headquarters in a little village called Flarincourt. There was a small white chateau a few hundred yards to the north where my staff and myself were housed. We arrived some days before the troops, and as the trains at the railhead disgorged them I myself took the "march past," sitting my horse at the roadside, my hand at the salute, while the doomed battalions tramped past me in columns of fours. There were motor-omnibuses waiting for them at the next village, and the men hated them as forerunners of disaster.

"'I had watched the last battalion of a brigade march past, and, knowing no other troops were due to arrive for some hours, rode off with an officer on my staff for lunch at the chateau. Opposite the chateau gates was a roadside Calvary, the Cross raised high and almost surrounded by poplars, but with an opening of the trees in front, made—so it seemed to me later—so that Christ might look down and marvel at the ways of men two thousand years after His own passion and death. Close against the Calvary, and in the shade of the poplars, a private soldier sprawled on the grass in an attitude of acute exhaustion. His face was pale and damp with sweat. To the sleeves of his tunic, below the numerals on his shoulder-straps, was sewn the divisional sign which marked him as one of my men and a straggler from one of the battalions which had just marched down the road.

"'Just then we were getting men from employment at the bases and from the non-combatant forces, men who had hitherto been declared unfit for service in the front line. They were hastily passed as "fit" by medical boards and drafted into fighting units after a few days' training. Some of them were fit for the work and others were not. I had a reputation to retain with men who came under my notice for falling out on the march. I reined up at once. "Hi, you, man" I shouted, "what are you doing there?"

"'He neither stirred nor answered, and in a trice I was off my horse and standing beside him, shouting and cursing. The man was clean-shaven, and his short hair was auburn-brown. I started a little when I saw his face, for I fancied I had seen him somewhere before. I knew the wide brow and the pair of large, deep, sorrowful brown eyes which he opened to look up into my face. The lower part of his face I did not recognize, but that brow and those eyes were strangely, insistently familiar. There was something else which affected me queerly. I put it down to some optical illusion, due to the sun's rays and the shrapnel helmet. When I first looked at him it seemed as if blood were trickling down his forehead. Then, as I looked closer, it was gone.

"'"Why can't you stand up," I bawled, "when an officer speaks to you? *What are you feigning, man?*"

"'"I must have fainted", he answered in a gentle cultured voice. One hand strayed round to his shoulders and touched the great square pack which was strapped upon them. "It is so heavy," he said.

"'I cursed and kicked him, told him to get up at once and go on, and stood over him while he struggled to his feet. I did not care if he were shamming or not. If he were, he would go on his way with a wholesome lesson. If he were not, he might drop down again and die for all I cared. He was no use to the Army in that event, and I cared nothing of what happened to men who could not march and shoot.

"'With great difficulty and much obvious suffering he rose to his feet. Then he stood still for a moment and looked at me. "This has happened before," he said very slowly and distinctly, and added: "You will remember."

"'Something—I do not know what—prevented me from questioning him as to his words. It seemed absurd at the time, but an unaccountable sensation of fear stole over me. The curse died on my lips as the man turned his back on me and began slowly and painfully to limp down the road. I remounted my horse and rode up to the chateau for lunch—wondering.

"'Next day occurred an incident which I forgot immediately afterwards for the time being. A party of men with a sergeant in charge was passing the chateau, proceeding on some duty or other. I came out immediately behind them so that, although they did not see me, I could hear them talking. "Your pack 'urts you, does it?" shouted the sergeant to one of them. "Well, you look up there." He nodded towards the Calvary. "Jesus Christ 'ad to carry something a blank sight 'eavier!" I do not know if he meant to be profane or if it were merely his rough way of offering conso- lation. But I remembered the incident later.

"'From the next day I was busy. Before dawn the muttering, rumbling and fluttering of gunfire began. It continued all day and the next night, increasing to drum-fire before the following dawn. Shortly afterwards the first reports came in. The day had gone ill with us. Our attack had broken down. I sent out the order: "Attack again immediately. Every objective must be taken." It was the sort of order that any of the great generals might have issued. It made me one with them—I, the Iron General.

"'All that day and the next panic reports came in from all the brigade headquarters. The enemy along our front was impregnably placed so long as he held out on the left and right. I knew it was so. I think a kind of madness seized me. To send the remnants of those battalions again and again to the attack was like flinging spray against a rock. But my pride weighed down all discretion. I was the Iron General who had never drawn back from what he set out to do. I cared for nothing but that reputation. From the safe distance of my chateau, far from the welter of mud and blood. I sent out the order repeatedly: "Attack again! Attack again!" And my big battalions melted and melted and melted, and long processions of Red Cross vans thundered past the chateau, and still I sent to my rebellious brigadiers the same mad command: "Attack again!"

"'You know how it ended, the thousands I sacrificed on the altar of my pride. That's ancient history now. When the final crash came, in the shape of a peremptory order from the Army Command, I was like a man dazed. Then, through my bewilderment streamed the light of old and dreadful memories. *He* had told me I should remember. I *did* remember! I *did* remember!'

"The General's voice rose to a scream. His face worked horribly and he clenched his hands and beat them upon the table, close by where I am sitting now, in a kind of frenzy.

"'What did you remember?' I asked him.

"'It was the soldier's face first of all—the soldier who had fainted under the weight of his pack beside the Calvary. I thought I knew it. I did know it. Everybody knows it. O God, have mercy—mercy!'

"I drew a long breath and sat still and staring. 'Ye did it unto Me.' The words shaped themselves in my brain and kept repeating themselves. The General's voice broke out again:

"'Don't you see? Don't you understand?' he snivelled. 'It was He I cursed and kicked as He lay fainting by the roadside, just as I had cursed and kicked Him on His way to that other death two thousand years ago. Oh, yes, I remembered that, too! It all came back so clearly across the centuries, even to the memory of how the blood-money in my pouch had jingled as I asked Him what He was feigning. I remembered all—all. How they laughed at me for a follower of Him... the leering High Priest of the Temple with his bag of money... the kiss in the Garden. And I remembered passages out of other lives since then, for death with me is scarcely a breathing space between one life and another. And in each of these lives I have betrayed my fellow-man because of the pride that is my heritage and curse through all the ages. I can look back until my mind reels upon betrayal after betrayal in my many lives, down to the day when, because of my pride, I betrayed those thousands in that hell upon the Somme. For that is my punishment!—to go on living and betraying, to live in many lands and under many names, but always to be Judas.'

"He fell forward and began to weep unpleasantly, great rending sobs that seemed to tear his throat. 'If I'd only known Him,' he whimpered, 'when He lay by the roadside outside Flarincourt, He might have forgiven me at last! I might have saved myself! But I must go on... I must go on to the same End which only marks another Beginning.'"

*

Standring brought his story to an abrupt conclusion. His cigar had gone out, and he sought for and lit another. Fitchett waited a little while, as if he expected more to come.

"Is that all?" he said at last.

"That is all the General's story, as he told it to me."

"But what about the end?"

"The end? Oh, you know that. I treated the General, and failed. You knew that from the beginning. I think you remarked that I wasn't infallible."

"But what did the General die of? One doesn't generally die of an hallucination, does one?"

"No. My dear fellow, surely you can guess. You remember what happened to Judas Iscariot, don't you?"

"Not—"

"Yes. The General hanged himself from that long beam out there in the hall."

BROWDEAN FARM

MOST people with limited vocabularies such as mine would describe the house loosely and comprehensively as picturesque. But it was more than beautiful in its venerable age. It had certain subtle qualities which are called Atmosphere. It invited you, as you approached it along the rough and narrow road which is ignored by those maps which are sold for the use of motorists. In the language of very old houses it said plainly: "Come in. Come in."

It said, "Come in" to Rudge Jefferson and me. In one of the front windows there was a notice, inscribed in an illiterate hand, to the effect that the house was to be let, and that the keys were to be obtained at the first cottage down the road. We went and got them. The woman who handed them over to us remarked that plenty of people looked over the house but nobody ever took it. It had been empty for years.

"Damp and falling to pieces, I suppose," said Rudge as we returned. "There's always a snag about these old places."

The house—Browdean Farm it was called—stood some thirty yards back from the road, at the end of a strip of garden not much wider than its façade. Most of the building was plainly Tudor, but part of it was even earlier. Time was when it had been the property of prosperous yeomen, but now its acres had been added to those of another farm, and it stood shorn of all its land save the small untended gardens in front and behind, and half an acre of apple orchard.

As in most houses of that description the kitchen was the largest room. It was long and lofty and its arched roof was supported by mighty beams which stretched across its breadth. There was a huge range with a noble oven. One could fancy, in the old days of plenty, a score of harvesters supping there after their work, and beer and cider flowing as freely as spring brooks.

To our surprise the place showed few signs of damp, considering the length of time it had been untenanted, and it needed little in the way of repairs. There was not a stick of furniture in the house, but we could tell that its last occupants had been people of refinement and taste. The wallpapers upstairs, the colours of the faded paints and distempers, the presence of a bathroom—that great rarity in old farmhouses—all pointed to the probability of its having been last in the hands of an amateur of country cottages.

Jefferson told me that he knew in his bones—and for once I agreed with his bones—that Nina would love the farm. He was engaged to my sister, and they were waiting until he had saved sufficient money to give them a reasonable material start in matrimony. Like most painstaking writers of no particular reputation Jefferson had to take care of the pence and the shillings, but like Nina's, his tastes were inexpensive, and it was an understood thing that they were to live quietly together in the country.

We inquired about the rent. It was astonishingly low. Jefferson had to live somewhere while he finished a book, and he was already paying storage for the furniture which he had bought. I could look forward to some months of idleness before returning to India. There was a trout stream in the neighbourhood which would keep me occupied and out of mischief. We laid our heads together.

Jefferson did not want a house immediately, but bargains of that sort are not everyday affairs in these hard times. Besides, with me to share expenses for the next six months, the cost of living at Browdean Farm would be very low, and it seemed a profitable speculation to take the house then and there on a seven years' lease. This is just what Jefferson did—or rather, the agreement was signed by both parties within a week.

Rudge Jefferson and I were old enough friends to understand each other thoroughly, and make allowances for each other's temperaments. We were neither of us morose but often one or both of us would not be anxious to talk. There were indefinite hours when Rudge felt either impelled or compelled to write. We found no difficulty in coming to a working agreement. We did not feel obliged to converse at meals. We could bring books to the table if we so wished. Rudge could go to his work when he chose, and I could go off fishing or otherwise amuse myself. Only when we were both inclined for companionship need we pay any attention to each other's existence.

And, from the April evening when we arrived half an hour after the men with the furniture, it worked admirably.

We lived practically in one room, the larger of the two front sitting-rooms. There we took our meals, talked and smoked and read. The smaller sitting-room Rudge commandeered for a study. He retired thither when the spirit moved him to invoke the muses and tap at his typewriter. Our only servant was the woman who had lately had charge of the keys. She came in every day to cook our meals and do the housework, and, as for convenience we dined in the middle of the day, we had the place to ourselves immediately after tea. The garden we decided to tend ourselves, but although we began digging and planting with the early enthusiasm of most amateurs we soon tired of the job and let wild nature take its course.

Our first month was ideal and idyllic. The weather was kind, and everything seemed to go in our favour. The trout gave me all the fun I could have hoped for, and Rudge was satisfied with the quality and quantity of his output. I had no difficulty in adapting myself to his little ways, and soon discovered that his best hours for working were in the mornings and the late evenings, so I left him to himself at those times. We took our last meal, a light cold supper, at about half-past nine, and very often I stayed out until that hour.

You must not think that we lived like two recluses under the same roof. Sometimes Rudge was not in the mood for work and hinted at a desire for companionship. Then we went out for long walks, or he came to watch me fish. He was himself a ham-handed angler and seldom attempted to throw a fly. Often we went to drink light ale at the village inn, a mile distant. And always after supper we smoked and talked for an hour or so before turning in.

It was then, while we were sitting quietly, that we discovered that the house, which was mute by day, owned strange voices which gave tongue after dark. They were the noises which, I suppose, one ought to expect to hear in an old house half full of timber when the world around it is hushed and sleeping. They might have been nerve-racking if one of us had been there alone, but as it was we took little notice at first. Mostly they proceeded from the kitchen, whence we heard the creaking of beams, sobbing noises, gasping noises, and queer indescribable scufflings.

While neither of us believed in ghosts we laughingly agreed that the house ought to be haunted, and by something a little more sensational than the sounds of timber contracting and the wind in the kitchen chimney. We knew ourselves to be the unwilling hosts of a colony of rats, which was in itself sufficient to account for most nocturnal noises. Rudge said that he wanted to meet the ghost of an eighteenth-century miser, who couldn't rest until he had shown where the money was hidden. There was some practical use in that sort of bogie. And although, as time went on, these night noises became louder and more persistent, we put them down to "natural causes" and made no effort to investigate them. It occurred to us both that some more rats had discovered a good home, and although we talked of trapping them our talk came to nothing.

We had been at the farm about a month before Rudge Jefferson began to show symptoms of "nerves." All writers are the same. Neurotic brutes! But I said nothing to him and waited for him to diagnose his own trouble and ease up a little with his work.

It was at about that time that I, walking homewards one morning just about lunch-time, with my rod over my shoulder, encountered the local policeman just outside the village inn. He wished me a good day which was at once hearty and respectful, and at the same time passed the back of his hand over a thirsty-looking moustache. The hint was obvious, and only a heart of stone could have refrained from inviting him inside. Besides, I believe in keeping in with the police.

He was one of those country constables who become fixtures in quiet, out-of-the-way districts, where they live and let live, and often go into pensioned retirement without bringing more than half-a-dozen cases before the petty sessions. This worthy was named Hicks, and I had already discovered that everybody liked him. He did not look for trouble. He had rabbits from the local poachers, beer from local cyclists who rode after dark without lights, and more beer from the landlord who chose to exercise his own discretion with regard to closing time.

P.C. Hicks drank a pint of bitter with me and gave me his best respects. He asked me how we were getting on up at the farm. Admirably, I told him; and then he looked at me closely, as if to see if I were sincere, or, rather, to search my eyes for the passing of some afterthought.

Having found me guileless, as it seemed, he went on to tell me of his length of service—he had been eighteen years on the one beat—and of how little trouble he had been to anybody. There was something pathetic in the protestations of the middle-aged Bobby that, to all the world, he had been a man and a brother. He seemed tacitly to be asking for reciprocity, and his own vagueness drew me out of my depth.

You know those beautifully vague men, who pride themselves for being diplomatists on the principle that a nod is as good as a wink to a blind horse? The people who will hint and hint and hint, the asses who will wander round and round and round the haystack with hardly a nibble at it? He was one of them. He wanted to tell me something without actually telling me, to exact from me a promise about something he chose not to mention.

I found myself in dialectical tangles with him, and at last I laughingly gave up the task of trying to follow his labyrinthine thoughts. I ordered two more bitters and then he said:

"Well, sir, if anything 'appens up at the farm, you needn' get talkin' about it. We done our best. What's past is past, and can't be altered. There isn't no sense in settin' people against *us*."

I knew from his inflection on the word that "us" was the police. He did not look at me while he spoke. He was staring at something straight across the counter, and I happened by sheer chance to follow the direction of his gaze.

Opposite us, and hanging from a shelf so as to face the customers, was a little tear-off calendar. The date recorded there was the nineteenth of May.

Two evenings later—which is to say the evening of May the twenty-first—I returned home at half-past nine full of suppressed excitement. I had a story to tell Rudge, and I was yet not sure if I should be wise in telling it. His nerves had grown worse during the past two days, but after all there are nerves and nerves, and my tale might interest without harming him.

It was only just dusk and not a tithe of the stars were burning as I walked up the garden path, inhaling the rank scents of those hardy flowers which had sprung up untended in that miniature wilderness. The sitting-room window was dark, but the subdued light of an oil lamp burned behind the curtains of Rudge's study. I found the door unbarred, walked in, and entered the study. You see, it was supper-time, and Rudge might safely be intruded upon.

Rather to my surprise the room was empty, but I surmised that Rudge had gone up to wash. That he had lately been at work was evident from the fact that a sheet of paper, half used, lay in the roller of the typewriter. I sat down in the revolving chair to see what he had written—I was allowed that privilege—and was astonished to see that he had ended in the middle of a sentence. In some respects he was a methodical person, and this was unlike him. The last word he had written was "the," and the last letter of that word was black and prominent as if he had slammed down the key with unnecessary force.

Two minutes later, while I was still reading, a probable explanation was revealed to me. I heard the gate click and footfalls on the path. Naturally I guessed that Rudge, temperamental as he was, had suddenly tired of his work and gone out for a walk. I heard the footsteps come to within a few yards of the house, when they left the path, fell softer on grass and weeds, and approached the window. The curtain obscured my view, but on the glass I heard the tap of finger-tips and the clink of nails.

I did not pause to reflect that Rudge, if he had gone out, must know that he had left the door on the latch, or that he could have no reason to suppose that I was already in the house. One does not consider these things in so brief a time. I just called out, "Right ho," and went round to the front door to let him in.

Having opened the front door I leaned out and saw him—Rudge, I imagined—peering in at the study window. He was no more than a dark, bent shadow in the dusk, crowned by a soft felt hat, such as he generally wore. "Right ho," I said again, and, leaving the door wide for him, I hurried into the kitchen. There was some salad left in soak which had to be shaken and wiped before bringing it to the table. I remember that, as I walked through to the sink, one of the beams over my head creaked noisily.

I washed the salad and returned towards the dining-room. As I turned into the hall a gust of air from the still open door passed like a cool caress across my face. Then, before I had time to enter the dining-room, I heard the gate click at the end of the garden path, and footfalls on the gravel. I waited to see who it was. It was Rudge—and he was bareheaded.

He produced a book at supper, and sat scowling at it over his left arm while he ate. This was permitted by our rules, but I had something to tell him, and after a while I forced my voice upon his attention.

"Rudge," I said, "I've made a discovery this evening. I know how you got this place so cheap."

He sat up with a start, stared at me, and winced.

"How?" he demanded.

"This is Stanley Stryde's old house. Don't you remember Stanley Stryde?"

He was pale already, but I saw him turn paler still.

"I remember the name vaguely," he said. "Wasn't he a murderer?"

"He was," I answered. "I didn't remember the case very well. But my memory's been refreshed today. Everybody here thought we knew, and the curious delicacy of the bucolic mind forbade mentioning it to us. It was rather a grisly business, and the odd thing is that local opinion is all in favour of Stryde's innocence, although he was hanged."

Rudge's eyes had grown larger.

"I remember the name," he said, "but I forget the case. Tell me."

"Well, Stanley Stryde was an artist who took this place. He was what we should call in common parlance a dirty dog. He'd got himself entangled with the daughter of a neighbouring farmer—the family has left here since—and then he found himself morally and socially compelled to marry her. At the same time he fell in love with another girl, so he lured the old one here and did her in. Don't you remember now?"

Rudge wrinkled his nose.

"Yes, vaguely," he said. "Didn't he bury the body and afterwards try to make out that she'd committed suicide? So this is the house, is it? Funny nobody told us before."

"They thought we knew," I repeated, "and nobody liked to mention it. As if it were some disgrace to *us*, you know! Oh, and, of course, the house is haunted."

Rudge stared at me and frowned.

"I don't know about 'haunted,'" he said, "but it's been a damned uncomfortable house to sit in for the past few evenings. I mean at twilight, when I've been waiting for you. My nerves have been pretty raw lately. Tonight I couldn't stand it, so I went out for a stroll."

"Left in the middle of a sentence," I remarked.

"Oh, so you noticed that, did you?"

"By the way," I asked, "what made you go out a second time?"

"I didn't."

"But my dear chap, you did! Because the first time you came in you wore a hat, and two minutes later I saw you walking up the garden path without one."

"That's when I did come back. I haven't worn a hat at all this evening."

"Then who—" I began.

"And that reminds me," he continued quickly, "when *you* come in of an evening you needn't sneak up to the window and tap on it with your fingers. It doesn't frighten me, but it's disconcerting. You can always walk into the room to let me know you've come back."

I sat and looked at him and laughed.

"But, my dear chap, I haven't done such a thing yet."

"You old liar!" he exclaimed with an uneasy laugh, "you've been doing it every evening for the past week—until tonight, when I didn't give you the chance."

"I swear I haven't, Rudge. But if you thought that, it explains why you did the same thing to me tonight."

I saw from his face that I had made some queer mistake, and interrupted his denial to ask:

"Then who was the man I saw peering in at the window? I saw him from the door. I thought you'd tapped at the window to be let in, not knowing that the door was open. So I went round and saw—I thought it was you—and called out, 'Right ho.'"

We looked at each other again and laughed uneasily.

"It seems we've got our ghost after all," Rudge said half jestingly.

"Or somebody's trying to pull our leg," I amended.

"I don't know that I should fancy meeting the ghost of a murderer. But, joking apart, the house *has* been getting on my nerves of late. And those noises we've always heard have been getting louder and more mysterious lately."

As if to corroborate a statement which needed no evidence so far as I was concerned we heard a scuffling sound from the kitchen followed by the loud creaking of timber. We laughed again puzzled uneasy laughter, for the thing was still half a joke.

"There you are!" said Rudge, and got upon his legs. "I'm going to investigate this."

He crossed the room and suddenly halted. I knew why. Then he turned about with an odd, shamed chuckle.

"No," he said, "there's no sense in it. I shall find nothing there. Why should I pander to my nerves?"

I had nothing to say. But I knew that in turning back he was pandering to cowardice, because just then I would have done almost anything rather than enter that kitchen. Had anybody asked me then where the murder was done I could have told them with as much certainty as if I had just been reading about it in the papers.

Rudge sat down again.

"Don't laugh at me," he said. "I know this is all rot, but I've got a hideous feeling that things hidden and unseen around us are moving steadily to a crisis."

"Cheerful brute," I said smiling.

"I know. It's only my nerves, of course. I don't want to infect you with them. But the noises we hear, and the fellow who comes and taps at the window—they want some explaining away, don't they?"

"Especially now that we know that somebody was murdered here," I agreed. "I'm beginning to wish we didn't know about that."

Rudge went early to bed that night, but I sat up reading. As often happens to me I fell asleep over my book, and when I woke I was almost in darkness, for the lamp needed filling. The last jagged, blue flame swelled and dwindled, fluttering like a moth and tapping against the glass. And as I watched it I became suddenly aware of the cause of my waking. I had heard the latch snap on the garden gate. And in that moment I began to hear them—the footfalls.

I heard the rhythmic crunch of gravel and then the swish of long grass and plantains, and then a shadow nodded on the blind. It loomed up large and suddenly became stationary. A loose pane rattled under the impact of fingers.

Perhaps there was a moon, perhaps not, but there was at least bright starlight in the world outside. The drawn blind looked like dim bluish glass, and the shadow of something outside was cut as cleanly as a silhouette clipped away with scissors. I saw only the head and shoulders of a man, who wore a dented felt hat. His head lolled over on to his left shoulder, just as I had always imagined a man's head would loll if—well, if he had been hanged. And I knew in my blood that he was a Horror and that he wanted me for something.

I felt my hair bristle and suddenly I was streaming with sweat. I don't remember turning and running, but I have a vague recollection of cannoning off the door post and stumbling in the hall. And when I reached my bed I don't know if I fainted or fell asleep.

No, I didn't tell Rudge next day. His nerves were in a bad enough state already. Besides, in the fresh glory of a May morning it was easy to persuade myself that the episode had been an evil dream. But I did question Mrs Jaines, our charwoman, when she arrived, and I saw a look half stubborn and half guilty cross her face.

Yes, of course, she remembered the murder happening, but she didn't remember much about it. Mr Stryde was quite a nice gentleman, although rather a one for the ladies, and she had worked for him sometimes.

Stryde's defence was that the poor girl had committed suicide and that he'd lost his head and buried the body when he found it. Lots of people thought that was true, but they'd hanged Mr Stryde for it all the same. And that was all I could get out of Mrs Jaines.

I smiled grimly to myself. As if the woman didn't remember every detail! As if the neighbourhood had talked of anything else for the two following years! And then I remembered the policeman's strange words and how he had been staring at the calendar while he spoke.

So that morning when I called at the inn for my usual glass of beer, I, too, looked at the calendar and asked the landlord if he could tell me the date of the murder.

"Yes, sir," he said, "it was May the—" And then he stopped himself. "Why, it was eight years ago, tonight!" he said.

I went out again that evening and came in at the usual hour. But that evening Rudge came down the path to meet me. He was white and sick-looking.

"He's been here again," he said, "half an hour ago."

"You saw him this time?" I asked jerkily.

"Yes, I did as you did and went round to the door." He paused and added quite soberly: "He *is* a ghost, you know."

"What happened?" I asked, looking uneasily around me.

"Oh! I went round to the door when I heard him tapping at the window, and there he was, as you saw him yesterday evening, trying to look through into the room. He must have heard me for he turned and stared. His head was drooping all on one side, like a poppy on a broken stem. He came towards me, and I couldn't stand that, so I turned and ran into the house and locked the door."

He spoke in a tone half weary, half matter of fact, and suddenly I knew that it was all true. I don't mean that I knew that just his story was true, I knew that the house was haunted and that the thing which we had both seen was part of the man who had once been Stanley Stryde.

When once one has accepted the hitherto incredible it is strange how soon one can adapt oneself to the altered point of view.

"This is the anniversary of the—the murder," I said quietly. "I should think something—something worse will happen tonight. Shall we see it through or shall we beat it?"

And almost in a whisper Rudge said:

"Poor devil! Oughtn't one to pity? He wants to tell us something, you know."

"Yes," I agreed, "or show us something."

Together we walked into the house. We were braver in each other's company, and we did not again discuss the problem of going or staying. We stayed.

I can pass over the details of how we spent that evening. They are of no importance to the story. We were left in peace until just after eleven o'clock, when once more we heard the garden gate being opened, and footfalls which by this time we were able to recognize came up the path and through the long grass to the window. We could see nothing, for our lamp was alight, but I knew what it looked like—the thing that stood outside and now tapped softly upon the glass. And in spite of having Rudge for company I lost my head and screamed at it.

"Get back to hell! Get back to hell, I tell you!" I heard myself shout.

And it was Rudge, Rudge the sensitive neurotic, who kept his head, for human psychology is past human understanding.

"No," he called out in a thin quaver, "come in. Come in, if we can help you."

And then, as if regretting his courage on the instant, he caught my hand and held it, drawing me towards him.

The front door was locked, but it was no barrier to that which responded to the invitation. We heard slow footfalls shuffling through the hall, the footfalls, it seemed to me, of a man whose head was a burden to him. I died a thousand deaths as they approached the door of our room, but they passed and died away up the passage. And then I heard a whisper from Rudge.

"He's gone through into the kitchen. I think he wants us to follow."

I shouldn't have gone if Rudge hadn't half dragged me by the hand. And as I went the sweat from the roots of my stiffened hair ran down my cheeks.

The kitchen door was closed, and we halted outside it, both of us breathing as if we had been running hard. Then Rudge held his breath for a moment, lifted the latch, and took a quick step across the threshold. And in that same instant he froze my chilled blood with a scream such as I had heard in wartime from a wounded horse.

He had almost fainted when he fell into my arms, but he had the presence of mind to pull the door after him, so that I saw nothing. I half dragged, half carried him into the dining-room and gave him brandy. And suddenly I became aware that a great peace had settled upon the house. I can only liken it to the freshness and the sweetness of the earth after a storm has passed. Rudge felt it, too, for presently he began to talk.

"What was he—doing?" I asked in a whisper.

"He? He wasn't there—not in the kitchen."

"Not in the kitchen? Then what—who—"

"It was She. Only She. She was kicking and struggling. From the middle beam, you know. And there was an overturned chair at her feet."

He shuddered convulsively.

"She was worse than he," he said presently—"far worse."

And then later:

"Poor devil! So he didn't do it, you see!"

Next morning we had it out with Mrs Jaines, and we did not permit her memory to be hazy or defective. She must have known that we had seen something and presently she burst into tears.

"He said he'd found her hanging in the kitchen, poor gentleman, and that he'd buried her because he was afraid people would say he'd done it. But the jury wouldn't believe him, and the doctors all said that it wasn't true, and that the marks on her neck were where he'd strangled her with a rope. I don't believe to this day he did it, I don't! But nothing can't ever bring him back." She paused at that and added. "Not back to life, I mean—real life, like you and me, I mean."

And that was all we heard and all we wished to hear.

Afterwards Rudge said to me:

"For his sake, the truth as we know it ought to be told to everybody. I suppose the police know?"

"Yes," I said, "the police know—now. But as Mrs Jaines said, it can't bring him back."

"Who wants to bring him back?" exclaimed Rudge with a shudder. "But perhaps if people knew—as we know—it might let him rest. I am sure that was what he wanted—just that people should know."

He paused and drew a long breath through his lips.

"You write it," he said jerkily. "I can't!"

And so I have.

THE GREEN SCARF

W HEN the Wellingford family became extinct the days of Wellingford Hall as one of the great country homes of England were already numbered. The estate passed into the hands of commercial-minded people who had no reverence for the history of a great house. The acres around the old Hall became too valuable as building sites to be allowed to remain as a park surrounding a country mansion. So the fat Wellingford sheep were driven elsewhere to pasture, and surveyors and architects heralded the coming of navvies and builders.

All this happened many years ago. The old park became crossed and criss-crossed by new roads, and perky little villas with names like "Ivyleigh" and "Dulce Domum" sprang up like monstrous red fungi. Even these have since mellowed, and grown their own ivy and Virginia creeper, and put on airs of respectable maturity. The Hall itself, forlorn and abandoned, like some poor human wretch deserted in his old age, began slowly to crumble into decay.

Wellingford Hall was no more than an embarrassment to the new owners of the estate, who were willing to let it or sell it at the prospective tenant's or purchaser's own price; but to dispose of a great house with no land attached to it and surrounded by a garden city is no easy matter. It was too big for its environment. After some vicissitudes as a private school and the home of a small community of nuns, it was abandoned to its natural fate: "for," said one of the directors of the Wellingford Estate, Limited, a gentleman not above mixing his metaphors, "what was the sense of keeping a white elephant in a state of repair?"

Three years before this present time of writing came Aubrey Vair, the painter, as poor as most other painters, a lover of old buildings and all the cobwebby branches of archæology, and took Wellingford Hall at a weekly rental of fewer shillings than might be demanded for the use of a gardener's cottage. He knew one of the directors, and he had discovered that a few rooms in the middle of the block of buildings were still habitable. The directors, I suppose, wondered why anyone should wish to live in the damp-ridden, rat-riddled old hole, but they did not despise shillings, and they let him come.

Vair wrote me several letters, begging me to come down and rough it with him. It was just the place for a writer, he assured me; it would give me ideas. He had been searching after priests'-holes and had discovered no less than five. One of the great rooms made the finest studio he had yet painted in. And really, as regards comfort, he avowed, it wasn't so bad, so long as one came there already warned to expect only the amenities of a poor bachelor establishment. And then, he added temptingly, there were the historical associations.

I already knew something about the latter, having discovered my facts in a book dealing with old English country houses. Charles the First had spent a night there during the Great Civil War. Charles the Second was supposed to have hidden there after the battle of Worcester. But best of all was the romantic tale of the capture and execution of Sir Peter Wellingford in 1649.

Briefly, Sir Peter was a proscribed Royalist who lived hunted and in hiding after the failure of the royal arms. A wiser man would have crossed the Channel, but Sir Peter had a young wife at Wellingford Hall. He had often visited her in safety, and might have continued to do so, but for a traitor in his own household. This fellow, so the story went, betrayed his master by waving a green scarf from one of the windows, this being a pre-arranged signal to inform a detachment of Parliamentary troops that the head of the house was secretly in residence. The soldiers burst in at night, and ransacked the house before Sir Peter Wellingford was discovered in a hiding-hole—or "privacie," as the old chronicle described it. The cavalier was dragged outside and shot in his own courtyard.

Here was a story romantic enough to inveigle the fancy of most men with a grain of imagination. I fully intended to visit Wellingford Hall, but circumstances caused me to defer my intention for the first summer and it was not until the following May, when Vair had been in residence a full year, that I paid him my deferred visit. I journeyed by road, driving myself in my small two-seater, so that Vair had no opportunity to meet me, and I had my first view of Wellingford Hall before I could be biased by his enthusiasms.

Holy writ speaks of the abomination of desolation standing where it ought not; and here was this grim, forbidding, crumbling old ruin still surrounded by its moat and standing in the midst of jerry-built "Chumleighs" and "Rosemounts." It was like finding the House of Usher in the middle of a new garden city. In spite of its moat the Hall had never been intended for a fortress and the bridge I crossed must have been nearly as old as the house itself.

Vair heard me coming and pushed open the great nail-studded door under the archway of the main entrance to come out and greet me with a grin and a handshake. He climbed up beside me and directed me round into the yard, where there was plenty of accommodation for a dozen cars. Strangely enough, the stables and coach-houses were in better repair than the old house itself.

The hall had once been magnificent, but most of the ceiling was gone, and the oak balustrade of the staircase, having had a commercial value, had been long since removed. A trail of sacking across broken paving stones pointed the way to Vair's apartments beyond. He ushered me into a fine room, in quite a reasonable state of repair, furnished with products of his speculations at country auctions. Although the month was May the weather was none too warm, and I was glad of the sight of the log fire which lent the room an additional air of comfort. Vair laughed to hear me exclaim, and asked if I were ready for tea.

He lived there, he explained, entirely alone, except that a charwoman came each morning to do the rough work and cook his one hot meal of the day.

"You won't mind putting up with cold stuff and tinned things of an evening?" he asked anxiously.

I hate tinned foods, but, of course, I could not say so.

After tea, Vair showed me the rest of the rooms which he had made habitable, and, really, he had managed to make himself much more comfortable than I had expected. He had contrived—Heaven knows how—to learn a lot of intimate history of the old place, and knew the name by which every room had been called in the house's palmy days of dignity and prosperity. My bedroom, for instance, was known as "Lady Ursula's Nursery," although history had long since forgotten who Lady Ursula was.

It was easy to see that Vair had a boyish enthusiasm for the place. He was a queer chap, with more than the average artist's share of eccentricities, and he believed in all manner of superstitions and pseudo sciences. He was one of those ageless men who might have been anything in the twenties, thirties, or forties. I happened to know that he was nearly fifty, but his thin wiriness of figure and boyish zest for life kept him youthful. Obviously his pleasure at having me down was not so much for my own sake as his. I was somebody to whom he could "show off" the house. He was clearly as proud of it as if it had been restored to its former dignity and he were the actual owner.

"For Heaven's sake, don't go about the place by yourself," he said, "or you'll break your neck. I've nearly broken mine a dozen times, and I'm beginning to know where it isn't safe to walk. It must be rather rare to find damp-rot and dry-rot in the same house, but we've got both here."

I promised faithfully that I wouldn't move without him. Even the main staircase did not appear too safe to me, but Vair assured me that it was all right.

After tea he took me over such parts of the house as it was safe to visit, but I shall make no attempt to describe most of this pilgrimage. My memory carries dreary pictures of damp and decay, of dust and dirt, and cobwebs, mouldering walls and crumbling floors. The old place must have been a warren of secret rooms and passages, and he showed me those he had discovered. All I can say is that the refugees of the bad old days must have been very uncomfortable, and those who escaped deserved to.

One large room under the roof, which we visited, had once been a secret chamber. It was called the Chapel, and here Mass had been said in defiance of the law throughout part of the sixteenth and seventeenth centuries.

"There must be a lot more secret rooms," Vair remarked. "Little Owen, who was a master at constructing such places, is known to have spent months here during the reign of Elizabeth. The house was always being raided, and the raiders had little satisfaction."

"They got the poor old cavalier," I laughed.

"Oh, yes. But he was given away, or sold, by a servant. I've shown you the place where I'm almost sure he hid—behind where the bed-head used to be in the room called the King's Chamber. We'll see if we can find some more while you're here, if you like."

It suddenly occurred to me that Vair had always called himself "sensitive," or psychic, and it was perhaps natural of me to put on the noncommittal smile of the polite sceptic and inquire if he had seen any ghosts. Rather to my surprise, he shook his head.

"No," he answered; "it isn't at all that kind of place. The house is quite friendly. I should have felt it at once if it had been otherwise."

"But I should have thought with its history—"

"Ah, it's seen troubled days, but they were always nice people who lived here. There are no dreadful legends of bloodshed and cruelty."

"There is the story of the cavalier," I objected. "Surely his ghost ought to haunt the place."

"Why? He was a good man from all accounts and he died a man's death. Only troubled or wicked people linger about the scenes of their earth-life. When he was taken out and slaughtered all the hatred and blood-lust came from *outside*. If any impressions of those spent passions remain, they're not inside the house, and I don't want them inside."

I smiled to myself, knowing that, from Vair's point of view, the house *ought* to be haunted, and his excuses for the non-appearance of a ghost or two struck me as ingenious but far-fetched.

"That's a pity," I said, tongue in cheek. "I quite hoped to be introduced to a Grey Lady or a Spectre Cavalier."

He frowned, knowing that I was laughing at him.

"Well, you won't be," he said, "unless—"

"Unless what?"

"Well, unless something happens to alter present conditions. If, for instance, we were to find something which someone long forgotten desired should remain hidden."

"I see."

"I doubt if you do. And I doubt if anything could be done now to disturb any of the Wellingfords in their long sleep. They seem to have been an ideal family; I haven't been able to find a word of scandal on any page of their history. Where there has once been bitterness and hatred, there you may look for ghosts. There was none here. All that came from outside. That frenzied desire, for instance, to trap and kill a man because he had fought for his king, long after his cause was well lost; that bitter bigotry which sought to prevent folk from worshipping according to their consciences. It all came from outside, I tell you!"

Vair's voice had risen. Like most men with no particular faith he respected all creeds, and religious intolerance always moved him to violent anger. Respect for his deadly seriousness kept my face grave.

"Do you mean just outside?" I asked.

"How do I know? And so long as they remain outside what does it matter? I assure you, I don't want them brought in."

To my relief, he then veered away from a subject which was hardly within my scope of conversation. There was little of the mystic in me. All the same, when at last I retired to bed in Lady Ursula's nursery, I was glad to remember that Vair had given the house a clean bill of health in the psychic sense. By the time I had been Vair's guest for twenty-four hours I had begun to feel with him that the old ruin had a kindly and friendly atmosphere, in spite of its apparent gloom, and that this might have been the legacy of good people who had lived and died within its walls.

At the risk of giving this narrative an air of being disconnected, I must pass hurriedly over the next two or three days of my visit, for they brought forth little that is worth recording. Sometimes Vair did a little painting, and then his preoccupation drove me to my own work, We did a little fishing and sometimes walked three-quarters of a mile to the Welling-ford Arms where, according to Vair, who accounted himself an expert, the bitter beer was better than the average. Sometimes we risked our necks on rickety stairs and crumbling floors, looking for more secret hiding-places, an occupation in which I soon became infected with some of Vair's schoolboy zest.

The place was quiet enough during the day, but the villas and bunga-lows which had marched almost to the edge of the moat made themselves audible at night. Every Lyndhurst and Balmoral seemed able to boast of a musical daughter or a powerful gramophone. The effect of sitting in one of those dignified old rooms with the windows open and hearing echoes from the musical comedies was grotesque in the extreme. Vair had evi-dently grown used to it, for he made no comment.

I had arrived on a Saturday, and it was on the afternoon of the Tuesday following that, between us, we made a discovery of historical interest; a discovery which we came afterwards bitterly to regret having made. We were on the first floor landing, where long windows, deep in a recess, looked out over the Wellingford Park estate, when Vair mentioned that he had never examined the window-seats.

"Sliding panels," he said, "certainly have existed, but they belong mostly to fiction. They were too hard to construct and too easily discovered. Take the five hiding-places you've seen in this house. Three of them are behind fireplaces, one under the stairs, and the other must have been masked at one time by the head of a bedstead. Window-seats were very often used, and this one looks likely. Let's try it."

We rapped it with our knuckles and, although it did not sound hollow, there was obviously an empty space beneath it. We pushed and tugged and teased the surface of the wood with our fingers. And suddenly I saw a crack widen, and part of the seat which had fitted into the rest of the woodwork as neatly as a drawer came away in my hands, and we stared at each other with laughter and curiosity in our eyes.

"Hallo, what's this!" Vair exclaimed.

The cavity disclosed was very small. It was obviously not the entrance to any place of concealment capable of holding a human being. I lit a match and thrust it down into the darkness. Then cheek by jowl we peered together into a cavity no more than three feet deep.

"Nothing here," I said, breaking cobwebs as I moved my wrist to and fro.

"Isn't there!" exclaimed Vair.

He brushed me aside and his arm disappeared up to the shoulder. His hand was black when he drew it forth, and an end of something like a black rag was between his fingers. It was an old piece of silk, so rotten with age that it almost crumbled under our touch; but when we had blown on it and brushed it with our fingers we saw that it owed its present colour to the dirt of ages, and that it had once been green. On the instant the old tale leaped into the minds of both of us, and we exclaimed together:

"The Green Scarf!"

I forget what we said for the first minute or two. We were both excited and elated. There is some peculiar pleasure, difficult to analyse or explain, in discovering a relic which serves to corroborate some old tale or passage of ancient history. We neither of us doubted that we had discovered the green scarf by which Sir Peter Wellingford had been betrayed nearly three hundred years before.

"The traitor must have kept it here in readiness," said Vair, his eyes dancing. "And when he'd signalled he dropped it back again, and there it's lain from that day to this."

"And most likely," I added, taking the relic from his hands, "this is the very window he waved from."

The window was open and I leaned out and let the dingy rag flutter from my hand in the warm afternoon breeze.

"Don't!" said Cair sharply, and pulled me back.

The silk was so rotten with age that even the weak breeze tore it slightly, and I thought at the time that Vair's sharp "Don't!" was uttered because of the damage I had unwittingly done. It was a relic of treachery and bloodshed, but we both regarded it with a queer sort of reverence, as if it were associated with something sacred.

I should think an hour must have passed before we mentioned anything else. We were both agreed that one of us should write to a newspaper announcing our discovery and that the scarf should be cleaned by an expert and offered to a museum. One remark of Vair's struck me at the time as a little strange, but the full force of it did not come to me until some hours later.

"I wish you hadn't waved it out of the window," he said. "It's what that damned traitor did. That's what made you do it, of course—trying to re-enact part of an old tragedy."

"I don't see that it matters," I returned lightly. "Nobody saw."

He turned on me at once.

"How do you know?" he demanded sharply.

I could not help laughing then.

"My dear fellow," I exclaimed, "are you afraid that the wife or daughter of one of your neighbours will think—"

"I wasn't thinking of *them,*" he returned curtly. "When that rag was waved out of that window nearly three hundred years ago, you know what happened, you know what it brought into the house."

I thought I had caught the drift of his meaning. Vair had always declined to walk under ladders or make the thirteenth of a party, and he was unhappy for days after he had spilled the contents of a salt-cellar.

"Oh, don't be an ass, Vair," I begged. "If there's any ill-luck about I give it leave to attack me and leave you alone."

He did not answer, and in a few minutes the incident had passed temporarily from my mind.

I have tried to tell this story so many times by word of mouth, and been compelled at this point to pause and hesitate, as now I am compelled to pause and think. It is not that my memory fails me; memory, indeed, serves me all too well. But hereabouts I am brought to realize the failure of my small command of words. A bad speaker can at least convey something otherwise unexpressed by look, gesture, hesitation, tone of voice. But with nothing but pen, ink, paper, and a limited vocabulary, I see little chance of giving an adequate account of what happened to us that night; of how with the twilight depression was laid upon us, straw by straw, and how with the coming of darkness horror was laid upon us, load by load.

Even before supper I found myself restless and ill at ease. Something began to weigh upon my spirit as if my mind carried the knowledge of some ordeal which I had presently to face. Of course, I put it down to an attack of "liver" and made up my mind to forget it. The intention was good, but it was unjustified by the desired result.

My discovery that Vair was suffering from a similar *malaise* did not help my own case. His spirits were far below normal, and I think our mutual discovery that the other was "below form" added weight to that which was already dragging at our hearts. To make matters worse we each began to act for the other's benefit, to force laughter, to crack heavy jokes, and make cumbersome epigrams. But when at twilight we lit the lamp and sat down to supper we tacitly agreed to give up pretending.

"Do you feel that there's a weight crushing you whenever there's thunder about?" Vair asked suddenly.

I was glad to think of some excuse to account for my mood and answered quickly:

"Yes, very often. And I wouldn't mind betting there's some thunder about tonight."

Vair looked at me and seemed suddenly to change his mind over what he had been about to say. He shook his head.

"The glass hasn't gone down."

I rose from the table without apology, went to the window, pulled aside the curtains, and looked out. It was just after sunset on a very perfect May evening. There was a red glow in the west, and around this glow there was an area of sky which was almost apple-green. This merged into a very deep blue in which one or two pale stars were already beginning to play hide-and-seek.

"No," I agreed grudgingly, "there isn't a cloud in the sky. Still, storms come up very quickly."

"Yes," said Vair, "and so do other things."

My lips moved to ask him what he meant, but I thought better of it. Whatever morbid imaginings he might be entertaining, they were scarcely likely to help my own mood. We ate in silence, continuing thus for a long time before I forced a laugh and exclaimed:

"Well, we're a jolly pair, aren't we? What the devil's the matter with us this evening? I only wish I knew."

"I only wish I didn't think I know," he answered strangely.

"Well, what do you think—"

"I think we ought to go out somewhere tonight and stay out."

"Why? You haven't felt like this before, have you?"

"No. And it's because I haven't felt like this before—"

He came to another sudden pause, and we looked into each other's faces for a moment before he lowered his gaze.

"Now, look here," I said, trying to keep my voice steady, "let's be as honest as we can and try to analyse this thing. I'll say it first. We're both afraid of something."

He went a step further.

"We're both afraid of the same thing," he said.

"Well, what is it, then? Let's find it out and confront it. When a horse shies at a tree you lead him up to it to show him that it's only a tree."

"If it happens to be a tree or something like a tree. But if it isn't... Look here, let's go out. Straight away now, while there's time. They've got bedrooms at the Wellingford Arms. Let's go and spend the night there."

With all my heart I wanted to. But Pride borrowed the voice of Reason and spoke for me.

"Oh, don't let's make fools of ourselves," I urged. "I for one don't want to truckle to my nerves. If we give way like this once we shall always be doing it."

He shrugged his shoulders.

"Let's have a drink."

He brought out the whisky. I am a temperate man with a weak head for spirits, and I admit that I exceeded my usual allowance, but it made no difference to me than if it were water. We sat facing each other gloomily in a silence which became increasingly difficult to break.

The unusual quality of this silence had already begun to impress me when Vair mentioned it, as if my thought had communicated itself to him.

"Don't you notice how extraordinarily still everything seems?" he asked presently.

"Yes," I agreed, and snatched suddenly at a straw. "The silence before the storm. There *is* a storm about, you see."

He shook his head.

"No," he said. "It isn't that kind of stillness."

And then, with a little leap of the heart and a tingling of the nostrils I suddenly realized a fact which seemed to me inexpressibly ugly. This stillness was not the hush of Nature before some electrical disturbance. For some time past we had heard no sound at all from the outer world. The gramophones and pianos in the little houses around us were all silent. It was the hour when at many houses on the estate hosts and guests were parting for the night, yet there was not the faint echo of a voice, nor the comfortable workaday sound of a car droning along a road. It may seem ludicrous, but I would have given a hundred pounds just then to hear the distant shunting of a train.

Vair rose suddenly, went to the window and looked out. I followed him. For some while now it had been completely dark. Overhead in a very clear sky the stars looked peacefully into our troubled eyes.

"No storm about," said Vair shortly.

He heard me catch my breath, and a moment later he was aware of what I had already perceived.

"Look! There aren't any lights! There isn't a light anywhere!"

It was true. The hour was not late, and yet from the rows of houses which began not so many yards distant, not a light was visible, nor was it possible to discern an outline of roof or chimney against the sky. We had been cut off from the lights and sounds of the outside world as completely as if we were in a cavern miles under the ground, save that our isolation—I can think of no other word—was lateral.

Vair's voice had risen high and thin. He made no effort to disguise the terror in it.

"There must be some fog about," I said; and I was so anxious lest my voice should sound like Vair's that I spoke out of the base of my chest.

"Fog! Look, man!"

I looked. Truly there was not the least sign of fog or mist. Until we raised our eyes to the sky we stared into impenetrable, featureless darkness.

Vair let the window curtains fall from his hand. He turned to me in the oppressive stillness, and his face worked until by an effort he controlled the muscles.

"Try to tell me," he said hoarsely, "*what* you've been feeling all the evening."

"How can I? The same as you, I suppose!" A reminiscence of soldiering came back to me. "It's been like waiting to go over the top. A horrible aching anxiety. No, something more than that. A sense of being trapped, of being surrounded—"

"Surrounded!" He caught up the word with a cry. "That's just what you are! That's just what we both are!"

I drew him away from the curtained window.

"Surrounded! By what?" I made myself ask.

He spread out his hands and shook them helplessly.

"The Powers of Darkness, Hatred, Blood-lust, Intolerance—they were all waiting, waiting for the signal. Do you think these things die like spent matches? Do you think the black act of treachery, which brought them into this house, left nothing behind it. *They* were waiting—all these years—I tell you!" Suddenly he bared his teeth at me. "You fool, to have waved that rag at them!"

Just for a moment I felt my brain turning like a wheel, but I made a fight for my sanity and won it back.

"Look here," I said, "for God's sake don't let's behave like madmen. Let's get out of it if the house is going to affect us like this."

He stared back at me, giving me a look which I could not read.

"No," he muttered; "you wanted to stay."

"Let's go down to the Wellingford Arms."

"They're closed now."

"It doesn't matter. They know you. They'll open for you."

I found myself lusting for the world beyond that unnatural girdle of darkness. The Wellingford Arms, with its vulgar tin advertisements of Somebody's Beer, and Somebody Else's Whisky, and its framed Christmas Number plates—at least there was sanity there.

But Vair suddenly turned on me the eyes of a hunted animal.

"You fool!" he burst out. "It's too late! We can't pass through *Them!*"

"What do you mean?" I faltered.

"They're all around us. You know it, too. They'll break in—in their own good time—as they did before. We're trapped, I tell you!"

Against my will, and Heaven knows how hard I fought for disbelief, Vair had captured my powers of reason. In theory, if not in action, I was now prepared to follow him like a child.

"What do they want?" I stammered.

"Us! One of us or both! What did Murder and Hatred and Blood-lust ever want but sacrifice?"

He fairly spat the words at me and I seized his arm.

"Come on," I said, "we're going to get out of this. We're going to run the gauntlet."

"Ah," said Vair thickly. "If we can."

We must have crossed the hall, although I do not remember it. My next recollection is of helping Vair in his fumbling with the bolts and lock of the great door. We wrenched it open and stood looking at an opaque wall of darkness.

I tried to force myself across the threshold, only to find myself standing rigid. As in a nightmare, my legs were shackled so that I could not move a step forward, but although terror clawed at me like a wild beast, my senses were keenly and even painfully alert.

I knew that this belt of darkness around the house was alive with whisperings and movements, with all manner of stealthiness, which lurked only just beyond the horizon of vision and the limits of hearing. And as I stood straining eyes and ears I knew that the barriers must soon break and that I should both see and hear.

We stood thus a long while on the edge of the threshold we could not pass, but whether it were seconds or minutes I could not say. To us it seemed hours ere the darkness passed, melting into the living forms of men. We could *see*, and there was movement everywhere; we could *hear*, and voices were shouting orders, although the actual words eluded us. They were human voices with strange nasal intonations, snarling and shouting. Even in my extremity I remembered having heard that the soldiery of Cromwell had affected a hideous nasal accent. And now the darkness was sundered and shivered by a score of lights, the lights of naked torches which nodded to the rhythm of men marching. I saw the glint of them on the metal heads of pikes, and on the long barrels of muskets outlined clearly now against a naked sky of stars.

Terror may bind a man to the spot, but another turn of the rack may torture him back into motion. So it was with us. Blind instinct alone made me slam the great door and shoot the nearest heavy bolt. I saw Vair groping for me like a tear-blinded child and I took his arm. We ran futilely back into the room we had vacated and crouched in the corner farthest from the door, while great noises like thunder began to reverberate through the house, as pike-handles and musket-butts crashed sickeningly on the great outer door.

We must both have taken leave of reason then, for neither Vair nor I can remember anything more until the great nail-studded door, smashed off its hinges, fell on to the broken flags of the hall with the loudest crash of all. The tramp of feet, mingled with the sound of arms carelessly handled, thudding against floor and wall, and with the sharp nasal snarling of voices. In a moment it seemed they were everywhere—in the hall, on the main staircase, in the room over our heads.

Vair had all this time the grip of a madman on my wrist, and suddenly he leaned to me and screamed into my ear:

"*The Chapel... under the roof... it's consecrated... there's a chance... there's a chance, I tell you...*"

"They're on the stairs!" I cried back in my despair.

"The back stairs! Come on!"

A second door in the old room gave access to a passage leading to the back stairs. Those stairs we knew to be unsafe, but ordinary human peril was something far beyond and beneath our consideration. I remember the rumble and murmur of sounds about the house as we rushed out into the passage. Footfalls and voices sounded everywhere, and musket-butts were smiting heavily against stairs and walls. As we stumbled and ran I expected at every step to be seized and overwhelmed by some horrible and nameless Power.

How we reached the attics I cannot now say. The narrow, crumbling staircase creaked and swayed under us, and once I went down thigh deep through a rotten stair, with splinters of hard wood tearing clothes and flesh. But we were near the top ere the hunt had scented their game and sounds of pursuit began to clamour behind us.

Vair forced open the door of the little room which had once been a chapel. I blundered in over his body, which lay prone just across the threshold. He had fallen unconscious, and I had to force his legs aside before I could close the door. I slammed it to in the faces of vague forms which filled the passage to the stair-head, and drove home the wooden bolt inside. And then it seemed to me that our pursuers recoiled from that closed door like a great wave from the base of a cliff, and ugly cries outside died down to uneasy whisperings; and instinctively I knew that we were safe.

I must have fainted then, for I remember nothing more until I woke in bright sunlight. Vair was sitting beside me, watching me, with a chalk-like face. We hardly spoke, but sought each other's hands like frightened children.

Eventually we nerved ourselves to go downstairs into the ruin and disorder of the old house, through which, one might have thought, a whirlwind had passed during the night.

SMEE

"No," said Jackson, with a deprecatory smile, "I'm sorry. I don't want to upset your game. I shan't be doing that because you'll have plenty without me. But I'm not playing any games of hide-and-seek."

It was Christmas Eve, and we were a party of fourteen with just the proper leavening of youth. We had dined well; it was the season for childish games, and we were all in the mood for playing them—all, that is, except Jackson. When somebody suggested hide-and-seek there was rapturous and almost unanimous approval. His was the one dissentient voice.

It was not like Jackson to spoil sport or refuse to do as others wanted. Somebody asked him if he were feeling seedy.

"No," he answered. "I feel perfectly fit, thanks. But," he added with a smile which softened without retracting the flat refusal, "I'm not playing hide-and-seek."

One of us asked him why not. He hesitated for some seconds before replying.

"I sometimes go and stay at a house where a girl was killed through playing hide-and-seek in the dark. She didn't know the house very well. There was a servant's staircase with a door to it. When she was pursued she opened the door and jumped into what she must have thought was one of the bedrooms—and she broke her neck at the bottom of the stairs."

We all looked concerned, and Mrs Fernley said:

"How awful! And you were there when it happened?"

Jackson shook his head very gravely. "No," he said, "but I was there when something else happened. Something worse."

"I shouldn't have thought anything could be worse."

"This was," said Jackson, and shuddered visibly. "Or so it seemed to me."

I think he wanted to tell the story and was angling for encouragement. A few requests which may have seemed to him to lack urgency, he affected to ignore and went off at a tangent.

"I wonder if any of you have played a game called 'Smee'. It's a great improvement on the ordinary game of hide-and-seek. The name derives from the ungrammatical colloquialism, 'It's me.' You might care to play if you're going to play a game of that sort. Let me tell you the rules.

"Every player is presented with a sheet of paper. All the sheets are blank except one, on which is written 'Smee'. Nobody knows who is 'Smee' except 'Smee' himself—or herself, as the case may be. The lights are then turned out and 'Smee' slips from the room and goes off to hide, and after an interval the other players go off in search, without knowing whom they are actually in search of. One player meeting another challenges with the word 'Smee' and the other player, if not the one concerned, answers 'Smee'.

"The real 'Smee' makes no answer when challenged, and the second player remains quietly by him. Presently they will be discovered by a third player, who, having challenged and received no answer, will link up with the first two. This goes on until all the players have formed a chain, and the last to join is marked down for a forfeit. It's a good noisy, romping game, and in a big house it often takes a long time to complete the chain. You might care to try it; and I'll pay my forfeit and smoke one of Tim's excellent cigars here by the fire until you get tired of it."

I remarked that it sounded a good game and asked Jackson if he had played it himself.

"Yes," he answered; "I played it in the house I was telling you about."

"And *she* was there? The girl who broke—"

"No, no," Mrs Fernley interrupted. "He told us he wasn't there when it happened."

Jackson considered. "I don't know if she was there or not. I'm afraid she was. I know that there were thirteen of us and there ought only to have been twelve. And I'll swear that I didn't know her name, or I think I should have gone clean off my head when I heard that whisper in the dark. No, you don't catch me playing that game, or any other like it, any more. It spoiled my nerve quite a while, and I can't afford to take long holidays. Besides, it saves a lot of trouble and inconvenience to own up at once to being a coward."

Tim Vouce, the best of hosts, smiled around at us, and in that smile there was a meaning which is sometimes vulgarly expressed by the slow closing of an eye. "There's a story coming," he announced.

"There's certainly a story of sorts," said Jackson, "but whether it's coming or not—" He paused and shrugged his shoulders.

"Well, you're going to pay a forfeit instead of playing?"

"Please. But have a heart and let me down lightly. It's not just a sheer cussedness on my part."

"Payment in advance," said Tim, "insures honesty and promotes good feeling. You are therefore sentenced to tell the story here and now."

And here follows Jackson's story, unrevised by me and passed on without comment to a wider public:—

Some of you, I know, have run across the Sangstons. Christopher Sangston and his wife, I mean. They're distant connections of mine—at least, Violet Sangston is. About eight years ago they bought a house between the North and South Downs on the Surrey and Sussex border, and five years ago they invited me to come and spend Christmas with them.

It was a fairly old house—I couldn't say exactly of what period—and it certainly deserved the epithet "rambling". It wasn't a particularly big house, but the original architect, whoever he may have been, had not concerned himself with economizing in space, and at first you could get lost in it quite easily.

Well, I went down for that Christmas, assured by Violet's letter that I knew most of my fellow-guests and that the two or three who might be strangers to me were all "lambs". Unfortunately, I'm one of the world's workers, and I couldn't get away until Christmas Eve, although the other members of the party had assembled on the preceding day. Even then I had to cut it rather fine to be there for dinner on my first night. They were all dressing when I arrived and I had to go straight to my room and waste no time. I may even have kept dinner waiting a bit, for I was last down, and it was announced within a minute of my entering the drawing-room. There was just time to say "hullo" to everybody I knew, to be briefly introduced to the two or three I didn't know, and then I had to give my arm to Mrs Gorman.

I mention this as the reason why I didn't catch the name of a tall dark, handsome girl I hadn't met before. Everything was rather hurried and I am always bad at catching people's names. She looked cold and clever and rather forbidding, the sort of girl who gives the impression of knowing all about men and the more she knows of them the less she likes them. I felt that I wasn't going to hit it off with this particular "lamb" of Violet's, but she looked interesting all the same, and I wondered who she was. I didn't ask, because I was pretty sure of hearing somebody address her by name before very long.

Unluckily, though, I was a long way off her at table, and as Mrs Gorman was at the top of her form that night I soon forgot to worry about who she might be. Mrs Gorman is one of the most amusing women I know, an outrageous but quite innocent flirt, with a very sprightly wit which isn't always unkind. She can think half a dozen moves ahead in conversation just as an expert can in a game of chess. We were soon sparring, or, rather, I was "covering" against the ropes, and I quite forgot to ask her in an undertone the name of the cold, proud beauty. The lady on the other side of me was a stranger, or had been until a few minutes since, and I didn't think of seeking information in that quarter.

There was a round dozen of us, including the Sangstons themselves, and we were all young or trying to be. The Sangstons themselves were the oldest members of the party and their son Reggie, in his last year at Marlborough, must have been the youngest. When there was talk of playing games after dinner it was he who suggested "Smee". He told us how to play it just as I've described it to you.

His father chipped in as soon as we all understood what was going to be required of us. "If there are any games of that sort going on in the house," he said, "for goodness' sake be careful of the back stairs on the first-floor landing. There's a door to them and I've often meant to take it down. In the dark anybody who doesn't know the house very well might think they were walking into a room. A girl actually did break her neck on those stairs about ten years ago when the Ainsties lived here."

I asked how it happened.

"Oh," said Sangston, "there was a party here one Christmas-time and they were playing hide-and-seek as you propose doing. This girl was one of the hiders. She heard somebody coming, ran along the passage to get away, and opened the door of what she thought was a bedroom, evidently with the intention of hiding behind it while her pursuer went past. Unfortunately it was the door leading to the back stairs, and that staircase is as straight and almost as steep as the shaft of a pit. She was dead when they picked her up."

We all promised for our own sakes to be careful. Mrs Gorman said that she was sure nothing could happen to her, since she was insured by three different firms, and her next-of-kin was a brother whose consistent ill-luck was a byword in the family. You see, none of us had known the unfortunate girl, and as the tragedy was ten years old there was no need to pull long faces about it.

Well, we started the game almost immediately after dinner. The men allowed themselves only five minutes before joining the ladies, and then young Reggie Sangston went round and assured himself that the lights were out all over the house except in the servants' quarters and in the drawing-room where we were assembled. We then got busy with twelve sheets of paper which he twisted into pellets and shook up between his hands before passing them round. Eleven of them were blank, and "Smee" was written on the twelfth. The person drawing the latter was the one who had to hide. I looked and saw that mine was a blank. A moment later out went the electric lights, and in the darkness I heard somebody get up and creep to the door.

After a minute or so somebody gave a signal and we made a rush for the door. I for one hadn't the least idea which of the party was "Smee". For five or ten minutes we were all rushing up and down passages and in and out of rooms challenging one another and answering, "Smee?—Smee!"

After a bit the alarums and excursions died down, and I guessed that "Smee" was found. Eventually I found a chain of people all sitting still and holding their breath on some narrow stairs leading up to a row of attics. I hastily joined it, having challenged and been answered with silence, and presently two more stragglers arrived, each racing the other to avoid being last. Sangston was one of them, indeed it was he who was marked down for a forfeit, and after a little while he remarked in an undertone, "I think we're all here now, aren't we?"

He struck a match; looked up the shaft of the staircase, and began to count. It wasn't hard, although we just about filled the staircase, for we were sitting each a step or two above the next, and all our heads were visible.

"…nine, ten, eleven, twelve—*thirteen*," he concluded, and then laughed. "Dash it all, that's one too many!"

The match had burned out and he struck another and began to count. He got as far as twelve, and then uttered an exclamation.

"There are thirteen people here!" he exclaimed. "I haven't counted myself yet."

"Oh, nonsense!" I laughed. "You probably began with yourself, and now you want to count yourself twice."

Out came his son's electric torch, giving a brighter and steadier light and we all began to count. Of course we numbered twelve.

Sangston laughed.

"Well", he said, "I could have sworn I counted thirteen twice."

From half-way up the stairs came Violet Sangston's voice with a little nervous trill in it. "I thought there was somebody sitting two steps above me. Have you moved up, Captain Ransome?"

Ransome said that he hadn't: He also said that he thought there was somebody sitting between Violet and himself. Just for a moment there was an uncomfortable Something in the air, a little cold ripple which touched us all. For that little moment it seemed to all of us, I think, that something odd and unpleasant had happened and was liable to happen again. Then we laughed at ourselves and at one another and were comfortable once more. There *were* only twelve of us, and there *could* only have been twelve of us, and there was no argument about it. Still laughing we trooped back to the drawing-room to begin again.

This time I was "Smee", and Violet Sangston ran me to earth while I was still looking for a hiding-place. That round didn't last long, and we were a chain of twelve within two or three minutes. Afterwards there was a short interval. Violet wanted a wrap fetched for her, and her husband went up to get it from her room. He was no sooner gone than Reggie pulled me by the sleeve. I saw that he was looking pale and sick.

"Quick!" he whispered, "while father's out of the way. Take me into the smoke room and give me a brandy or a whisky or something."

Outside the room I asked him what was the matter, but he didn't answer at first, and I thought it better to dose him first and question him afterward. So I mixed him a pretty dark-complexioned brandy and soda which he drank at a gulp and then began to puff as if he had been running.

"I've had rather a turn," he said to me with a sheepish grin.

"What's the matter?"

"I don't know. You were 'Smee' just now, weren't you? Well, of course I didn't know who 'Smee' was, and while mother and the others ran into the west wing and found you, I turned east. There's a deep clothes cupboard in my bedroom—I'd marked it down as a good place to hide when it was my turn, and I had an idea that 'Smee' might be there. I opened the door in the dark, felt round, and touched somebody's hand. 'Smee?' I whispered, and not getting any answer I thought I had found 'Smee'.

"Well, I don't know how it was, but an odd creepy feeling came over me, I can't describe it, but I felt that something was wrong. So I turned on my electric torch and there was nobody there. Now, I swear I touched a hand, and I was filling up the doorway of the cupboard at the time, so nobody could get out and past me." He puffed again. "What do you make of it?" he asked.

"You imagined that you had touched a hand," I answered, naturally enough.

He uttered a short laugh. "Of course I knew you were going to say that," he said. "I must have imagined it, mustn't I?" He paused and swallowed. "I mean, it couldn't have been anything else *but* imagination, could it?"

I assured him that it couldn't, meaning what I said, and he accepted this, but rather with the philosophy of one who knows he is right but doesn't expect to be believed. We returned together to the drawing-room where, by that time, they were all waiting for us and ready to start again.

It may have been my imagination—although I'm almost sure it wasn't—but it seemed to me that all enthusiasm for the game had suddenly melted like a white frost in strong sunlight. If anybody had suggested another game I'm sure we should all have been grateful and abandoned "Smee". Only nobody did. Nobody seemed to like to. I for one, and I can speak for some of the others too, was oppressed with the feeling that there was something wrong. I couldn't have said what I thought was wrong, indeed I didn't think about it at all, but somehow all the sparkle had gone out of the fun, and hovering over my mind like a shadow was the warning of some sixth sense which told me that there was an influence in the house which was neither sane, sound nor healthy. Why did I feel like that? Because Sangston had counted thirteen of us instead of twelve, and his son had thought he had touched somebody in an empty cupboard. No, there was more in it than just that. One would have laughed at such things in the ordinary way, and it was just that feeling of something being wrong which stopped me from laughing.

Well, we started again, and when we went in pursuit of the unknown "Smee", we were as noisy as ever, but it seemed to me that most of us were acting. Frankly, for no reason other than the one I've given you, we'd stopped enjoying the game. I had an instinct to hunt with the main pack, but after a few minutes, during which no "Smee" had been found, my instinct to play winning games and be first if possible, set me searching on my own account. And on the first floor of the west wing following the wall which was actually the shell of the house, I blundered against a pair of human knees.

I put out my hand and touched a soft, heavy curtain. Then I knew where I was. There were tall, deeply-recessed windows with seats along the landing, and curtains over the recesses to the ground. Somebody was sitting in a corner of this window-seat behind the curtain. Aha, I had caught "Smee!" So I drew the curtain aside, stepped in, and touched the bare arm of a woman.

It was a dark night outside, and, moreover, the window was not only curtained but a blind hung down to where the bottom panes joined up with the frame. Between the curtain and the window it was as dark as the plague of Egypt. I could not have seen my hand held six inches before my face, much less the woman sitting in the corner.

"Smee?" I whispered.

I had no answer. "Smee" when challenged does not answer. So I sat down beside her, first in the field, to await the others. Then, having settled myself I leaned over to her and whispered:

"Who is it? What's your name, 'Smee?'"

And out of the darkness beside me the whisper came back: "Brenda Ford."

I didn't know the name, but because I didn't know it I guessed at once who she was. The tall, pale, dark girl was the only person in the house I didn't know by name. Ergo my companion was the tall, pale, dark girl. It seemed rather intriguing to be there with her, shut in between a heavy curtain and a window, and I rather wondered whether she was enjoying the game we were all playing. Somehow she hadn't seemed to me to be one of the romping sort. I muttered one or two commonplace questions to her and had no answer.

"Smee" is a game of silence. "Smee" and the person or persons who have found "Smee" are supposed to keep quiet to make it hard for the others. But there was nobody else about, and it occurred to me that she was playing the game a little too much to the letter. I spoke again and got no answer, and then I began to be annoyed. She was of that cold, "superior" type which affects to despise men; she didn't like me; and she was sheltering behind the rules of a game for children to be discourteous. Well, if she didn't like sitting there with me, I certainly didn't want to be sitting there with her! I half turned from her and began to hope that we should both be discovered without much more delay.

Having discovered that I didn't like being there alone with her, it was queer how soon I found myself hating it, and that for a reason very different from the one which had at first whetted my annoyance. The girl I had met for the first time before dinner, and seen diagonally across the table, had a sort of cold charm about her which had attracted while it had half angered me. For the girl who was with me, imprisoned in the opaque darkness between the curtain and the window, I felt no attraction at all. It was so very much the reverse that I should have wondered at myself if, after the first shock of the discovery that she had suddenly become repellent to me, I had no room in my mind for anything besides the consciousness that her close presence was an increasing horror to me.

It came upon me just as quickly as I've uttered the words. My flesh suddenly shrank from her as you see a strip of gelatine shrink and wither before the heat of a fire. That feeling of something being wrong had come back to me, but multiplied to an extent which turned foreboding into actual terror. I firmly believe that I should have got up and run if I had not felt that at my first movement she would have divined my intention and compelled me to stay, by some means of which I could not bear to think. The memory of having touched her bare arm made me wince and draw in my lips. I prayed that somebody else would come along soon.

My prayer was answered. Light footfalls sounded on the landing. Somebody on the other side of the curtain brushed against my knees. The curtain was drawn aside and a woman's hand, fumbling in the darkness, presently rested on my shoulder. "Smee?" whispered a voice which I instantly recognized as Mrs Gorman's.

Of course she received no answer. She came and settled down beside me with a rustle, and I can't describe the sense of relief she brought me.

"It's Tony, isn't it?" she whispered.

"Yes," I whispered back.

"You're not 'Smee' are you?"

"No, she's on my other side."

She reached a hand across me, and I heard one of her nails scratch the surface of a woman's silk gown.

"Hullo, 'Smee'! How are you? *Who* are you? Oh, is it against the rules to talk? Never mind, Tony, we'll break the rules. Do you know, Tony, this game is beginning to irk me a little. I hope they're not going to run it to death by playing it all the evening. I'd like to play some game where we can all be together in the same room with a nice bright fire."

"Same here," I agreed fervently.

"Can't you suggest something when we go down? There's something rather uncanny in this particular amusement. I can't quite shed the delusion that there's somebody in this game who oughtn't to be in it at all."

That was just how I had been feeling, but I didn't say so. But for my part the worst of my qualms were now gone; the arrival of Mrs Gorman had dissipated them. We sat on talking, wondering from time to time when the rest of the party would arrive.

I don't know how long elapsed before we heard a clatter of feet on the landing and young Reggie's voice shouting, "Hullo! Hullo, there! Anybody there?"

"Yes," I answered.

"Mrs Gorman with you?"

"Yes."

"Well, you're a nice pair! You've both forfeited. We've all been waiting for you for hours."

"Why, you haven't found 'Smee' yet," I objected.

"*You* haven't, you mean. I happen to have been 'Smee' myself."

"But 'Smee's' here with us," I cried.

"Yes," agreed Mrs Gorman.

The curtain was stripped aside and in a moment we were blinking into the eye of Reggie's electric torch. I looked at Mrs Gorman and then on my other side. Between me and the wall there was an empty space on the window-seat. I stood up at once and wished I hadn't, for I found myself sick and dizzy.

"There *was* somebody there," I maintained, "because I touched her."

"So did I," said Mrs Gorman in a voice which had lost its steadiness. "And I don't see how she could have got up and gone without our knowing it."

Reggie uttered a queer, shaken laugh. He, too, had had an unpleasant experience that evening. "Somebody's been playing the goat," he remarked. "Coming down?"

We were not very popular when we arrived in the drawing-room. Reggie rather tactlessly gave it out that he had found us sitting on a window-seat behind a curtain. I taxed the tall, dark girl with having pretended to be "Smee" and afterwards slipping away. She denied it. After which we settled down and played other games. "Smee" was done with for the evening, and I for one was glad of it.

Some long while later, during an interval, Sangston told me, if I wanted a drink, to go into the smoke room and help myself. I went, and he presently followed me. I could see that he was rather peeved with me, and the reason came out during the following minute or two. It seemed that, in his opinion, if I must sit out and flirt with Mrs Gorman—in circumstances which would have been considered highly compromising in his young days—I needn't do it during a round game and keep everybody waiting for us.

"But there was somebody else there," I protested, "somebody pretending to be 'Smee'. I believe it was that tall, dark girl, Miss Ford, although she denied it. She even whispered her name to me."

Sangston stared at me and nearly dropped his glass.

"Miss *Who?*" he shouted.

"Brenda Ford—she told me her name was."

Sangston put down his glass and laid a hand on my shoulder.

"Look here, old man," he said, "I don't mind a joke, but don't let it go too far. We don't want all the women in the house getting hysterical. Brenda Ford is the name of the girl who broke her neck on the stairs playing hide-and-seek here ten years ago."

THE SWEEPER

IT seemed to Tessa Winyard that Miss Ludgate's strangest characteristic was her kindness to beggars. This was something more than
a little peculiar in a nature which, to be sure, presented a surface like
a mountain range of unexpected peaks and valleys; for there was a thin
streak of meanness in her. One caught glimpses of it here and there to be
traced a little way and lost, like a thin elusive vein in a block of marble.
One week she would pay the household bills without a murmur; the next
she would simmer over them in a mild rage, questioning the smallest
item, and suggesting the most absurd little economies which she would
have been the first to condemn later if Mrs Finch the housekeeper had
ever taken her at her word. She was rich enough to be indifferent, but old
enough to be crochetty.

Miss Ludgate gave very sparsely to local charities, and those good busy-
bodies who went forth at different times with subscription lists and tales
of good causes often visited her and came empty away. She had plausible,
transparent excuses for keeping her purse-strings tight. Hospitals should
be state-aided; schemes for assisting the local poor destroyed thrift; we had
heathen of our own to convert, and needed to send no missionaries abroad.
Yet she was sometimes overwhelmingly generous in her spasmodic charities
to individuals, and her kindness to itinerant beggars was proverbial among
their fraternity. Her neighbours were not grateful to her for this, for it was
said that she encouraged every doubtful character who came that way.

When she first agreed to come on a month's trial Tessa Winyard had
known that she would find Miss Ludgate difficult, doubting whether

she would be able to retain the post of companion, and, still more, if she would want to retain it. The thing was not arranged through the reading and answering of an advertisement. Tessa knew a married niece of the old lady who, while recommending the young girl to her ancient kinswoman, was able to give Tessa hints as to the nature and treatment of the old lady's crochets. So she came to the house well instructed and not quite as a stranger.

Tessa came under the spell of the house from the moment when she entered it for the first time. She had an ingrained romantic love of old country mansions, and Billingdon Abbots, although nothing was left of the original priory after which it was named, was old enough to be worshipped. It was mainly Jacobean, but some eighteenth-century owner, a devotee of the then fashionable cult of Italian architecture, had covered the facade with stucco and added a pillared portico. It was probably the same owner who had erected a summer house to the design of a Greek temple at the end of a walk between nut bushes, and who was responsible for the imitation ruin—to which Time had since added the authentic touch—beside the reedy fishpond at the rear of the house. Likely enough, thought Tessa, who knew the period, that same romantic squire was wont to engage an imitation "hermit" to meditate beside the spurious ruin on moonlight nights.

The gardens around the house were well wooded, and thus lent the house itself an air of melancholy and the inevitable slight atmosphere of damp and darkness. And here and there, in the most unexpected places, were garden gods, mostly broken and all in need of scouring. Tessa soon discovered these stone ghosts quite unexpectedly, and nearly always with a leap and tingle of surprise. A noseless Hermes confronted one at the turn of a shady walk; Demeter, minus a hand, stood half hidden by laurels, still keeping vigil for Persephone; a dancing faun stood poised and caught in a frozen caper by the gate of the walled-in kitchen garden; beside a small stone pond a satyr leered from his pedestal, as if waiting for a naiad to break the surface.

The interior of the house was at first a little awe-inspiring to Tessa. She loved pretty things, but she was inclined to be afraid of furniture and pictures which seemed to her to be coldly beautiful and conscious of their own intrinsic values. Everything was highly polished, spotless and speckless, and the reception rooms had an air of state apartments thrown open for the inspection of the public.

The hall was square and galleried, and one could look straight up to the top storey and see the slanting balustrades of three staircases. Two suits of armour faced one across a parquet floor, and on the walls were three or four portraits by Lely and Kneller, those once fashionable painters of court beauties whose works have lost favour with the collectors of today. The dining-room was long, rectangular and severe, furnished only with a Cromwellian table and chairs and a great plain sideboard gleaming with silver candelabra. Two large seventeenth-century portraits by unknown members of the Dutch School were the only decorations bestowed on the panelled walls, and the window curtains were brown to match the one strip of carpet which the long table almost exactly covered.

Less monastic, but almost as severe and dignified, was the drawing-room in which Tessa spent most of her time with Miss Ludgate. The boudoir was a homelier room, containing such human things as photographs of living people, work-baskets, friendly armchairs and a cosy, feminine atmosphere; but Miss Ludgate preferred more often to sit in state in her great drawing-room with the "Portrait of Miss Olivia Ludgate," by Gainsborough, the Chippendale furniture, and the cabinet of priceless china. It was as if she realized that she was but the guardian of her treasures, and wanted to have them within sight now that her term of guardianship was drawing to a close.

She must have been well over eighty, Tessa thought; for she was very small and withered and frail, with that almost porcelain delicacy peculiar to certain very old ladies. Winter and summer she wore a white woollen

THE LITTLE BLUE FLAMES

shawl inside the house, thick or thin according to the season, which matched in colour and to some extent in texture her soft and still plentiful hair. Her face and hands were yellow-brown with the veneer of old age, but her hands were blue-veined, light and delicate, so that her fingers seemed over-weighted by the simplest rings. Her eyes were blue and still piercing, and her mouth, once beautiful, was caught up at the corners by puckerings of the upper lip, and looked grim in repose. Her voice had not shrilled and always she spoke very slowly with an unaffected precision, as one who knew that she had only to be understood to be obeyed and therefore took care always to be understood.

Tessa spent her first week with Miss Ludgate without knowing whether or not she liked the old lady, or whether or not she was afraid of her. Nor was she any wiser with regard to Miss Ludgate's sentiments towards herself. Their relations were much as they might have been had Tessa been a child and Miss Ludgate a new governess suspected of severity. Tessa was on her best behaviour, doing as she was told and thinking before she spoke, as children should and generally do not. At times it occurred to her to wonder that Miss Ludgate had not sought to engage an older woman, for in the cold formality of that first week's intercourse she wondered what gap in the household she was supposed to fill, and what return she was making for her wage and board.

Truth to tell, Miss Ludgate wanted to see somebody young about the house, even if she could share with her companion no more than the common factors of their sex and their humanity. The servants were all old retainers kept faithful to her by rumours of legacies. Her relatives were few and immersed in their own affairs. The house and the bulk of the property from which she derived her income were held in trust for an heir appointed by the same will which had given her a life interest in the estate. It saved her from the transparent attentions of any fortune-hunting nephew or niece, but it kept her lonely and starved for young companionship.

It happened that Tessa was able to play the piano quite reasonably well and that she had an educated taste in music. So had Miss Ludgate, who had been a performer of much the same quality until the time came when her rebel fingers stiffened with rheumatism. So the heavy grand piano, which had been scrupulously kept in tune, was silent no longer, and Miss Ludgate regained an old lost pleasure. It should be added that Tessa was twenty-two and, with no pretensions to technical beauty, was rich in commonplace good looks which were enhanced by perfect health and the freshness of her youth. She looked her best in candlelight, with her slim hands—they at least would have pleased an artist—hovering like white moths over the keyboard of the piano.

When she had been with Miss Ludgate a week, the old lady addressed her for the first time as "Tessa." She added: "I hope you intend to stay with me, my dear. It will be dull for you, and I fear you will often find me a bother. But I shan't take up all your time, and I daresay you will be able to find friends and amusements."

So Tessa stayed on, and beyond the probationary month. She was a soft-hearted girl who gave her friendship easily but always sincerely. She tried to like everybody who liked her, and generally succeeded. It would be hard to analyse the quality of the friendship between the two women, but certainly it existed and at times they were able to touch hands over the barrier between youth and age. Miss Ludgate inspired in Tessa a queer tenderness. With all her wealth and despite her domineering manner, she was a pathetic and lonely figure. She reminded Tessa of some poor actress playing the part of Queen, wearing the tawdry crown jewels, uttering commands which the other mummers obeyed like automata; while all the while there awaited her the realities of life at the fall of the curtain—the wet streets, the poor meal and the cold and comfortless lodging.

It filled Tessa with pity to think that here, close beside her, was a living, breathing creature, still clinging to life, who must, in the course of nature, so soon let go her hold. Tessa could think: "Fifty years hence I shall be seventy-two, and there's no reason why I shouldn't live till then." She wondered painfully how it must feel to be unable to look a month hence with average confidence, and to regard every nightfall as the threshold of a precarious tomorrow.

Tessa would have found life very dull but for the complete change in her surroundings. She had been brought up in a country vicarage, one of seven brothers and sisters who had worn each other's clothes, tramped the carpets threadbare, mishandled the cheap furniture, broken everything frangible except their parents' hearts, and had somehow tumbled into adolescence. The unwonted "grandeur" of living with Miss Ludgate flavoured the monotony.

We have her writing home to her "Darling Mother" as follows:

"I expect when I get back home again our dear old rooms will look absurdly small. I thought at first that the house was huge, and every room as big as a barrack-room—not that I've ever been in a barrack-room! But I'm getting used to it now, and really it isn't so enormous as I thought. Huge compared with ours, of course, but not so big as Lord Branbourne's house, or even Colonel Exted's.

"Really, though, it's a darling old place and might have come out of one of those books in which there's a Mystery, and a Sliding Panel, and the heroine's a nursery governess who marries the Young Baronet. But there's no mystery that I've heard of, although I like to pretend there is, and even if I were the nursery governess there's no young baronet within a radius of miles. But at least it ought to have a traditional ghost, although, since I haven't heard of one, it's probably deficient even in that respect! I don't like to ask Miss Ludgate because, although she's a dear, there are questions I couldn't ask her. She might believe in ghosts and it might scare her to talk about them; or she mightn't, and then she'd be furious with me for talking rubbish. Of course, I know it's all rubbish but it would be very nice to know that we were supposed to be haunted by a nice Grey Lady—of, say—about the period of Queen Anne. But if we're haunted by nothing else, we're certainly haunted by tramps."

Her letter went on to describe the numerous daily visits of those nomads of the English countryside, who beg and steal on their way from workhouse to workhouse; those queer, illogical, feckless beings who prefer the most intense miseries and hardships to the comparative comforts attendant on honest work. Three or four was a day's average of such callers, and not one went empty away. Mrs Finch had very definite orders and she carried them out with the impassive face of a perfect subject of discipline. When there was no spare food there was the pleasanter alternative of money which could be transformed into liquor at the nearest inn.

Tessa was for ever meeting these vagrants in the drive. Male and female they differed in a hundred ways; some still trying to cling to the last rags of self-respect, others obscene, leering, furtive, potential criminals who lacked the courage to rise above petty theft. Most faces were either evil or carried the rolling eyes and lewd loose mouth of the semi-idiot, but they were all alike in their personal uncleanliness and in the insolence of their bearing.

Tessa grew used to receiving from them direct and insolent challenges of the eyes, familiar nods, blatant grins. In their several ways they told her that she was nobody and that if she hated to see them, so much the better. They knew she was an underling, subject to dismissal, whereas they, for some occult reason, were always the welcome guests. Tessa resented their presence and their dumb insolence and secretly raged against Miss Ludgate for encouraging them. They were the sewer-rats of society, foul, predatory and carrying disease from village to village and from town to town.

The girl knew something of the struggles of the decent poor. Her upbringing in a country vicarage had given her intimate knowledge of farm hands and builders' labourers, the tragic poverty of their homes, their independence and their gallant struggles for existence. On Miss Ludgate's estate there was more than one family living on bread and potatoes and getting not too much of either. Yet the old lady had no sympathy for them, and gave unlimited largess to the undeserving. In the ditches outside the park it was always possible to find a loaf or two of bread flung there by some vagrant who had feasted more delicately on the proceeds of a visit to the tradesmen's door.

It was not for Tessa to speak to Miss Ludgate on the subject. Indeed, she knew that—in the phraseology of the servants' hall—it was as much as her place was worth. But she did mention it to Mrs Finch, whose duty was to provide food and drink, or, failing those, money.

Mrs Finch, taciturn through her environment but still with an undercurrent of warmth, replied at first with the one pregnant word, "Orders!" After a moment she added: "The mistress has her own good reasons for doing it—or thinks she has."

It was late summer when Tessa first took up her abode at Billingdon Abbots, and sweet lavender, that first herald of the approach of autumn, was already blooming in the gardens. September came and the first warning gleams of yellow showed among the trees. Spiked chestnut husks opened and dropped their polished brown fruit. At evenings the ponds and the trout stream exhaled pale, low-hanging mists. There was a cold snap in the air.

By looking from her window every morning Tessa marked on the trees the inexorable progress of the year. Day by day the green tints lessened as the yellow increased. Then yellow began to give place to gold and brown and red. Only the hollies and the laurels stood fast against the advancing tide.

There came an evening when Miss Ludgate appeared for the first time in her winter shawl. She seemed depressed and said little during dinner, and afterwards in the drawing-room, when she had taken out and arranged a pack of patience cards preparatory to beginning her evening game, she suddenly leaned her elbows on the table and rested her face between her hands.

"Aren't you well, Miss Ludgate?" Tessa asked anxiously.

She removed her hands and showed her withered old face. Her eyes were piteous, fear-haunted and full of shadows.

"I am very much as usual, my dear," she said. "You must bear with me. My bad time of the year is just approaching. If I can live until the end of November I shall last another year. But I don't know yet—I don't know."

"Of course you're not going to die this year," said Tessa, with a robust note of optimism which she had found useful in soothing frightened children.

"If I don't die this autumn it will be the next, or some other autumn," quavered the old voice. "It will be in the autumn that I shall die. I know that. I know that."

"But how can you know?" Tessa asked, with just the right note of gentle incredulity.

"I know it. What does it matter how I know?... Have many leaves fallen yet?"

"Hardly any as yet," said Tessa. "There has been very little wind."

"They will fall presently," said Miss Ludgate. "Very soon now..."

Her voice trailed away, but presently she rallied, picked up the miniature playing cards and began her game.

Two days later it rained heavily all the morning and throughout the earlier part of the afternoon. Just as the light was beginning to wane, half a gale of wind sprang up, and showers of yellow leaves, circling and eddying at the wind's will, began to find their way to earth through the level slant of the rain. Miss Ludgate sat watching them, her eyes dull with the suffering of despair, until the lights were turned on and the blinds were drawn.

During dinner the wind dropped again and the rain ceased. Tessa afterwards peeped between the blinds to see still silhouettes of trees against the sky, and a few stars sparkling palely. It promised after all to be a fine night.

As before, Miss Ludgate got out her patience cards, and Tessa picked up a book and waited to be bidden go to the piano. There was silence in the room save for intermittent sounds of cards being laid with a snap upon the polished surface of the table, and occasional dry rustlings as Tessa turned the pages of her book.

... When she first heard it Tessa could not truthfully have said. It seemed to her that she had gradually become conscious of the sounds in the garden outside, and when at last they had so forced themselves upon her attention as to set her wondering what caused them it was impossible for her to guess how long they had actually been going on.

Tessa closed the book over her fingers and listened. The sounds were crisp, dry, long drawn out and rhythmic. There was an equal pause after each one. It was rather like listening to the leisurely brushing of a woman's long hair. What was it? An uneven surface being scratched by something crisp and pliant? Then Tessa knew. On the long path behind the house which travelled the whole length of the building somebody was sweeping up the fallen leaves with a stable broom. But what a time to sweep up leaves!

She continued to listen. Now that she had identified the sounds they were quite unmistakable. She would not have had to guess twice had it not been dark outside, and the thought of a gardener showing such devotion to duty as to work at that hour had at first been rejected by her subconscious mind. She looked up, with the intention of making some remark to Miss Ludgate—and she said nothing.

Miss Ludgate sat listening intently, her face half-turned towards the windows and slightly raised, her eyes upturned. Her whole attitude was one of strained rigidity, expressive of a tension rather dreadful to see in one so old. Tessa not only listened, she now watched.

There was a movement in the unnaturally silent room. Miss Ludgate had turned her head, and now showed her companion a white face of woe and doom-ridden eyes. Then, in a flash, her expression changed. Tessa knew that Miss Ludgate had caught her listening to the sounds from the path outside, and that for some reason the old lady was annoyed with her for having heard them. But why? And why that look of terror on the poor white old face?

"Won't you play something, Tessa?"

Despite the note of interrogation, the words were an abrupt command, and Tessa knew it. She was to drown the noise of sweeping from outside, because, for some queer reason, Miss Ludgate did not want her to hear it. So, tactfully, she played pieces which allowed her to make liberal use of the loud pedal.

After half an hour Miss Ludgate rose, gathered her shawl tighter about her shoulders, and hobbled to the door, pausing on the way to say good night to Tessa.

Tessa lingered in the room alone and reseated herself before the piano. A minute or two elapsed before she began to strum softly and absent-mindedly. Why did Miss Ludgate object to her hearing that sound of sweeping from the path outside? It had ceased now, or she would have peeped out to see who actually was at work. Had Miss Ludgate some queer distaste for seeing fallen leaves lying about, and was she ashamed because she was keeping a gardener at work at that hour? But it was unlike Miss Ludgate to mind what people thought of her; besides, she rose late in the morning, and there would be plenty of time to brush away the leaves before the mistress of the house could set eyes on them. And then, why was Miss Ludgate so terrified? Had it anything to do with her queer belief that she would die in the autumn?

On her way to bed Tessa smiled gently to herself for having tried to penetrate to the secret places of a warped mind which was over eighty years old. She had just seen another queer phase of Miss Ludgate, and all of such seemed inexplicable.

The night was still calm and promised so to remain.

"There won't be many more leaves down tonight," Tessa reflected as she undressed.

But when next morning she sauntered out into the garden before breakfast the long path which skirted the rear of the house was still thickly littered with them, and Toy, the second gardener, was busy among them with a barrow and one of those birch stable brooms which, in mediæval imaginations, provided steeds for witches.

"Hullo!" exclaimed Tessa. "What a lot of leaves must have come down last night!"

Toy ceased sweeping and shook his head.

"No, Miss. This 'ere little lot come down with the wind early part o' the evenin.'"

"But surely they were all swept up. I heard somebody at work here after nine o'clock. Wasn't it you?"

The man grinned.

"You catch any of us at work after nine o'clock, Miss!" he said. "No, Miss, nobody's touched 'em till now. 'Tes thankless work, too. So soon as you've swept up one lot there's another waitin.' Not a hundred men could keep this 'ere garden tidy this time o' the year."

Tessa said nothing more and went thoughtfully into the house. The sweeping was continued off and on all day, for more leaves descended, and a bonfire built up on the waste ground beyond the kitchen garden wafted its fragrance over to the house.

That evening Miss Ludgate had a fire made up in the boudoir and announced to Tessa that they would sit there before and after dinner. But it happened that the chimney smoked, and after coughing and grumbling, and rating Mrs Finch on the dilatoriness and inefficiency of sweeps, the old lady went early to bed.

It was still too early for Tessa to retire. Having been left to herself she remembered a book which she had left in the drawing-room, and with which she purposed sitting over the dining-room fire. Hardly had she taken two steps past the threshold of the drawing-room when she came abruptly to a halt and stood listening. She could not doubt the evidence of her ears. In spite of what Toy had told her, and that it was now after half-past nine, somebody was sweeping the path outside.

She tiptoed to the window and peeped out between the blinds. Bright moonlight silvered the garden, but she could see nothing. Now, however, that she was near the window she could locate the sounds more accurately, and they seemed to proceed from a spot further down the path which was hidden from her by the angle of the window setting. There was a door just outside the room giving access to the garden, but for no reason that she could name she felt strangely unwilling to go out and look at the mysterious Worker. With the strangest little cold thrill she was aware of a distinct preference for seeing him—for the first time, at least—from a distance.

Then Tessa remembered a landing window, and, after a little hesitation she went silently and on tiptoe upstairs to the first floor, and down a passage on the left of the stair-head. Here moonlight penetrated a window and threw a pale blue screen upon the opposite wall. Tessa fumbled with the window fastenings, raised the sash softly and silently and leaned out.

On the path below her, but some yards to her left and close to the angle of the house, a man was slowly and rhythmically sweeping with a stable broom. The broom swung and struck the path time after time with a soft, crisp *swish*, and the strokes were as regular as those of the pendulum of some slow old clock.

From her angle of observation she was unable to see most of the characteristics of the figure underneath. It was that of a working man, for there was something in the silhouette subtly suggestive of old and baggy clothes. But apart from all else there was something queer, something odd and unnatural, in the scene on which she gazed. She knew that there was something lacking, something that she should have found missing at the first glance, yet for her life she could not have said what it was.

From below some gross omission blazed up at her, and though she was acutely aware that the scene lacked something which she had every right to expect to see, her senses groped for it in vain; although the lack of something which should have been there and was not, was as obvious as a burning pyre at midnight. She knew that she was watching the gross defiance of some natural law, but what law she did not know. Suddenly sick and dizzy, she withdrew her head.

All the cowardice in Tessa's nature urged her to go to bed, to forget what she had seen and to refrain from trying to remember what she had *not* seen. But the other Tessa, the Tessa who despised cowards, and was herself capable under pressure of rising to great heights of courage, stayed and urged. Under her breath she talked to herself, as she always did when any crisis found her in a state of indecision.

"Tessa, you coward! How dare you be afraid! Go down at once and see who it is and what's queer about him. He can't eat you!"

So the two Tessas imprisoned in the one body stole downstairs again, and the braver Tessa was angry with their common heart for thumping so hard and trying to weaken her. But she unfastened the door and stepped out into the moonlight.

The Sweeper was still at work close to the angle of the house, near by where the path ended and a green door gave entrance to the stable yard. The path was thick with leaves, and the girl, advancing uncertainly with her hands to her breasts, saw that he was making little progress with his work. The broom rose and fell and audibly swept the path, but the dead leaves lay fast and still beneath it. Yet it was not this that she had noticed from above. There was still that unseizable Something missing.

Her footfalls made little noise on the leaf-strewn path, but they became audible to the Sweeper while she was still half a dozen yards from him. He paused in his work and turned and looked at her.

He was a tall, lean man with a white cadaverous face and eyes that bulged like huge rising bubbles as they regarded her. It was a foul,

suffering face which he showed to Tessa, a face whose misery could—
and did—inspire loathing and a hitherto unimagined horror, but never
pity. He was clad in the meanest rags, which seemed to have been cast at
random over his emaciated body. The hands grasping the broom seemed
no more than bones and skin. He was so thin, thought Tessa, that he
was almost—and here she paused in thought, because she found herself
hating the word which tried to force itself into her mind. But it had its
way, and blew in on a cold wind of terror. Yes, he was almost transparent,
she thought, and sickened at the word which had come to have a new and
vile meaning for her.

They faced each other through a fraction of eternity not to be meas-
ured by seconds; and then Tessa heard herself scream. It flashed upon
her now, the strange, abominable detail of the figure which confronted
her—the Something Missing which she had noticed, without actually
seeing, from above. The path was flooded with moonlight, but the Visitant
had no shadow. And fast upon this vile discovery she saw dimly *through* it
the ivy stirring upon the wall. Then as unbidden thoughts rushed to tell
her that the Thing was not of this world, and that it was not holy, and the
sudden knowledge wrung that scream from her, so she was left suddenly
and dreadfully alone. The spot where the Thing had stood was empty save
for the moonlight and the shallow litter of leaves.

Tessa had no memory of returning to the house. Her next recollection
was of finding herself in the hall, faint and gasping and sobbing. Even as
she approached the stairs she saw a light dancing on the wall above and
wondered what fresh horror was to confront her. But it was only Mrs
Finch coming downstairs in a dressing-gown, candle in hand, an incon-
gruous but a very comforting sight.

"Oh, it's you, Miss Tessa," said Mrs Finch reassured. She held the candle
lower and peered down at the sobbing girl. "Why, whatever is the matter?
Oh, Miss Tessa, Miss Tessa! You haven't never been outside, have you?"

Tessa sobbed and choked and tried to speak.

"I've seen—I've seen—"

Mrs Finch swiftly descended the remaining stairs, and put an arm around the shuddering girl.

"Hush, my dear, my dear! I know what you've seen. You didn't ought never to have gone out. I've seen it too, once—but only once, thank God."

"What is it?" Tessa faltered.

"Never you mind, my dear. Now don't be frightened. It's all over now. He doesn't come here for you. It's the mistress he wants. You've nothing to fear, Miss Tessa. Where was he when you saw him?"

"Close to the end of the path, near the stable gate."

Mrs Finch threw up her hands.

"Oh, the poor mistress—the poor mistress! Her time's shortening! The end's nigh, now!"

"I can't bear any more," Tessa sobbed; and then she contradicted herself, clinging to Mrs Finch. "I must know. I can't rest until I know. Tell me everything."

"Come into my parlour, my dear, and I'll make a cup of tea. We can both do with it, I think. But you'd best not know. At least not tonight, Miss Tessa—not tonight."

"I must," whispered Tessa, "if I'm ever to have any peace."

The fire was still burning behind a guard in the housekeeper's parlour, for Mrs Finch had only gone up to bed a few minutes since. There was water still warm in the brass kettle, and in a few minutes the tea was ready. Tessa sipped and felt the first vibrations of her returning courage, and presently looked inquiringly at Mrs Finch.

"I'll tell you, Miss Tessa," said the old housekeeper, "if it'll make you any easier. But don't let the mistress know as I've ever told you."

Tessa inclined her head and gave the required promise.

"You don't know why," Mrs Finch began in a low voice, "the mistress gives to every beggar, deserving or otherwise. The reason comes into what

I'm going to tell you. Miss Ludgate wasn't always like that—not until up to about fifteen years ago.

"She was old then, but active for her age, and very fond of gardenin'. Late one afternoon in the autumn while she was cutting some late roses, a beggar came to the tradesmen's door. Sick and ill and starved, he looked— but there, you've seen him. He was a bad lot, we found out afterwards, but I was sorry for him, and I was just going to risk givin' him some food without orders, when up comes Miss Ludgate. 'What's this?' she says.

"He whined something about not being able to get work.

"'Work!' says the mistress. 'You don't want work—you want charity. If you want to eat,' she says, 'you shall, but you shall work first. There's a broom,' she says, 'and there's a path littered with leaves. Start sweeping up at the top, and when you come to the end you can come and see me.'

"Well, he took the broom, and a few minutes later I heard a shout from Miss Ludgate and come hurryin' out. There was the man lyin' at the top of the path where he'd commenced sweeping, and he'd collapsed and fallen down. I didn't know then as he was dying, but he did, and he gave Miss Ludgate a look as I shall never forget.

"'When I've swept to the end of the path,' he says, 'I'll come for you, my lady, and we'll feast together. Only see as you're ready to be fetched when I come.' Those were his last words. He was buried by the parish, and it gave Miss Ludgate such a turn that she ordered something to be given to every beggar who came, and not one of 'em to be asked to do a stroke of work.

"But next autumn, when the leaves began to fall, he came back and started sweeping, right at the top of the path, round about where he died. We've all heard him and most of us have seen him. Year after year he's come back and swept with his broom which just makes a brushing noise and hardly stirs a leaf. But each year he's been getting nearer and nearer to the end of the path, and when he gets right to the end—well, I wouldn't like to be the mistress, with all her money."

*

It was three evenings later, just before the hour fixed for dinner, that the Sweeper completed his task. That is to say, if one reposes literal belief in Mrs Finch's story.

The servants heard somebody burst open the tradesmen's door, and, having rushed out into the passage, two of them saw that the door was open but found no one there. Miss Ludgate was already in the drawing-room, but Tessa was still upstairs, dressing for dinner. Presently Mrs Finch had occasion to enter the drawing-room to speak to her mistress; and her screams warned the household of what had happened. Tessa heard them just as she was ready to go downstairs, and she rushed into the drawing-room a few moments later.

Miss Ludgate was sitting upright in her favourite chair. Her eyes were open, but she was quite dead; and in her eyes there was something that Tessa could not bear to see.

Withdrawing her own gaze from that fixed stare of terror and recognition she saw something on the carpet and presently stooped to pick it up.

It was a little yellow leaf, damp and pinched and frayed, and but for her own experience and Mrs Finch's tale she might have wondered how it had come to be there. She dropped it, shuddering, for it looked as if it had been picked up by, and had afterwards fallen from, the birch twigs of a stable broom.